M. Dean Wright

Published by M. Dean Wright, 2023.

This is a work of fiction. Similarities to real people, places, or events are entirely coincidental.

WELCOME, CALLER

First edition. January 17, 2023.

Copyright © 2023 M. Dean Wright.

ISBN: 979-8201332921

Written by M. Dean Wright.

For all of you who yearn to be your true self, but fear every day that you might be "faking it."

You're not.

1

In a town as small as Bugswick, Malcolm's surprised it's taken this long for him to bump into his self-proclaimed archnemesis. He just didn't think the *bumping into* part would be so literal.

There's orange juice spreading down the front of his shirt, seeping into the cracked tiles of the grocery store, and a bruise forming on his backside that probably would have been worse if it weren't for the loaf of bread that broke his fall. He draws the squished loaf out from beneath him and frowns. He was going to make ham and cheese sandwiches with that.

A muttered curse draws his attention, and he looks up to find high top curls and brown eyes. The source of his grocery catastrophe.

Peter Tollemache sits in an inelegant heap on the floor, legs spread out like a newborn giraffe while his groceries (an unfortunate amount of soup products) marinate in his lap. Malcolm throws his head back and groans, clenching his eyes shut to block out the buzzing fluorescent lights that have only been adding to his growing annoyance since this *situation* began. Malcolm brings his head back down when he hears Peter let out a pointedly long-suffering sigh.

"Were you dropped on the head as a kid?" Peter asks slowly, his voice low and livid.

Peter clenches his jaw, then swipes his tongue over his teeth. He does that when he's especially irritated. Malcolm noticed it in college. Peter had seemed to hate Malcolm's guts before they'd even had the chance to exchange pleasantries, so Malcolm ended up wasting hours of precious study time glaring at Peter across the room instead, as if staring at the backside of his head would somehow unlock the mystery of what crawled up his ass and died there. It's a puzzle Malcolm has long since given up on solving.

"You're the one who bumped into me, asshole," Malcolm barks back, gathering his groceries in his arms.

"God, this is gonna take ages to get out," Peter mumbles, like a prick. An employee with impressively dark bags under their eyes comes by and hands him several paper towels. Peter is considerably nicer to the worker than he is to Malcolm, accepting the help with a quiet nod and a soft thanks.

Malcolm waits for Peter to use up his share of paper towels and hand over the extra, but he seems content to use every piece for himself. Malcolm can feel the orange juice seeping further into his shirt and down his chest. It starts to drip down to his boxers, and he bristles.

"Hey," Malcolm says, but Peter ignores him, using the rest of the paper towels to wipe at his jeans. Half of them are still dry. Malcolm reaches out to grab one, but Peter holds it out of the way. "Hey! I need some of those!"

"Go ask for more, then," Peter says without a second glance to Malcolm. He continues to pat down his legs and arms, the latter of which had been most certainly *untouched* by the soup. He's doing this on purpose.

"This wouldn't have happened if you'd just watch where you're going," Malcolm says, hoping the venom in his voice disguises the fact that he isn't actually sure who bumped into whom. Malcolm's friends know how oblivious and clumsy he can be, but *Peter* doesn't know that, and Malcolm doesn't intend to apologize now that he's blamed Peter so vehemently.

After a lot more paper towels and twice as much complaining, Malcolm finally pays for his items (ignoring Peter's dirty looks from the aisle over) and marches down the street toward his apartment with his groceries in hand, including a new carton of orange juice and the squished loaf of bread that seems to be steadily un-squishing itself.

Malcolm pulls out his phone and opens up the only group chat on his messaging app. It's currently titled **Got Bees?** He suspects Jazz is the one who changed the name.

you will not believe what just happened

Goby's phone is perpetually attached to their palm when they aren't working, so their reply comes the quickest.

A HEIST!!!

You think everything is a heist, Goob, Mona texts back.

nah i agree with goby. it's definitely a heist this time, Jazz says.

THANK YOU JAZMINE, Goby says, and before anyone can reply, they shoot out another text:

someone is probably on their way to
steal the queens jewels...its up to you
to save the country mal...SAVE US ALL!!!!

goby, we don't have a queen

yea we do she's right here, Jazz replies.

The text is followed by a picture Jazz seems to have just taken of Mona. It's slightly blurry; Jazz must have snuck the photo before Mona noticed. Mona's socked feet are propped up on Jazz's lap, Jazz's hand resting gently on her ankle. Mona's smiling absently at her own phone.

Aw, my darling, Mona replies, along with several heart emojis.

BARF, Goby says, **NOT IN FRONT OF THE CHILD**

what child?

ME!

don't be a homophobe, Jazz says.

homo-gobe, Goby replies. It takes Malcolm a second to realize they were trying to make a play on their own name. It didn't work.

that was awful, Jazz says.

that was genius, Goby replies.

all of you give me gray hairs.

Malcolm takes a second look at the photo Jazz sent to the chat and grins, saving it to his phone. Mona and Jazz are sitting comfortably on his old pea-green leather couch, a hand-me-down from his cousin that he had to convince Goby and Mona to let him keep in their shared apartment. The black Ragamuffin Malcolm rescued several years back, lovingly named Lady Governor, can be made out in the corner of the screen, her tail brushing against the golden-brown skin of Mona's leg.

Despite the warmth in his chest, he can't help but tease them:

if you do anything on my couch
i'm kicking you both out

Malcolm, sweetheart, I adore you, but I would rather die than do anything of the sort on this thing, Mona says.

Malcolm's jaw drops, even as he feels his lips draw up into a smile against his will. He clicks the group FaceTime button, rearranging his expression until he looks more offended than he really feels. Everyone answers right away, their faces popping up onto the screen one by one.

"It's not that bad!" Malcolm says immediately, adjusting his grip on the groceries so he can hold them all in one hand and the phone in the other. "She's just a little worn out, that's all!"

"Malcolm, this thing has, like, eighteen holes in it," Jazz says. She turns the camera towards her hand, where he can see one of her ringed fingers start to dig into a hole in his couch. Her finger sinks through to the knuckle. "It's dead meat, dude. Pretty sure I can feel it deteriorating under my ass. You're lucky I'm not dragging it out to the curb right now."

"I think it's charming," Goby chimes in, close enough to the camera that the bottom half of their face gets cut off. Malcolm can tell that they're smiling from their squinty eyes and the risen apples of their cheeks, pale and freckled.

"Of course you would," Jazz says, "you'd call a dirty sewer tire *'perfectly delightful!'*" Jazz waves her hand into the air and puts on a voice that's probably supposed to be an imitation of Goby, but sounds more like some kind of Muppet.

Goby starts to say something along the lines of "I'll show you perfectly delightful," when Mona cuts in.

"What was it you wanted to tell us, Malcolm?" Mona says, a laugh in her voice as her socked foot emerges from the corner of Jazz's portion of the screen and pokes at her cheek. Jazz swats it away, wrinkling her nose, and Mona sticks her tongue out in return.

"Right, yeah," Malcolm says right as he gets the keys into the apartment door and swings through. Mona, Jazz and Goby look up at the sound of his entrance. "You will *never* guess who I ran into at the grocery store."

"The President," Goby guesses from where they sit on the countertop of the kitchen island. Lady Governor tries stubbornly to catch one of the drawstrings from Goby's sweatpants with her paws as Goby swings their feet back and forth. Goby wiggles their toes at her, and Lady Governor latches onto their ankle.

"No, not the President," Malcolm says, pinching lightly and affectionately at Goby's ear as he passes. They huff and kick out at his leg, which he just barely manages to swivel around before he can trip and drop his groceries. Again.

"Steve Buscemi," Jazz shouts out a guess. She's risen from her spot on the couch to replace the album that was playing on the living room record player (something by The Who, Malcolm thinks) with a new one.

"Uh, no, not quite," Malcolm says, unpacking the groceries just as The Clash begins to play. Jazz is familiar enough with the album to know exactly where to place the needle, and Malcolm isn't surprised when the distinct notes of "Brand New Cadillac" start to fill the room. Jazz bops her head to the beat as she returns to the couch, this time sitting herself between Mona's legs so that her back rests against Mona's chest.

"Was it Mr. Lu?" Mona asks as she wraps her arms around Jazz's middle. Jazz's locs have been wrapped into a bun at the top of her head, so Mona rests her chin on Jazz's shoulder in order to better look at Malcolm.

"Thank you for the proper guess, Mona. This is why you're my favorite," Malcolm says, ignoring Goby's indignant gasp. Mr. Lu works at the only Asian supermarket in town. He has a mean face, but that never fools the people who have grown to know him. He has a granddaughter named Miranda that he loves to spoil, and he brags about her to any customer willing to listen. Malcolm and the rest of the group have always had a soft spot for the old man. "He's not who I wanted to talk about, but I actually did run into him on the way home; he's invited us to Miranda's soccer game next week."

"*Score*," Goby says earnestly. "Free snow cones."

"No snow cones until the players get them first this time, you cretin," Jazz says, pointing a stern finger at Goby.

"They'll take all the good flavors!" Goby complains.

"They're *eleven*!"

"Back to me," Malcolm says, and everyone returns their attention to him (except for Lady Governor, who is now leaning over the top of the couch to paw at one of the many pins and patches on Jazz's jean jacket). "I ran into..." Malcolm pauses, letting the suspense build. "Peter Tollemache."

The others blink.

"Who?" Mona says.

"Your college crush?" Jazz says, her lips quirking up.

Malcolm flusters, sputtering out a number of nonsensical half-words before he can get out a full sentence. "What? I'm—I didn't—*no*. I did not have—" Malcolm realizes his voice has climbed up in volume and quickly lowers it. "I did not have a *crush* on Peter

Tollemache." He spits out the name like a particularly sour orange slice, then scoffs. "He hates me."

"This is the guy you stare at all the time, yeah?" Goby says, hopping down from the kitchen island. They grab an apple out of the fridge and bite into it with a satisfying crunch. When Malcolm furrows his eyebrows at them, they continue through a mouthful of chewed up Honeycrisp, "Whenever he's out on a run you stare at the dude like he's got sunbeams shooting out of his butt."

"I only stare at him because he hates me!" Malcolm says, and he curses when he feels the burn of a blush at the tips of his ears. "We're enemies."

"If you're enemies, why don't you just ignore him?" Mona says. Her voice is smooth and warm, like tea and honey. She sounds so sensible, and it frustrates Malcolm to no end when he just wants to be irrational.

He turns to unpack the rest of his groceries while he thinks of a good reason for his actions, but before he can, Jazz interrupts.

"You just hate the thought of anyone not liking you, huh?" Jazz says with a sly grin.

Malcolm grumbles, "You know for a fact that plenty of people have hated me over the course of my life. You've seen it yourself."

This is true. Jazz is the only one in the group who has known Malcolm since before college. They'd become friends in elementary school, when Malcolm had told her he didn't think it was weird that she wanted to kiss girls like boys did, and she had let him borrow her beanie to tuck his hair up into since his mother refused to cut it any shorter than shoulder length.

They were also the first people either of them had come out to.

"Do you know what transgender means?" Jazz had asked at a sleepover with Malcolm in middle school, back when she still regularly went by Jazmine instead of Jazz.

Malcolm was standing in front of his floor length mirror, tying his mother's scarf around his chest to see if it would make him look a bit more like his male classmates. He put a hoodie on top, but it just made him look like he was hiding lumpy grocery bags under his shirt. He glanced at Jazz through the mirror, but she wasn't looking at him. She was reading a book on his bed, her legs crossed and her tight curls pushed out of her face with a headband. He couldn't see the full title of the book from where he stood, but he thought he saw the words "and Human Sexuality" peeking out from behind her hands. He had never seen the book in his house, so she must have brought it with her.

"I don't think so," Malcolm said, slumping when the scarf unraveled and fell out from the bottom of his hoodie.

Jazz had explained the term to him, reading the definition straight out of the book. Then she talked about a relative of hers who was transgender, and how he had transitioned after high school. Throughout the whole conversation, she kept her eyes on her book, overly casual. Now Malcolm knows that her feigned disinterest in the conversation had been her way of being supportive.

"Huh," Malcolm had said when she was finished. "That...that sounds like me."

"Okay," Jazz had said, finally looking up from the book.

Malcolm had shuffled over to Jazz, sitting daintily on the edge of the bed. He blinked once, then said, "I think I'm transgender."

Jazz had smiled and said, "Alright. I think I'm a lesbian."

They spent the rest of the night watching Labyrinth (Jazz's favorite), and fell asleep holding each other. Malcolm asked to borrow Jazz's book the next day, and he read all about bisexuality, eventually coming to terms with that side of his identity as well. (Malcolm wouldn't come out to anyone else for years, as either trans or bi—but knowing that Jazz knew, and loved him nonetheless, was enough.)

Many years later, at the start of college, Jazz showed up at Malcolm's doorstep with that same book, along with a frantic look in her eye.

"I need to figure something out," she had said, planting herself at his dining room table. She had both the book and her laptop open, and she would periodically switch between the two platforms throughout the evening. Malcolm hadn't said much; just sat with her while she read, occasionally giving her fruit slices when she went too long without eating.

That night, she came out as asexual. (Malcolm needed a bit of explanation about the difference between sexual and romantic attraction, and how being asexual didn't make Jazz any less of a lesbian. He did a little more soul searching after that and came to the conclusion that he was definitely still bi—in both the romantic and sexual sense.)

They've been together through every identity crisis, through every confusing and frustrating moment. They've been there to protect one another from the world when the only people who seemed to care about them were themselves.

The current Jazz softens a bit. Remembering the years of bullying and loneliness they've both had to endure, however, isn't enough to stop her from mocking him when the chance arises, and her insufferable grin grows wider.

Damn. He had hoped pulling the Queer Trauma card would work.

"I'm not talking about high school assholes," Jazz says to Malcolm. "Peter isn't a bigot, he just doesn't like you. But you don't know *why* he doesn't like you, and that bugs the shit out of you, huh?"

Malcolm groans deep in the back of his throat, dragging his hands down his face. "Okay fine, yes, of course it bugs me. Why wouldn't he like me? I'm a fucking delight!"

"How do you even know he doesn't like you? I've never seen you two actually talk," Goby says, taking a seat in the chair next to the couch. Malcolm sits himself down on the carpet, leaning his elbows on the coffee table.

"That's because they *don't* talk," Jazz says. She strokes a hand down Lady Governor's back as the old cat settles on top of her thighs, and Mona leans forward from behind Jazz to scratch at Lady's chin. "I think they spoke, like, once in college? But apart from that Malcolm just glares at him."

"He glares first!" Malcolm flings his arms out for (unneeded) emphasis. "And we *didn't* talk. Not until today, that is."

"You spoke to him?" Mona says, the only one in the group who has yet to tease him about his nemesis. He doesn't keep his hopes up, though; Mona can be just as bad as the other two, she's just better at hiding it. The dimple in her cheek tells him she's finding his dilemma just as amusing as the others.

"More like shouted," Malcolm says. He scratches at the scruff on his cheek. "I kinda...dumped his soup in his lap."

"Pardon?" Mona says, eyes wide.

Jazz snorts once before dissolving into a fit of giggles, her whole body moving with the effort, and Lady Governor darts out of her lap to escape the noise. Goby has joined in as well, gripping at their stomach as great big guffaws leave their mouth.

"You fucking *what*?" Jazz manages to say through an almost painful sounding wheeze.

"I didn't do it on purpose!" Malcolm insists, his cheeks burning. He tugs at the front of his beanie and pulls it over his eyes. "I always end up zoning out when I'm at the store and I never bump into people, but of course the one time I do it's my archnemesis! And I tried explaining that it was an accident but he wouldn't listen, just stole all the damn paper towels for himself." Okay, the part about him trying to explain himself is a bit of a fib, but they don't need to know that. It's *basically* what happened.

"Well, he is the one who got soup in his lap," Goby points out. Malcolm rips off his beanie so he can frown at Goby.

"And I got soaked in OJ!" Malcolm says, picking at the sticky front of his shirt where a large stain has developed from the spill. He doesn't normally wear white shirts in fear of sweat stains (his high school gym class had forced students to wear white shirts that always stained yellow in the pits after the first week), but it was cool enough outside today that he figured stains could be avoided. How foolish he had been.

"I've always said you look good in orange," Mona says, bringing her hand up in a vain attempt to stifle a laugh.

"Monaaa," Malcolm whines, drawing out the vowels. "Don't laugh at me, you're the nice one! You're supposed to be on my side."

"Babes, when are you going to learn," Jazz says, "we will always be on the side that involves laughing at your misfortune."

Malcolm sighs, making a great big show of it just to be dramatic. (He spots an exaggerated eye roll from Jazz but resolutely ignores it.)

"Alright then, guess I'll just get fucked," Malcolm says, standing from the floor.

"You should! Maybe it'll help you loosen up a bit," Jazz says, and she laughs as Malcolm picks up a pen and flings it at her head.

2

When Malcolm wakes, it takes him several long minutes of wondering why his blanket is so hairy and warm before he realizes that Lady Governor has just planted her rear on his chest, leaving her tail to rest right along his face. He grunts and shifts as much as he can without disrupting her, squinting his eyes at the harsh light in the room.

They've all fallen asleep in the living room again. Living room slumber parties have been a regular occurrence since even before they became roommates, so Malcolm isn't surprised to find himself waking up on the floor with a crick in his neck and someone's knee jabbing his back.

Jazz is the only one of them who doesn't actually live in the apartment, although Malcolm suspects it's only a matter of time before Mona is moving out to go live with her. They've only been dating for a few months, but they knew each other for years before that. Malcolm was surprised when Jazz didn't pop the question by their one-month anniversary.

"I refuse to be a stereotype, Mal," Jazz had said. He wasn't familiar enough with lesbian stereotypes to be sure which one she was referring to, but he was kind enough not to push (and he definitely didn't mention that he had caught Jazz looking at hand crafted rings on her laptop after her and Mona's second date).

Malcolm sniffs at the air, and his eyes open fully at the delicious scent.

"Rise and shine, darlings," Mona says from the kitchen. Jazz and Goby begin to stir from beside Malcolm. He grimaces when he feels Goby unstick their clammy palm from where it had been placed against his calf. Jazz burrows deeper into her makeshift nest of blankets, making a noise similar to that of a disturbed cat. "Malcolm and I have work in thirty and I know you two aren't going to eat breakfast if I don't make it, so get up and help yourself."

God bless Mona's love for cooking. If he were a less selfish person, Malcolm would insist that she quit her job at the pub with him and become a chef. Thankfully, he doesn't have to be selfish; Mona has said time and time again that cooking as a profession would ruin her love for it. He could understand that, although he can't help but feel like a villain depraving the world of her amazing culinary adventures.

"What's on the menu, chef?" Goby asks in their best Gordon Ramsay, although the effect is ruined when they yawn halfway through.

"I thought I'd try this new steamed bun recipe I found online," Mona says, placing a large bowl in the middle of the kitchen island. "The filling I made isn't exactly traditional, but I wanted to experiment. Don't worry, love, I made a few without meat for you," she adds, pushing a smaller bowl towards Jazz, who's been trying to go vegetarian on and off for several weeks. (This is her fourth attempt after she gave in to Mona's pigs in a blanket last Saturday.)

Malcolm's on his feet in seconds, his mouth watering. Goby lets out a delighted *"oooh,"* and Jazz leaves her blanket cave to snatch a fresh bun before Goby can eat any of hers. She's kept one blanket wrapped snugly around herself, leaving only her head to poke out like a particularly crabby turtle.

"I also made one with Nutella for you, Goob," Mona said.

Goby looks on the verge of tears, snatching up the steamed bun that Mona was holding out to them and stuffing a large portion into their mouth. They let out a whimper, slumping backwards as if the taste were enough to knock them off their feet.

"Will you marry me?" Goby says, their mouth a disgusting cave of Nutella that they don't even bother to hide with their hand. "I'm pretty sure this is grounds for marriage. We can elope, go wherever you like."

"Only if you promise not to tell Mr. Lu I've ruined his perfectly good bao buns with cheap hazelnut filling," Mona says, dragging her thumb across Goby's chin to catch the drop of Nutella that had fallen there, only to wipe it off on Goby's shirt.

"Oi, I'm right here," Jazz cuts in, properly waking up at the prospect of her girlfriend eloping without her.

"You should've asked first, then," Mona teases, leaning over to kiss the pout off of Jazz's face.

Goby turns to Malcolm and fakes a gag, sticking their finger at their tongue for full effect. Malcolm smiles and drags a hand through their hair, ruffling the top. Their hair is too short and choppy to possibly mess up, but he's been doing it since their hair was shoulder length (and blue, not a vibrant pumpkin-orange like it is now) back in college, and Goby grunts in annoyance at the familiar brotherly gesture.

Mona and Malcolm make quick work of getting ready for their shift after breakfast. Mona kisses both Jazz and Goby on the way out, Jazz on the lips and Goby on the forehead. Malcolm gives Goby a playful cuff against the chin before flipping Jazz the bird, which she returns with a laugh.

Setting up the pub never takes long, but Malcolm always insists on going in thirty minutes before his shift technically starts just to make sure he isn't late (which is practically impossible when you live right above your workplace), and Mona is kind enough to putz around in the empty pub just so he isn't alone.

"Good morning, sweetheart," Mona crouches and coos at the small terrarium sitting amongst the bottom shelf bourbon. "Did you miss me?"

"You know we're going to get an OSHA violation one of these days because of that thing," Malcolm says as he wipes down at a table with a questionable stickiness on its surface.

"Loads of establishments have pets! You see cats in bodegas and fish tanks in restaurants all the time, what's so different?" Mona says.

"I'm pretty sure they're planning on cooking those fish."

She looks so genuinely distraught for a moment that Malcolm almost feels bad.

"Mona, you eat fish!" Malcolm says.

"Not *those* fish!" Mona says, then turns back to place a gentle finger against the glass of the terrarium. "And I would never eat *you*, Terrance."

Malcolm blows a raspberry and scrubs harder at the table.

"So," Mona says, considerably closer than before. Malcolm looks up to see her leaning against the bar counter across from him. "Has she called again?"

Malcolm hums. "Last night. You were asleep, but Goby woke up and threw my phone in the freezer before I could answer."

Mona cracks a smile. "Good job, Goob."

"I can make my own choices."

"Of course you can, love," Mona says softly. "You know we wouldn't be doing this if you hadn't specifically asked us to help you."

"Wish helping me didn't involve freezing my phone," Malcolm grumbles.

"Would you have answered otherwise?"

Malcolm frowns and looks down at the table. Mona pats his hand, a gesture that would have felt patronizing if it were anyone else in that moment. He places his other hand on top of hers, so that it's sandwiched in between his own.

"Alright, enough about that," Mona chirps, and Malcolm's thankful for the subject change for about a millisecond before she keeps talking. "Tell me more about this college crush Jazz was talking about."

"*Nemesis*," Malcolm says emphatically, turning away to hide the color in his cheeks.

"Jazz seemed pretty sure that there was more to it than that, at least in college," Mona says with a grin.

"Jazz once went two weeks without a shower in seventh grade. Don't trust a single thing that woman says."

Before Mona can reply, Malcolm turns away and heads towards the other side of the pub. He turns on the portable radio that sits at the far end of the bar, just so he has something to do with his hands. They've never actually used the old thing since the pub has built-in speakers, but he turns up the volume anyway before Mona can accuse him of avoiding the conversation (which he is most definitely doing).

The first station he lands on that isn't filled with static has surprisingly decent music; it's similar to what Jazz plays on his record player whenever she comes over. (She never grew out of her punk phase. It's been Doc Martens and the Sex Pistols for almost as long as he's known her.) He remembers the song that's playing—remembers Jazz back in high school, blasting it in her room as she smudged her mother's eyeliner around her eyes, shouting the lyrics at Malcolm until he knew the song by heart. His taste in music today is entirely thanks to what she's introduced him to (or, more accurately, forced him to listen to over and over).

"That was 'Kiss Off' by the Violent Femmes," a voice on the radio says as the song fades out. It's an older man, by the sounds of it. His voice is low and sticky, and Malcolm gets the urge to call the station just to ask the man to clear his throat of whatever phlegm seems to be stuck in there. "Next up, we have The Kinks."

The man goes into a bit of backstory about the band, but he sounds disinterested. Detached. Malcolm scrunches his nose, wishing the music would return quicker. Or for someone to replace Mr. Phlegm Voice, at the very least.

"Have you been to that new record shop?" Mona says from behind Malcolm, and he jumps.

"New—huh?" Malcolm says.

"The new record shop, down the street from Mr. Lu?" She leans forward and turns down the volume on the radio a notch. "Can't remember what the place is called, but I went by there a couple days ago on my board and it looked pretty cool."

Malcolm lifts his eyebrows in interest. "We could use some new records. Jazz has been on my ass about updating our collection."

Mona scrunches her nose. "It is a bit sad, isn't it?"

Malcolm sighs, "Yeah, it is." He has precisely six records—hardly enough to even consider it a collection. Two of them were gifts from Jazz, which included a passive aggressive note implying that if he didn't buy more music for his record player, then she would steal it in the middle of the night since she clearly knew its worth better than him. "Maybe I'll go this week, pick up something to surprise her."

Mona makes a thoughtful noise. "Good. I think you'll like it there."

She heads towards the front door to flip the sign to OPEN. Malcolm follows her with his eyes, and when she turns around with a calculatedly neutral expression, he squints at her.

"What?" She says, placing her hands on her hips.

"What are you up to?" Malcolm says.

"Nothing!"

"Uh-uh," Malcolm shakes his head, "you've got your scheming face on."

"I don't have a scheming face! Like you said, I'm the nice one, Mal—I don't *scheme*."

"Oh fuuuck off, you absolutely do," Malcolm laughs. "I trust you about as much as those other two fuckheads."

Mona scoffs in offense, but her dimples are popping out in her effort not to smile. She straightens out the cuffs of her black button-up shirt, eyes downcast as she says, "If you *must* know, there's an employee at the record shop that I think you'd get along with."

Malcolm squints harder. Mona rolls her eyes.

"He's cute," she says.

Malcolm gapes. "You're trying to set me up with someone!"

"I just think you could get out some more," Mona says. "When's the last time you went out on a date?"

He looks down, chewing at the inside of his cheek. He doesn't want to admit that the last time he went out with someone was before he started using the men's restrooms—before his name was even Malcolm.

"Mal," Mona says, her voice softening. Her eyes are far too knowing, and it makes his skin itch.

"I'm good, Mona," he says. "I don't need someone else to make me feel complete. I don't need sex or—or *romance* to feel whole."

"Of course you don't, babes," Mona says kindly. "All of that stuff about relationships making us whole, that's bullshit. We're whole people all on our own."

"Exactly."

"However," Mona holds up a finger, "while you don't *need* a relationship, you do *want* one. You are the most hopeless romantic I know. Don't argue, I've seen you watch *Pride and Prejudice*."

Malcolm squawks indignantly, but Mona ignores him and continues.

"You just need to know," she says, "that while you don't need romance or a Jane-Austen-level love life to be whole, you still deserve it. It's there if you want it. You just have to go out and get it."

Go out and get it.

As if it's that easy.

"Thanks, Mona," Malcolm says. "But I just don't think romance is in the cards for me."

3

Roisin Records. That's what the record shop is called.

The whole store is probably the flashiest thing in town, with its bright neon lettering and colorful LED lights in the window. While the rest of Bugswick looks worn down and well on its way to being reclaimed by nature, Roisin Records is vibrant and electrifying, breathing life into whatever and wherever its light touches.

He can hear the music playing in the store from outside, can feel it thumping inside his chest. (He doesn't recognize the song. He's never heard Jazz play it, and if Jazz doesn't introduce it to him, it's unlikely to end up on his radar.)

It's gray and muggy outside, making the orange glow of the shop's interior even more inviting.

Then he enters the store.

The music roots itself into his lungs. It invades his senses in the best possible way, drowning out every worry. It's a solid weight in his body that feels like warmth. Like comfort. Like safety.

He lets his eyes flutter shut, breathing in.

"Can I help you?"

He doesn't recognize the voice immediately. He squints his eyes open, and it's like missing a step on the stairs, the way Malcolm's stomach swoops so violently at the sight of the man in front of him. He blinks slowly, praying for the universe to lend him some patience.

"Are you following me?" Malcolm asks Peter.

Peter lifts an eyebrow, which Malcolm refuses to be jealous about. (He's spent countless hours practicing a single-eyebrow-lift in the mirror, but it only ever makes him look like he's trying too hard.)

"I work here," Peter says slowly, like he's talking to a child. Malcolm feels his neck prickling at Peter's condescending tone. He's suddenly very glad that he's wearing shoes that give him an extra inch in height; he'd explode if Peter were looking down at him figuratively *and* literally.

"Well, how was I supposed to know that? It's not like you're wearing a uniform," Malcolm says, waving his hand flippantly at Peter.

Peter looks down at his outfit. He has this whole vintage aesthetic going on, a loose green sweater French tucked into a pair of black slacks. A white button-up peaks out of the collar and sleeves of the sweater. Malcolm wishes that it didn't work so well on him.

"So, your next guess wasn't that I'm shopping, but that I'm...stalking you?" Peter asks, almost smiling. He's obviously holding in a laugh, and Malcolm feels his cheeks color.

"Don't laugh at me."

"No, you're right, that's a very reasonable assumption," Peter says, nodding.

Malcolm folds his arms together. "What kind of name is Raisin Records anyway?"

"Roisin," Peter corrects. "It's Irish."

"It's dumb." It's not that dumb, but he can't come up with anything clever to say. "Why is it Irish? Who came up with that?"

"How am I supposed to know? I'm not the owner," Peter says.

"Who *is* the owner? Are *they* Irish?" Malcolm looks around at the empty store. "Are they even here? Is *anyone* here?"

"No, it's just me right now. Travis works in the back usually, but he's not in today."

"*Travis*," Malcolm says, testing the name out. "He sounds like a prick."

Peter sighs, but it sounds more amused than Malcolm was expecting. "He's nice enough, just a bit of a dip."

They stand for a moment, both looking around at anything but the other. Malcolm isn't entirely sure what to do. This is the most they've ever actually talked before, and he wasn't prepared to find them sitting in this—what even is this? Would he call it a friendly atmosphere? It's amiable, at the very least. He doesn't know what to do with an amiable Peter Tollemache. The world might implode.

"So, are you in my store for a reason, or...?"

Malcolm presses his thumb to his temple, his irritation returning as quickly as it had vanished. "Well, obviously I'm here for music," he says, gesturing at the rows of records and CDs.

"Right," Peter says. "Very specific."

"Oh, buzz off, Peter," Malcolm finally says, storming off. Unfortunately, the store is very small, so he doesn't get very far.

He looks back once just to see Peter roll his eyes, and his whole body moves with it as he walks back behind the counter. He starts flipping through a magazine, his chin propped up in his hand. Malcolm forces himself to look away.

He spends a long time browsing through the records, coming back to a few that seem like Jazz's style. After a while, though, he realizes just how lost he is. He knows Jazz, he knows what she likes, but which one should he pick? He can't remember if this album from The Who was one that she liked or if this was the album she refused to listen to because it didn't have their lead drummer in it anymore...or maybe it was the guitarist. Or was that Pink Floyd?

He doesn't know music like she does. There are *so* many options to choose from, far more than he was prepared for, and he can only afford one or two right now, and he *sucks* at making decisions. He doesn't get paid until next week. Maybe he should have waited. Maybe he should have—

A record is suddenly shoved in front of his face, and he takes a surprised step back. He looks up, eyes wide. Peter is in front of him, holding the record. His face is the epitome of neutrality. When Malcolm continues to stare at him, his eyes wide and calculating, Peter gives him an annoyed frown.

"You kept coming back to the Modern Lovers," he explains. "This is their best album. You should get this one."

Malcolm looks down at it. It does look familiar. He thinks he's seen Jazz pull up this exact album on her phone to play in the car once.

"And this, if you're looking to buy a few," Peter says, holding out another record. His slender fingers wrap delicately around the album.

"Buzzcocks," Malcolm reads slowly, holding back a snort. Goby is definitely rubbing off on him; they'd be on the ground laughing right now.

"God, you're one of those people," Peter grumbles to himself. He sets the two records down next to Malcolm, then walks back towards the front counter. "Get them or don't, I don't care."

Malcolm spends a few more minutes browsing just out of spite, but in the end chooses to buy the records Peter recommended. If Jazz doesn't like them then at least he'll have someone to blame.

"Good choice," Peter mutters cheekily when Malcolm brings the records to the counter. Malcolm makes a disgruntled noise and looks away, fiddling with his hoodie sleeve as Peter rings him up.

"Are these for someone?" Peter asks.

"Yeah," Malcolm says, handing over his card. "My friend, Jazz. She really likes music."

"Ah. I figured you were a bit too clueless to be shopping for yourself."

"Hey!" Malcolm starts, straightening up. "I'll have you know, I own a record player."

"Oh yeah?"

"Yeah."

"Why?"

"Wh—" Malcolm falters. "Why? What do you mean, why?"

"Why do you own one? What do you like about record players? About records?" Peter says, sliding Malcolm's records into a sleek yellow bag.

"I—" Malcolm shifts, shuffling his feet. He chews at his cheek for a second, wishing he paid more attention to any of Jazz's rants about how record players preserved the authenticity of music or whatever. "They—they, y'know, preserve the authenticity of music."

Peter purses his lips and squints at Malcolm. He holds the bag of records in one hand, not moving. Malcolm reaches for it and Peter pulls the bag away. Malcolm tries again, and Peter shifts the bag over to his other hand.

Malcolm groans, dragging a hand through his hair before snapping, "They look cool! They look really fucking cool, okay? I genuinely cannot tell a difference between listening to music on Spotify and listening to it on a record player but owning one makes me feel cool as fuck, so. Yeah. Fuck off." (The last remark was made as more of an afterthought, but he needed to feel like he got the last word somehow.)

Malcolm takes a deep breath at the end of his rant and huffs it out, his cheeks slightly more flushed than they were before. The smallest of grins pulls at Peter's lips, and Malcolm knows he's mocking him. (There's a thin scar along Peter's top lip that Malcolm deliberately doesn't focus on.)

Peter hands over Malcolm's bag, his expression returning to its infuriatingly neutral state.

"Have a good day, Malcolm."

Malcolm grunts, turning away quickly, but he stops when he gets to the doors. The blare of the music in the store had masked the sound of the pouring rain outside. Malcolm curses and turns back around.

"Do you have an extra umbrella I can borrow?" Malcolm asks.

There's a folded umbrella sitting on the counter, and Peter slowly drags it off the counter and out of sight. "Nope," he says, his face the picture of customer service.

Malcolm rolls his eyes harder than he thought was physically possible and turns to brace the storm.

4

Luck never seems to be on Malcolm's side. Not only did the storm leave Malcolm drenched and shivering, but it cut out the power in his apartment. He walks in to find Goby sitting on the couch in the dark, huddled under several blankets as the light of a single candle flickers against their pale skin.

"Hey, Goob," Malcolm says, shoving his wet shoes off of his feet. "Give me just a minute, I'm gonna dry off."

They hum without looking up. Malcolm pauses, taking a closer look at Goby. They're staring into the candlelight, their expression blank. Malcolm forgoes drying off and shuffles carefully to the couch, picking up the blankets surrounding Goby and burrowing in next to them.

"Ugh, you're sopping wet, dude," Goby says, irritated, but they snuggle in closer to him anyway. "You're getting water all over the couch."

"It's falling apart anyway, what's a little water going to do?" Malcolm says.

"Grow mold?"

Malcolm shrugs, "It's an old couch anyway, we can always replace it."

Goby shifts back, staring at him with furrowed eyebrows. "You *love* this couch. What's up with you?"

"What's up with you?" Malcolm retorts.

Goby blinks, turning back to stare at the candle. Malcolm does the same. They remain silent for a few minutes before Goby speaks again.

"I dunno what's going on with me tonight, Mal," Goby says quietly, almost a whisper. "I dunno if it's the power being out, or the fact that no one else was home, but I just..."

They trail off, but Malcolm knows what they mean well enough. This sort of thing happens with Goby, on particularly quiet days when they have nothing but their thoughts to occupy their time. They'll shut down, and sometimes it takes a while to bring them back. Sometimes days. Luckily it doesn't seem too bad this time around—Malcolm must have come home just in time.

"What can I do?" Malcolm says, keeping his voice low. Something about the darkness in the house makes him feel like he should stay quiet, but maybe Goby needs something else.

"Talk to me," Goby says, leaning their cheek against Malcolm's shoulder. "Please?"

It's times like these that Malcolm remembers Goby's age. He's only a few years older than them, but he can't help but think of them as the baby sibling he's never had. He kisses their hair, smoothing down the stray pieces that stick to his mouth.

"I ran into Peter again today," Malcolm says calmly.

Goby gasps softly. There's not as much energy in it as there could be, but it's something. "Peter 'Cute Butt' Tollemache?"

Malcolm laughs, willing to endure the teasing if it means Goby will feel a little lighter. "I have *never* said—"

"You don't *need* to say anything, I can see it in your eyes," Goby says, wiggling their fingers in the air for emphasis. "You wanna give him a big 'ol smooch. A big juicy kiss on the lips."

"Gross," Malcolm snorts. He tucks his feet further under his thighs to warm up his freezing toes. He's starting to dry, but the chill of the rain still seeps into his bones. "It's really not like that, honest. But..."

"Buuut...?"

"Well," Malcolm says. "I think maybe we could...do away with all this stupid archenemy shit. Possibly. I don't know, maybe I'm being dumb, but—when I ran into him today, it was like I got a glimpse at what it would be like to be...not *friends*, that would be asking too much, but. Oh, I don't know."

Goby makes a noise of interest, reaching over to pet Lady Governor's head as she hops up in between them. She stretches and starts to make biscuits on their blanket, purring noisily.

"Why do you guys hate each other again?" Goby asks.

Malcolm swallows, joining Goby in petting Lady Governor's soft fur.

"You know what, Goob," Malcolm says softly, "I'm not really sure. It's just...always been like that. He's always hated me, and I guess I just wasn't sure what to do except hate him back."

"Maybe it's a misunderstanding," Goby says. They reach out and poke Malcolm in the cheek. "I can't imagine anyone hating you once they get to know you, Mal."

"That's the thing, Goob, he *doesn't* know me. He decided he hated me before even giving me a chance."

Goby sits up so quickly that Lady Governor nearly goes toppling over the side of the couch.

"Well, that's it, then!" Goby shouts, much louder than their previously peaceful atmosphere called for.

"What's it?"

"You just need to talk to Peter more, and then he'll see what a cool dude you are and you guys will be best friends forever."

Malcolm barks out a loud laugh. "I doubt that. I *might* be able to swing a reluctant acquaintanceship. Best friends is stretching it. Besides," he adds, ruffling Goby's hair, "*you're* my best friend."

"Jazz is your best friend," Goby corrects.

"I can have more than one."

"You *just* said you couldn't be best friends with Peter because you already had a best friend!"

"I mean, I have *enough* best friends. I don't need another," Malcolm says, throwing himself backward so he can stick his feet up on the coffee table. "I think three best friends is enough, don't you? Three seems like enough."

Goby laughs, pushing Malcolm's face with their palm. When Malcolm retaliates with a yank at their ankle, the two dissolve into a wrestling match on the floor. He taps out when Goby traps his arm behind his head as they sit on his shoulders.

Once the sun has gone down far past the horizon, leaving the living room even darker than it was before, Malcolm invites Goby to sleep in his room with him. Malcolm sets up his phone to play music since neither of them can fall asleep easily to silence. (Goby requests the Muppet Movie soundtrack, and Malcolm complies with only a little complaint.)

"Hey Malcolm?" Goby whispers into the dark. Malcolm feels their breath against his cheek and scrunches his nose. They didn't brush their teeth.

"You reek," he says.

Goby chuckles, breathing more sour air into Malcolm's face, but he doesn't mind.

"Thank you," they say.

He knows they're not referring to the comment he made about their breath. He wraps his arm around their waist, tucking their head under his chin. "Of course."

It's silent for a moment, before Goby tacks on, "Loser."

Malcolm smiles. "Nerd."

With the rain pattering against his window and Kermit crooning into his ear about lovers and dreamers, Malcolm falls asleep quickly.

5

"Mal...Mal. *Malcolm*!"

Malcolm jolts awake, catching himself just before he can topple over the edge of the bed. He can already feel a bruise on his leg where Goby must have kicked him in their sleep.

"Malcolm, dude, I'm so sorry," Goby's saying frantically, and Malcolm finds himself waking quickly as he registers the panic in their voice. They're standing at the edge of the bed, bouncing from foot to foot. "You're not *technically* late, but I know you like to get there early and—well, you're definitely not gonna be early, but if you hurry you might—"

Malcolm's arm shoots out like the strike of a viper in his hurry to grab his phone from the nightstand. Dead. It must have died sometime in the night. He usually charges it while he sleeps, but since the storm took out the power that wasn't an option. *Dammit.*

He shouldn't have fallen asleep playing music last night, it completely drained the battery. That means he missed his alarms.

"*Shit*," Malcolm hisses. "What time is it?"

"Uh," Goby scratches their cheek. "9:52."

Malcolm spits out a creative string of obscenities, hurling himself out of bed. If he skips the shower, brushes his teeth quickly, maybe skips the hair product too...

Goby helps him, scrambling to get his clothes ready. They throw him his work shirt as he jumps into his slacks, and he haphazardly shoves his arms into the sleeves as Goby sprints to the toaster. He shoves his feet into his work shoes, cursing when the backs pinch his heels.

"Hold up," Goby says as he's darting out the door.

Malcolm turns around, still doing up the top buttons of his shirt, and Goby shoves an unevenly buttered piece of toast into his mouth.

"Okay, gogogo!" Goby says, waving their hands at him in a shoo-ing motion.

"Hm-hmph!" Malcolm says, crumbs flying out of his mouth.

"You're welcome!" Goby shouts as he sprints off.

He bounds down the stairs, taking them two at a time, and crashes into the pub. His phone is still dead so he's not sure what time it is, but the few regulars occupying the pub's corner tables let him know that he's properly late for the first time in his life. He swallows the bite of toast left in his mouth and tries to ignore the fact that he's begun to shake.

"Oh, there you are! I was getting worried you might have decided to play hookie without me," Mona smiles as Malcolm makes his way to her. She pauses to look him over, her brows furrowing. "You okay, love?"

Malcolm tries to catch his breath as he walks behind the bar. His heart is beating harder than it should, and his palms are definitely sweating. He wipes them down on his pants. "I'm fine."

"Are you sure?" Mona says, reaching over to hold his arm. He pulls it away. "You seem a bit...all over the place."

No, he's not fine. He knows he's not.

But he *should* be fine, because this isn't a big deal, and it's pissing him off even more that he's reacting to such a small thing because it's *not a big deal* and something's touching his skin—

"Malcolm?"

—and there's music playing over the speakers and people across the pub talking and one of the lights overhead keeps flickering and he needs to call someone to fix it and something keeps *touching his fucking skin*—

Malcolm's arm darts up and behind his head, yanking vigorously at the shirt tag that's been scratching at his neck.

"Stupid—*fucking*—" Malcolm tugs at it harshly, but it won't budge.

"Settle, Malcolm, don't rip it," Mona says, bringing a hand up to his neck. "I'll get it."

Malcolm clenches his jaw, teeth grinding. Her feather-light touch is just as bad as the tag. She seems to sense the way his shoulders tense, and she takes her hand away from his neck so she's only touching his shirt collar. A moment later he hears a *snip!* and the irritating tag is gone.

Malcolm sighs. "Thank you."

"Are you sure you're alright, Mal?" Mona asks, her voice quieter than before.

"I'm fine," he says, dragging a hand down his face. "Just woke up late. My phone died in the middle of the night, so none of my alarms worked."

"Oh, hun, I'm sorry," she says, and she brings a hand up to lightly touch his arm.

He flinches from the touch and snaps, "Well, if you were actually *here* this morning then I might have—"

He cuts himself off with a sharp inhale, but he can already see the hurt in Mona's eyes.

"I'm sorry," she says quietly, and he knows she genuinely means it. "I slept over at Jazz's place. I should've—"

"No, no, don't apologize," Malcolm says. He taps the tips of his fingers to his thumb, from forefinger to pinky and then back again, trying to calm himself. "I'm sorry. That was unfair. She's your girlfriend, there's no reason for you to stay at the apartment just to make sure I wake up on time. You're not my mom."

Mona stays carefully silent for a moment, keeping her hands clasped in front of her. She glances over Malcolm, then says kindly, "Do you need to go back home? Take the day off? It's definitely going to be a slow day, I can handle it myself."

Malcolm's already shaking his head before she's finished. "No, I'm alright, really. Just need to...collect myself."

Mona nods her head. "Alright, well, at least take a break to cool down. This place is practically empty, so take as long as you need."

Malcolm hesitates for a moment, but Mona gives him a stern look until he finally nods. "Alright. Alright. But get me if you need me, okay?"

"Same to you, darling," Mona says.

He leaves through the back of the store and into the alley off the side of the building, all the while praying that none of the patrons saw him snap like that. He probably looked rabid when he came in, and blowing up at Mona didn't help.

He sits down, dragging his legs up until his arms rest on his knees. He lets his head fall back until it bumps against the brick wall behind him. He breathes in. The air is always rank out here thanks to the garbage bins, but it's somehow better than inside, where everything is just. *Too much.*

He never knows why that happens. Why suddenly lights are too bright and music is too loud and talking and touching and *everything* is just far, far too much. It's like a switch being flipped in his brain, and he never knows what to do to make things better but to shut himself away and wait for things to feel calm again. Otherwise he erupts, and sometimes the people he cares about get stuck in the fire.

He feels his eyes begin to sting, and he lets the tears fall now that he's alone. This helps sometimes, too. Crying. But sometimes it just makes him feel worse. Puffy, burning eyes and that awful clogged feeling in your throat.

He hopes that's not the case this time. It's a bit too late to stop.

"Malcolm?"

You have got to be kidding me, Malcolm thinks.

Malcolm looks towards the entrance of the alleyway, where Peter stands with one hand in his pocket and the other hand awkwardly hovering at his side. Malcolm isn't quite sure what to do, but he knows if he talks that his voice will crack or something equally as embarrassing, so he stays quiet.

Do not come closer. Don't you dare come closer.

Peter comes closer. Malcolm curses the universe.

"What's wrong with you?" Peter says.

It might be the fact that Malcolm can't tell if Peter's saying it out of concern or out of judgment, or maybe the fact that Malcolm knows Peter can see the redness in his eyes and the dampness of his cheeks, but he feels every nerve in his body explode with rapidfire anger, and he snaps.

"Would you just fuck *off*, Peter!" Malcolm shouts. "I would literally rather you be anywhere else right now. Just fucking *go*."

"You—"

"*GO!* Leave me the *fuck alone.*"

Peter teeters backwards, eyes wide. Malcolm can feel his heartbeat in his neck, his chest rising and falling rapidly. He lets his head fall back rougher than he should, jaw clenched against the brief stab of pain that knocks through his skull when his head meets the wall. He keeps his eyes shut tight. He doesn't want to see whatever expression Peter has on his face. He doesn't want to see what other hurt he's caused today.

Peter doesn't say anything else. Malcolm hears his footsteps as he leaves the alleyway, fading until they've disappeared completely. It's what Malcolm wanted, but for some ridiculous and idiotic reason it still makes his heart sink.

The ground is still damp from yesterday's storm, and the coldness of it seeps into Malcolm's clothes. A drop of rain falls from a pipe above Malcolm and drips into the puddle next to his feet.

He lowers his head into his arms and cries.

6

The portable radio from the pub is never used, as far as Malcolm is aware, so he's pretty sure it's only barely considered stealing to take it from the pub and bring it to his apartment late that night. It's like taking home furniture someone's left on the curb, sort of. It was Mona's suggestion in the first place anyway. He was so worried about his phone dying again the next time he fell asleep to music, she insisted he take the radio to ease his mind. (She had originally suggested moving the record player into his bedroom, but Malcolm said Jazz would riot if it was removed from the living room.)

He didn't tell Mona about what happened with Peter in the alleyway. He has to physically shake his head to keep the memory from replaying over and over in his mind, his face burning with shame every time he thinks of Peter's stricken face. He could apologize, he *wants* to apologize, but that's just not what the two of them *do*. They glare and they scowl and they move on. They don't apologize. Do they?

No wonder the guy hates him.

Malcolm sets up the radio on his nightstand, letting the music play as he strips off his clothes and shimmies into a pair of Spider-Man pajama pants. The dial is still turned to the station he had set up from before. (He's not surprised to find out he was the last person to touch the old thing.)

The station is playing a song he recognizes but can't quite pinpoint. He's brushing his teeth in the bathroom connected to his room, occasionally inspecting his face for acne (thank you, testosterone injections), when the music fades out and a voice fills the room.

"That was 'Roadrunner' by the Modern Lovers," a man says. Malcolm pauses with the toothbrush still in his mouth, listening to the new voice. It's not the phlegmy old guy from before, thank god.

"I used to listen to the *Modern Lovers* album on repeat throughout my freshman year in high school, right when I was getting more passionate about music. I remember saving up to buy that album and digging my dad's old record player out of storage just to play it all the time. Drove him absolutely up the *wall*." He pauses to laugh a little bit, the sound altered and crackly on the radio. "Pops, if you're listening, that one was for you. Thought you'd finally escaped it, huh?"

The man laughs again, and Malcolm finds himself smiling along with him. He likes this new guy's voice. Youthful. Happy. Actually interested in what he's talking about. It's almost familiar.

He spits into the sink and shuffles over to the radio, turning up the volume.

"For all you insomniacs out there just tuning in, I'm your host for the evening, Max Rebo," the man says. "I'm new at the station, but don't worry, I've still got all your favorites lined up for the night. And for any of you night owls who are interested in stopping by sometime tonight, you can call in at—"

Malcolm's not sure what exactly compels him to do it, but in an instant his phone is in his hand, and he's typing the number in as the host calls it out. His phone rings, and someone who isn't the man on the radio answers first. He assumes it's a screener to make sure he isn't a troll of some sort, but the speaker doesn't ask him any questions past his name, just boredly tells him to hold until the host is ready.

"Oh, shit," the man on the radio mutters, a note of surprise in his voice, his professional demeanor slipping for half a moment. "Looks like we have a caller already!"

There's a click on the phone Malcolm has pressed to his ear, and suddenly Max Rebo is right there, his voice on Malcolm's phone as well as the radio.

"Welcome, welcome, caller," he says, an almost nervous lilt to his voice. He sounds young, possibly close to Malcolm's age. He did say he was new—perhaps he's new not just to the station, but to radio entirely. The thought helps calm Malcolm's nerves.

"Hey," Malcolm says after a pause.

The man laughs easily, and Malcolm's shoulders lose some of their tension at the sound. "Hello. How are we doing tonight, caller?"

Malcolm panics for a moment, wondering why exactly he called. Instead of answering the question like any sane person would, with a 'Fine' or maybe a 'Not too bad, and you?' he blurts out the first thing that he had on his mind before calling in.

"What kind of name is Max Rebo?" Malcolm says, blushing brilliantly as soon as the words have left his mouth. He grips the fabric of his pants with his free hand, fighting the urge to smack his forehead with his palm. It's silent for several unbearable seconds.

Luckily, Rebo seems to find Malcolm's comment more amusing than insulting. A bright laugh filters through the speaker before it's quickly muffled, almost as if Rebo hadn't meant to do it, and Malcolm turns down the radio so he can hear it better through his phone. Rebo's voice is clearer than it was on the radio when he responds, "Well, that's just not fair! I don't even know your name and here you are trashing mine."

"There is no way that's your real name," Malcolm says as his brain shouts *why the fuck are you still talking!*

"It's a nickname, actually," Rebo explains. Malcolm wonders if he's smiling.

"Oh," Malcolm says a bit awkwardly. He rubs his neck, eyebrows furrowing. "Hang on, is the whole thing a nickname or just the Rebo part?"

"Nuh-uh. My turn for questions, caller." His voice is low and teasing when he asks, "With whom do I have the pleasure of speaking?"

Malcolm clears his throat, standing from his bed. He's never been good at sitting still.

"Um, well," Malcolm falters. He stands next to his window and lets his eyes follow a pedestrian as they jaywalk, waiting until they've safely made it across to look away. "Is it a requirement to give my real name?"

"Absolutely not," Rebo says. "As we've established, Max Rebo isn't exactly the name I've got on my birth certificate."

Malcolm murmurs, "Neither is mine." He sputters then, remembering he's live on the radio, and says, "Clark. You can call me Clark, if you'd like."

"Like Clark Kent?" Rebo's definitely smiling now. Malcolm can hear it in his voice.

"Something like that," Malcolm says.

"Cute name."

Cute? Malcolm purses his lips, his cheeks flushing. Is he being flirted with? Is that what's happening?

Is he going to flirt back?

"Wish I could say the same about yours, Rebo," Malcolm says.

Rebo laughs, and he doesn't try to stifle it this time. "Ouch. I'll tell you what, Clark, if you can figure out where I got the name 'Max Rebo'—*without Googling it*—I'll give you my real name. And don't go looking up the radio station's website, either. That's cheating."

"So your name isn't actually Max?"

"Nope," he says, popping the p. "Not even close."

"Yeah, you don't sound like a Max," Malcolm says, and it makes no sense but he's smiling anyway.

"What the hell does a Max sound like?"

"Cuter, probably."

He can hear Rebo gasp in offense, and he smiles. "I'll have you know, I'm incredibly handsome. Dazzling smile, sparkling eyes, the whole nine yards."

"Is that why they stuck you on the radio?"

"Jeez, you're full of fire tonight, Clark," Rebo's laughter leaks through his words, and Malcolm can't help but laugh along with him. "You know, I'm surprised anyone actually called in. The audience for this station doesn't actually include a whole lot of night owls—fans of classic rock are either young enough to use Spotify or old enough to be dead asleep by this hour—and being a newbie at the station and all, I didn't really...expect anyone."

"Well," Malcolm hesitates, not entirely sure what to say to that. Sorry? "I'm sure there's someone out there listening in, shouting at their radio for us to get a move on with the music."

"Ah, they'll just have to wait their turn."

Malcolm bites at his pinky, the force of his smile jostling the phone. "How long am I allowed to, uh...?"

"Oh! Oh, um, hang on." There's a short pause and the squeaking noise of a chair turning. When his voice returns, it starts out quieter, almost as if his head was turned away from the mic before he remembered himself. "Uh, my supervisor just shrugged, so...yeah, not entirely sure what that means."

Malcolm returns to his seat at his bed, and Lady Governor hops up into his lap. He pets her back and chews at the inside of his cheek before letting it go and saying, "If I have to go, I can always call back in. If you aren't busy with your dozens of other callers, of course."

The laugh Rebo lets out is short and soft. It might be Malcolm's favorite so far. "That would be nice. You're a pretty interesting guy, Clark."

"All I've done is make fun of you," Malcolm says. "Do you have a thing for humiliation?"

"Nah," he says. "I just like a guy with some spark in him, that's all."

Malcolm licks his bottom lip, ducking his head as his cheeks flame. Lady Governor looks at him curiously, and he shields her eyes with his free hand.

Definitely flirting, then.

7

The clock reads 12:13pm when Malcolm wakes up the next day, and a brief spike of panic races through his chest before he remembers he has work off today. He stretches out, starfishing across the bed and groaning noisily. He takes a moment to come to his senses, sleep still fogging his mind, before throwing his legs over the bed and making his way to the kitchen.

Taped to the fridge, he finds a note. It's decorated with several strawberry stickers and a fairly decent doodle of Lady Governor. The real Lady Governor curls around his ankle, purring in interest.

> *Malcolm,*
>
> *Goby's at work and I'm going to the skate park. There are banana waffles in the fridge. Please use the toaster, you'll ruin them in the microwave.*
>
> *Love,*
>
> *Your favorite roommate*

"God bless Mona Greene," Malcolm says, grabbing the leftover waffles out of the fridge. Lady Governor chirps at his feet in agreement, knowing she'll get to have some as well. He can never deny her a nibble of whatever he's eating, as much as Jazz says he's spoiling her.

As if the thought summoned her, the front door suddenly bangs open and Jazz strides through. Malcolm jumps at the force of her entrance.

"Shit, Jazz!" Malcolm yelps. "Don't do that, you nearly made me drop my waffles."

WELCOME, CALLER 41

"Did you just wake up?" Jazz says, closing the door with the sole of her boot. "You look like shit."

"Thanks," he grumbles, popping the cold waffles into the toaster. He grabs whipped cream from the fridge and peanut butter from the pantry, throwing the latter to Jazz. She catches it easily, grabbing a spoon from the drawer and plunging it into the jar before shoving it into her mouth.

"Seriously, dude, your eye bags have eye bags," she says, noisily smacking her way through the peanut butter. "How late did you stay up?"

Malcolm grumbles, "Like, 2? 2:15?"

Jazz makes a noise, something like *pfft*. "Rookie."

"Some of us need sleep, Jazz," he responds. "We can't all be little gremlins who thrive off Red Bulls and jars of Skippy."

"Why'd you stay up if you're such a sleep slut, then?" Jazz says, hopping up onto the kitchen island.

Malcolm shrugs. "I was listening to music."

Jazz puckers her mouth, her top lip jostling her septum piercing as she squints at him. He hates how easily people can get him to talk if they just wait him out. For Jazz, it never takes longer than a few seconds for her to wear him down.

"There's this radio show I started listening to," Malcolm explains. His waffles pop out, and he turns away to lay them out on a napkin and spray an unhealthy amount of whipped cream on them, thankful for the excuse to not look Jazz in the eye. "You can, like, call in and stuff."

"You called in on a radio show?" Jazz says, and he can hear the incredulity in her voice. "Why?"

"I dunno, it seemed like it'd be fun. Plus the host seemed...nice."

There's a pause, and he can imagine the face Jazz is making. The slow dawning realization.

"Nice," Jazz repeats slowly.

Malcolm nods, finally turning around with a bite of waffle in his mouth. Jazz has her eyes narrowed and her lips quirked up into a smirk.

"And what did this host sound like?"

Malcolm shrugs again, wishing his body remembered how to do anything else. "I dunno. Nice."

"Uh huh," Jazz nods, tossing her spoon into the sink and leaning forward, her elbows on her knees.

Malcolm tuts and heads into the living room. "Shut up."

"I didn't say anything!"

"You were going to!"

"Well, of course I was *going* to," Jazz relents, hopping off of the counter to follow him. "Baby boy's got a new crush!"

"I do *not*."

"You absolutely do." She plops down on the floor, next to where Malcolm had flopped belly-first onto the couch, hiding his blush in the cushion. "Would you say their voice was more Han Solo, Ferris Bueller or Elizabeth Swann?"

Malcolm looks up at her and scowls. "How dare you use my bisexual awakenings against me."

Jazz waits in silence, eyebrows raised.

Malcolm sighs. "Han Solo."

Jazz lets out an '*oooh*,' biting her lip mockingly. "Hot."

"Shut up!"

"Give me a name, I need a name."

Malcolm closes his eyes, accepting that this is his fate now. "Max Rebo is the name he uses."

Jazz pauses for a moment, her eyebrows furrowing. "That sounds really familiar, actually."

Malcolm turns his head to her, excitement bubbling in his gut before he can stamp it down. "Really? Do you know where it's from? He said if I can guess where it's from then he'll tell me his real name."

Jazz leans back from where Malcolm had steadily gotten closer, nearly falling off the couch in the process. "Well, now I'm definitely not gonna tell you."

"What?" Malcolm's face falls. "Why not?"

"I can't just ruin his weird attempt at flirting right off the bat!" Jazz says. "That's some cute shit, dude. He obviously made up this game so that you'd have a reason to come back! No, you have to figure it out yourself."

Malcolm falls back onto the couch, the old leather squeaking. "I don't know if it's flirting."

"Don't be stupid," Jazz says. "That's flirting."

"I don't even know if he's queer! He could be straight and I'm just looking into something that isn't even there."

Jazz purses her lips and picks up the stack of googly eyes that Goby left on the coffee table. She starts taking them off and sticking them on her leather jacket. "Ask him next time."

"What?"

"You're calling in again next time, right? Ask him if he's straight or not."

"Jazz," Malcolm says seriously. "I can't just ask someone—someone on *live radio*—if they're gay. What if he is gay but he's in the closet? Or what if he's straight and I just make an absolute fool of myself?"

"There are ways to go about it without directly saying, 'Hey, do you happen to be a raging homo by any chance?'" Jazz says. "Just, like, ask him about his dating life or something. Slip it in there, all casual-like."

"Casual-like," Malcolm repeats. He hates that he's starting to warm up to the idea. Dating could potentially come up as a topic of conversation on a late-night radio show, yeah? It's possible. This could work.

Jazz nods her head seriously. "Casual-like."

Malcolm pauses then. "Hang on, why are you here?"

"What the fuck, man?" Jazz says, lifting her arms in offense.

Malcolm laughs, throwing a pillow at her that she dodges with ease. "No, I mean, Mona's at the skatepark. You'd usually be tripping over yourself to watch your girlfriend look cool on a board, what are you doing at the apartment?"

Jazz pauses, using Lady Governor's presence at her side as a distraction. She takes off a googly eye from her jacket and places it on Lady's forehead.

When she doesn't respond, Malcolm says sternly, "Jazmine."

"Mona said you might need a distraction," Jazz finally says, sticking another googly eye on Lady's chin. She's a surprisingly patient cat. "She told me about what happened at the pub."

Malcolm momentarily worries that she's talking about what happened in the alleyway with Peter—but no, Mona didn't know about that.

"I'm sorry," Malcolm says, eyes downcast. "I'm so sorry, I shouldn't have said all that to Mona. I was way over the line."

"I mean, yeah, you shouldn't have," Jazz says, nodding. "But she said you've already apologized, like, a hundred times. I'm not mad, dude, and neither is she. We're just worried about you."

"You have nothing to worry about. I was just tired."

"It was more than that," Jazz says sternly. "She says you looked like your world was falling apart when you came into the pub. Like you'd crumble at the drop of a hat."

Malcolm stays silent.

"Is it happening more often?" Jazz asks, her voice far kinder than it usually is.

He wants to tell her to stop, to say something crass and loud. He needs her to be normal with him. He can't deal with everyone changing up their routines. First Peter being companionable, and now Jazz being nice. He can't handle all of these changes—but he knows he owes her an explanation.

"It's not like how it was in school," he says, and she relaxes.

His episodes (he's never sure what else to call them) happened pretty frequently in school. He spent the majority of his weekdays on edge, feeling like a soda can getting shaken up as he squeezed through the crowded halls to get to their classrooms where everything was just too bright and loud, and it would build and build until he'd lash out. He was usually able to keep it in until he got home, punching at his pillow and at his arms and legs until all of that energy drained out of him. But sometimes he'd let it out on his friends. On Jazz. It's a wonder how he kept any of them.

"What can we do?" Jazz says.

"You know I don't know the answer to that," Malcolm says. He reaches over and plucks one of the googly eyes off of Jazz's jacket, sticking it onto Lady Governor's ear, which flicks a few times in response. "I just keep it bottled up the best I can until I can go somewhere to calm down."

"I hate that you have to go through it at all," Jazz says, and he looks up at her curiously.

"Me? I'm the one hurting people when I get like that."

"You hurt people the way a wounded animal hurts people, dude," Jazz says. "You don't mean to hurt anyone, you're just in pain. I see it in your face, in your whole fuckin' body, everytime it happens. I just hate that we can't help."

Malcolm slides off of the couch and sits down next to Jazz, bumping his forehead against her shoulder. The leather of her jacket is cool and solid against his skin. She pats at his knee, sighing. He wishes it didn't sound so defeated.

He doesn't say anything. He wishes he could say that they'll figure something out. That there *is* something they can do to help. But he doesn't know a single thing about why it happens or how to change it, how to cope with it other than by isolating himself or exploding.

Jazz seems to notice him retreating into his head, and she kindly changes the subject.

"You've got a pretty rad cat, man," she says, sticking yet another googly eye on Lady Governor. She's starting to look more and more like a biblically accurate angel.

Malcolm smiles weakly. Lady Governor always had a way of dragging him out of his pity parties. "Yeah, she's pretty neat."

Lady Governor meows, a pitiful high-pitched sound that was one of the reasons why he took her in when he first found her. She steps over into his lap carefully and makes herself comfortable, still ignoring the plethora of sticky eyeballs on her fur.

"You gonna call Mr. Rebo again?" Jazz asks.

Malcolm makes a face. "Don't call him that, it makes him sound like a dad."

"Are you saying you wouldn't be interested if he were a DILF?"

"You shouldn't be allowed to speak," Malcolm says, and Jazz shoves at his shoulder with her own. He laughs and continues, "Yeah, I think I'm gonna call in again. He said his segment is every weekend, including Fridays."

Jazz perks up. "Are you gonna call tonight then? It's Saturday!"

"I know it's Saturday." Malcolm hesitates for a moment, poking his tongue against his bottom lip. "Should I not wait? Would that be too, like, clingy?"

"Don't fucking wait, dude! You're probably the best thing that blessed his boring night," Jazz says. "Can I listen in? I want to listen in."

"No, you may not," Malcolm says.

"Why not?"

"Because if he *does* like men and is also somehow interested in me of all people, I don't need you ruining my chances by dicking around while I talk to him."

"I'll be silent as a mouse! Cross my heart and hope to die," Jazz says. She swipes her finger across her chest in a slicing motion, complete with surprisingly accurate slicing sound effects, before letting her head fall to the side with her tongue rolled out dramatically.

Malcolm shakes his head, "Not tonight, at least. Maybe another time."

"I'm holding you to that."

Malcolm smiles, but it falters when his phone buzzes in his pocket. He feels his face pale, and Jazz sits up.

"Is it—"

"I don't know," he says, digging the phone out of his pocket. His shoulders relax when he sees the contact. "No. No, it's just Mona."

Jazz nods, relaxing as Malcolm answers the phone.

"Mona Lisa," Malcolm says as a greeting.

"Never heard that one before," Mona says. "Are you available tonight, love?"

"Uh, yeah," Malcolm says, looking at Jazz, who raises a quizzical eyebrow at him. Why can everyone do that but him? "What do you need?"

Apparently, Mona needs him at work tonight. Two of the night workers gave up their shifts, so the pub will be short staffed. Mona, being too kind for her own good, had already said she and him could fill in for them.

"I'm so sorry," Mona says. "I shouldn't have said you could do it without asking, especially after the day you had yesterday—you need *rest*, and here I am making you do even more work—"

Malcolm has to shout her name a few times for her to relax, but he eventually convinces her he's fine enough to work.

"Can't pause my life every time I have a breakdown," Malcolm says. "I'll be there."

Jazz doesn't seem as convinced.

"Are you *sure* you're alright to go in?" Jazz says. "I know you said this episode wasn't as bad as in school, but from what Mona told me—"

"Mona hasn't seen me during an episode like you have, remember?" Malcolm says. "By the time she knew me in college, I was having episodes every few months instead of every other day. She was just surprised, that's all."

Jazz still seems unconvinced, so Malcolm touches her cheek until she looks him in the eye with no small amount of reluctance.

"I promise you," he says emphatically, "I'm fine."

8

He should've said no. He should've hung up on Mona and stayed home.

Barely ten minutes after he's started his shift, he looks outside and sees the very last person he wants to see. The arrogant bastard's collar is coolly pulled up against the wind, his eyes squinted as he shoves at the front door. (It's been storming on and off all week—seems like it'll be on again soon enough.) Malcolm hits the deck and hides underneath the bar counter just as Peter enters the pub.

Mona is a saint for keeping her cool. She throws him a curious look before glancing up at who can only be Peter and saying, "Hey there, stranger!"

"Oh, hey!" Peter says, pleasantly surprised. Malcolm can sort of see the two of them in the mirror along the shelves. Mona is taller than either of them and blocks most of Peter's body, but Malcolm can see his hands resting on the bar. His skin is a cooler, deeper brown than Mona's. "Sorry, was it...Mary?"

"Mona," she corrects, waving her hand to dismiss Peter's embarrassment before it's even there.

"That's a cool name," he says, voice laced with genuine interest.

Malcolm can see part of Peter's smile in the mirror, crinkling his eyes. He's so much nicer to Mona than he ever is with Malcolm. Or maybe he's just happier. Malcolm doesn't know why the thought tugs unpleasantly at his chest.

"Thank you very much! I chose it myself," she says, placing a hand on her hip. "Can I get you anything?"

Peter taps his fingers against the counter twice. "What would you give someone to ease their nerves?"

Nerves? Malcolm thinks. *What's he up to?*

His back is starting to ache, and he suddenly wishes he had the brains to pick a more comfortable hiding spot before getting stuck in this crouched position.

Mona makes a curious noise as she prepares a drink. "You've got something big tonight?"

"Nah, not big," he says, and now that Malcolm thinks about it, he does sound a bit nervous. "Just got my hopes up to talk to someone later, and I'm not sure how it's gonna go. Or if he'll even show up."

Someone? What kind of someone? An employer kind of someone? A *date* kind of someone?

"I'm sure it'll be fine," Mona says. He sees her in the mirror, reaching over to place a comforting hand on Peter. He relaxes under her touch. She always has that effect on people. "You seem like a pretty cool guy. Whatever it is you're worried about, you're gonna kick ass."

She hands him his drink, something auburn (Malcolm wasn't paying enough attention to see what she made). Peter laughs, and tips the drink to her. "Thanks," he says, before taking a sip. His eyes widen and he looks at the glass in his hand with delighted surprise.

"Good, right?" Mona says. Peter barely has a chance to respond before Mona is perking up, turning away excitedly. "Oh! I know what'll help distract you."

Malcolm watches her reach over to the terrarium that's currently hidden underneath the counter. His eyes go wide and he shakes his head at her furiously, and she throws him a mischievous smile before turning back to Peter.

"This is Terrance."

There's a moment of silence. In the mirror, Malcolm can see Peter leaning in close to the terrarium, looking slightly confused.

"All I see are leaves and sticks."

"Hang on, he's good at hiding," Mona says, before opening up the terrarium and dipping her hand inside. She brings her hand back out, holding it out to Peter. "Ta-da! Isn't he gorgeous?"

Peter's eyes are wide, but in interest rather than alarm. "Holy shit," he breathes. "That is *cool*."

"Right?" Mona says, twisting her arm as the stick bug crawls across her palm and her fingers. "He's the pub mascot."

He's definitely not.

"I love him," Peter says. He holds out his own hand hesitantly, drink forgotten. "Can I?"

"Of course!" Mona says, placing her hand near Peter's so Terrance can slowly crawl across their palms. "Just don't tell my coworker, he's always making a fuss about OSHA."

"Well, he isn't here, is he?" Peter says. "Nothing he can do about it."

"Precisely, my friend," Mona says, poking at Malcolm's leg with her toe. "If he *really* cared about OSHA violations, he'd be stopping me right now. Guess he doesn't mind as much as we thought."

Malcolm rolls his eyes, wishing Mona would look down at him again just so he can send her his most devastating glare.

The two of them talk for far longer than Malcolm was prepared to crouch for. By the time Peter has left, Malcolm's arm has gone numb where he had been putting most of his weight, and his neck has developed a painful crick. Mona reaches down and hauls him to his feet, already talking.

"That was the guy from the record shop I was telling you about!" Mona says. "He's just your type, don't you think? Hell, if I were straight, he'd be my type too."

"*Him?*" Malcolm says. "Mona, that's Peter!"

Mona blinks at him. "Yes, Peter from the record shop."

"No, Mona," Malcolm says slowly. "Peter, my archnemesis."

Her head snaps towards the front door, even though Peter is long gone. "*He's* the guy you poured soup on? But he's so sweet!"

"I didn't do that on purpose!"

"We need to get you back on his good side," Mona says in a way that makes Malcolm suspect she's already strategizing in her head.

"Who says I'm the one who needs to get on his good side? Maybe *he* needs to get on *my* good side," Malcolm argues.

"You have to let me teach you how to skate," Mona says, ignoring his protests entirely. "He'll see you outside his shop and won't be able to resist your rebellious charm."

"With my luck, he'll see me wipe out and break my nose first."

Mona looks like she's about to argue, but Malcolm shuts down the conversation as another patron enters the pub. Mona is undeterred; she continues to throw several suggestive winks his way throughout the night, including a few not-so-subtle (and slightly inaccurate) hand gestures that leave him flustered and whipping a cleaning cloth at her hip. He should have never introduced her to Jazz.

He tries to race to his room as quietly as he can knowing Goby might be asleep. The shift he took kept him until midnight, making him an hour late to Rebo's show. The show will be on for a couple more hours, but Malcolm doesn't want to waste a second of it. Mona was kind enough to clean up for the both of them, seeing how antsy he was to get home. He'll never be able to repay her for all of the favors she's done him.

When he finally leaps into bed, still fully clothed and panting, it's twelve minutes past midnight. He slaps the on button for the radio, and it buzzes to life just as a song fades out.

"That was 'Should I Stay or Should I Go' by the Clash," a familiar voice says, and Malcolm relaxes back into his bed. Rebo delves into a short story about the band and his experience with their music; his sister is a bigger fan of them than he is, apparently, and he dedicates that song to her. Malcolm likes that he talks about his family so much. It makes him feel warm.

"Now, I know I haven't had much luck so far tonight, but we're gonna give this another try," Rebo says, and Malcolm sits up. "If there's anyone—maybe even, uh...never mind, just—if there's anyone who'd like to call in tonight, here's our number."

Malcolm whips out his phone, punching in the numbers. This time he saves it to his contacts. The screener answers him first, like last time, and he's told to hold until the host is ready. There's a click over the receiver, and Malcolm swallows despite the desert that his mouth has become.

"Welcome, welcome, to the Marvelous Max Rebo show!"

There's a voice in the distance that sounds like it says, "*That's not what it's called!*"

"Not yet, but it'll catch on, just you wait," Rebo replies to them. Then his attention is back on Malcolm. "Welcome to the show, caller! Don't mind my supervisor, she's a stick in the mud. Who do we have here?"

"You really don't get calls often, do you?" Malcolm says, and he's already breaking out into a smile.

There's a second of silence before Rebo is speaking again, sounding just short of elated. "Oh, please. Please tell me this is who I think it is."

Malcolm sighs, hoping he sounds more put out than he truly feels. "It's Clark."

"Clark Kent!" Rebo shouts, and there's a sharp sound like he's clapped his hands together in triumph. "I was hoping you'd come back!"

"I told you I would," Malcolm says. He grabs a pillow from behind his head and hugs it to his chest. "Sorry I'm a bit late to the show. I haven't lost my spot as your favorite caller have I?"

Rebo makes a dismissive noise. "Never."

The call goes well into the night, far longer than their last. He learns that Rebo's favorite animal is a panda, and Malcolm confides that iguanas are his. Rebo's favorite color is green, and Malcolm's is orange. It isn't until the call is over that Malcolm remembers Jazz's advice on how to ask Rebo about his sexuality, but there's a strong part of him that knows this won't be his last chance to ask about it. He can wait.

Even after his call has long ended, Malcolm stays up until Rebo is signing off from the show at 2am. "Goodnight and sleep well, everybody," Rebo says in a warm, low voice, as if he were lulling the audience to sleep himself.

Malcolm thinks about Rebo as he closes his eyes, his walls lowered in the early morning. It's safe to have feelings for him, Malcolm rationalizes in his mind. He's just a voice. An untouchable dream. Nothing could really happen—so it's safe.

Malcolm wakes only once within the night to the boom of thunder and Lady Governor jumping from her place on his chest to scamper out of his room in alarm. Apart from this, he sleeps soundly through the night.

9

Malcolm was 19 and freshly moved out of his childhood home when he found Lady Governor during one of the worst weeks of his life. It was raining when he found her. (He considered it an appropriate reflection of his mood at the time, not yet realizing that rain in Bugswick was just about as common as smog in LA.)

He had spotted her in an alley, her frail black form hiding in between some crates in an attempt to shelter herself from the cold weather. His eyes had already been burning and his throat was thick with excess emotion, but for a moment, he had something to worry about other than himself. So he went to her.

He sat in front of her, several feet away. He didn't mind that his pants were getting wet and the gravel was uncomfortable beneath his palms. It was probably nothing compared to what she had gone through.

"Hello," he said, barely a whisper.

She meowed, small and broken, as if she hadn't used her voice in days. His chest ached..

"Do you have a family?" he asked. He looked around the alleyway. No one seemed to be around. "How long have you been out here?"

There was an indent around her neck, as if a collar that was far too tight had been left on her for far too long. She licked at the spots where her skin showed through her fur, gnawing at some of the raw areas. She meowed again, and Malcolm wiped at his eyes.

"You hang right here," he said, rising from his seat. She jumped back, hissing, and he kept his palms up as he backed away. "I'll be right back. It's gonna be alright."

He returned quickly with some leftover chicken from his apartment, and sat an inch closer to her than he did before. He ripped off a small piece and placed it close to her before leaning away again.

"I'm Malcolm," he said, folding his hands into his lap. "I'll come up with a name for you eventually."

She mewled and blinked at him, her ears flattened to her skull.

"It's okay. Take your time."

After several minutes of hesitation, she stepped forward. She had a limp in one foot that Malcolm couldn't see before. She grabbed the chicken quickly with her teeth, pulling it back to her in between the crates so she could eat in the shadows.

Malcolm smiled in triumph, tearing off another piece and placing it on the ground a couple of inches closer to himself. She stared at him.

Malcolm sat back further, resting his back against the wall opposite the poor cat. She was too small for her age—a fully grown adult, maybe even a senior if the gray around her eyes were any indication. He could see her ribs through her skin. He could take care of her.

He felt his eyes stinging again, and he swiped away any tears that managed to escape.

"My dad died."

She blinked at him, stone still.

"It wasn't a shock, really," he said as he drew up his knees, wrapping his arms around his legs. "Lung cancer. We knew it was coming. Honestly, that's not even why I'm crying." He laughed at himself harshly, and the cat flinched back. He fell silent, whispering an apology.

"We didn't have the best relationship, but it wasn't the worst, really," he said. He pulled at one of his shoelaces, letting it come nearly undone. "But my mom..."

He trailed off. The cat took a step towards the chicken.

"My mom has never really accepted...any of this stuff about me. Honestly, the sexuality thing was easier for her than the gender thing. At least the sexuality thing was easier to ignore."

She grabbed the chicken with her teeth like before. This time she stayed where she was. Malcolm smiled for a moment, but it fell quickly.

"When I showed up to the funeral in a suit, she said—" he felt his throat close up and he cleared it, looking away so he wouldn't startle the cat again. "She said...uh, to quote her," —he laughed bitterly, quietly, before continuing— "'it's bad enough I lost a husband. I don't need you rubbing in the fact that I've lost a daughter, too.'"

He sniffed. The cat stared at him.

"She said some really awful stuff. Some bullshit about how dad wouldn't recognize me if he were alive, that I was—*disrespecting* his memory of me." It was getting difficult to speak through his tears, but at that point he couldn't seem to stop. He dropped his head, a sob ripping out of his throat.

"It's just so fucking hard sometimes," he said into his lap, his voice watery and uneven. He kept his eyes shut, breathing through clenched teeth. "Just. *So* fucking hard."

He counted his breaths, in and out.

In for 1...2...3...4...

Hold.

Out for 1...2...3...4...5...6—

He felt something soft bump at his hand, and he looked up quickly. The cat jumped back, so he froze. Her pupils dilated, waiting for him to make another sudden move. When he stayed still for several long moments, she gradually made her way back to him, stretching her neck out hesitantly until she could sniff at his knuckle. He slowly unfurled his fist, and she rubbed against his palm. He could feel her purring against his skin. He stared, unblinking.

"Hello," he said for the second time, more of an exhale than a word.

She stepped closer to him, and he lowered his legs to the ground. (The careful calculation of his movements reminded him of playing Operation. Slow and steady. Don't fuck up your patient.) She cautiously stepped into the V of his open legs, placing a paw against his thigh and meowing that pitiful meow.

"You're an awfully good listener," he said, smoothing his hand down her back. He could feel every bump in her spine. She purred again, loud and strong, stronger than he thought her frail body would be capable of.

"We've got a lot in common, I think," he said softly, rubbing behind her ears. She closed her eyes in content. "Both rejected. Both super cute. I think we're going to get along quite well."

10

Malcolm wakes far later than usual, and it takes him a moment to realize that the quiet noise he hears is coming from the radio—he must have forgotten to turn it off when he fell asleep. He turns it up a bit. (Rebo might not be hosting, but the music's still good.) It sounds like the Clash again, but it may be something else.

He stumbles into the kitchen, scratching at his chest as he yawns. The apartment is quiet apart from the music and the slapping of his feet against the hardwood floors. There's a note taped to the fridge again, this time to let him know about the sausage biscuits in the fridge. He blinks, rubbing at his eyes.

The extra hours of sleep leaves Malcolm feeling extra fogged and slow that afternoon, which is why it takes him so long to realize that something is wrong. He hasn't seen Lady Governor at all since he woke up.

His eyebrows furrow. He makes a clicking sound with his mouth. "Lady?" he calls out. "Lady Governooor! My lovely Lady!" He makes a few exaggerated kissing sounds. She usually wanders out at that. Nothing happens.

He shuffles into his room to turn off the radio, trying to listen for the soft *pap pap pap* of her paws against the floor. Still nothing.

He checks Goby and Mona's rooms. Empty. He checks the bathroom. Empty. Underneath his bed, behind the couch, inside every closet and cupboard. Empty. Empty. Empty.

He stops when he finally sees the front door. It's cracked open an inch.

He calls Mona.

"Lady's gone," Malcolm says as soon as the line clicks, panting as he races around the apartment. "She's—I woke up and I didn't see her anywhere and I've checked fucking *everywhere*—"

"Hold on," Mona says, her voice more serious than he's ever heard it, and after a moment he can hear two other voices on the line.

"Hey, what's going on?" Goby says.

"Lady Governor's missing," Jazz says. She must have already been with Mona to know.

"I've looked everywhere, I swear, and she's just not *here*," Malcolm says, pulling at his hair. "She's not—she's not—the front door was open, she must've—"

"Malcolm, breathe," Jazz says, solid and comforting. "We're going to find her. She's a strong girl, she'll be okay."

Malcolm nods even though he knows she can't see him. If he speaks, he might fall apart. In the background of the call, he can hear Goby speaking to someone. They're at work, he thinks.

"Malcolm, darling, we're on our way now," Mona says. "Just stay put."

"No, no," Malcolm says, "we have to start looking now, I don't know how long she's been gone, she could be—she could—"

"I'll go then," Goby says. "I'm closer to the apartment. Mona, Jazz, you guys start searching the roads. Malcolm and I can start covering the nearby buildings as soon as I get there."

"Aren't you at work?" Jazz asks.

"I got it covered," Goby says. "Ain't no way I'm gonna work on some dumb cars while my girl is missing. Malcolm, I'll be there in two minutes—wait for me, okay?"

Malcolm opens his mouth, wanting to protest, but he knows he's in no state to start searching on his own. Mona and Jazz have already voiced their agreements to the plan, but everyone is staying on the call. Malcolm leans against the kitchen counter and drags a hand over his eyes.

Goby arrives in record breaking time, panting heavily.

"Did you run here?" Malcolm says, already out the door and following Goby down the steps.

"Of course I did," Goby says. "Now where do we start?"

Before they head anywhere, Malcolm grabs Goby and pulls them into a fierce hug. He sniffles, burying his face in their neck. They wrap their arms around him tightly.

"Thank you," Malcolm mutters. "I know she's just a cat, but—"

"Hey," Goby says sharply, drawing away from Malcolm to hold him by the shoulders. "She's not just a cat. That's our girl out there, and we're gonna find her. Yeah?"

Malcolm blinks, wiping his hand over his eyes. "Yeah."

"My man," Goby says with a smile, patting Malcolm once. "Now where do you wanna start?"

They start at the pub. Malcolm circles the perimeter of the building while Goby checks inside. They meet up at the entrance, and Malcolm deflates when Goby says that no one inside had seen her. They migrate to the building over, checking inside storm drains along the way. It starts to rain, and Malcolm spits a curse as he pulls up his hood. Goby does the same, shuffling closer to him.

"She hates storms," Malcolm says.

"I know."

"She hates being wet."

"I know."

"She can't stand being cold."

"Malcolm," Goby says, stopping. Malcolm doesn't want to stop. "She's gonna be okay."

Malcolm shakes his head. "She's gonna think I abandoned her, Goby. Just like her last family. I can't do that to her."

"Which is exactly why we're gonna find her," they say, starting their trek down the sidewalk again.

They've searched five different stores and an entire apartment complex by the time Jazz and Mona pull up in the truck. The sun has begun to set, the inky night bleeding out over the sky like a bruise.

The rain has gotten worse, and there's a flash of white before thunder cracks overhead.

"Malcolm!" Mona shouts over the rain, leaning out of the passenger side window, getting her hair drenched in seconds.

"Did you guys find anything?" Malcolm calls back. He and Goby stand outside of Mr. Lu's, their arms shoved into their pockets, shrinking into themselves in an attempt to stay dry beneath their raincoats.

Mona shakes her head, blinking water out of her eyes. "Nothing. I think we need to go back."

"Back where?"

"Back home!" Jazz says from the driver's side. "It's a nightmare out here, there's no way we're going to find her in this!"

"And just leave her in the storm?" Malcolm says, stepping back in disbelief. "No! No fucking way!"

"She might have run back home to escape the weather," Mona says. "We should at least check!"

Malcolm's ready to say no, but Goby pulls at his sleeve. "They're right," they say. "We should at least check to see if she's there. If not, then we can take a break inside, get some food, and try again."

Malcolm twists his mouth to the side, turning back to look at Jazz and Mona. They're waiting on his answer. He turns his face to the ground, closing his eyes and bringing a hand up to tap at his chest. He sighs and nods his head.

"Fine," he says. "Fine. Let's go."

The drive back to the apartment is short. Malcolm leaps out of the truck before it's even fully stopped. He looks around outside the pub first, double checking every crevice and corner that he may have missed before. He bounds up the stairs to the apartment, taking them two at a time. He hopes to find a mound of black fur sitting at the welcome mat, but when he gets there, there's nothing waiting outside their door.

Lady Governor didn't come home.

Malcolm drags himself into the apartment. He didn't even bother to lock the door when he left. He collapses into a chair at the kitchen island as soon as he's passed through the door. He lets his head fall into his hands.

The others stay silent. What else can they say that hasn't already been said? He knows she's out there somewhere, that she's a strong girl, that she can protect herself. But she might still be lost. She might not make it back home. As old and nearly deaf as she is, she probably won't.

Jazz reaches him first, bringing her arms around his waist from behind. Mona comes up on his left, placing a hand on his arm and kissing his hair comfortingly. Goby comes in on the right, resting their temple against his head and holding onto his raincoat like a child. They stay like that, leaving an ever-growing puddle of water on their hardwood floor, breathing together.

He's not quite sure what he'll do if she's gone. Lady Governor is—was—*is* his family. He needs her to be safe; but more selfishly, he just needs her *here*. He needs her to hold, to calm him down.

Just as Malcolm feels the tug of emotion in his throat draw fresh tears to his eyes, the doorbell rings. They all startle at the sound, staring at the door. Malcolm looks around him. One, two, three...yes, they're all here. They don't have any other friends, at least none who visit. So who could be here? And in the middle of a storm, no less?

"Did any of you teach Lady how to ring the bell, by chance?" Jazz asks.

"I wouldn't put it past her," Mona says. "She's clever."

"Not that clever," Malcolm says.

Goby is the one who finally jumps to action, opening the door slowly at first, then all at once. Malcolm isn't sure who he had expected to see on the other side, but it isn't Peter. He shouldn't be surprised, really, but he is.

"Uh, hi?" Goby says.

"Peter?" Malcolm says, walking up to the door. As he gets closer, he sees that Peter's holding something close to him, his raincoat gently draped around its form.

"I'm really glad you all are the type to put your address on pet collars," Peter says, and he carefully opens his coat to reveal a wet and trembling Lady Governor sitting in the crook of his arm.

Malcolm really hates how much he's been crying for the past few days, but he can't help but dissolve into tears of relief at the sight of her. He rushes up to Peter and scoops Lady out of his arms, holding her close to his face, breathing in the musty smell of her drenched fur. She smells like dirt and rain and trash, but he doesn't pull away for a second. He's sobbing into her coat, but she doesn't seem to mind. She's clinging onto his shoulder, still shivering either from the cold or the fear of being lost for so long.

"Thank you," Jazz is saying next to him. "Thank you so much, you have no idea how much this means to us."

"Of course," Peter says. He sounds far, and Malcolm looks up to see that he's still standing at the entrance, hands in his pockets now that he doesn't have an elderly cat to hold onto. "I used to have a dog as a kid that I would do anything for. I get how scary it is to lose them."

"Where did you find her?" Mona asks. She still has a hand on Malcolm. He can't for the life of him remember why he once snapped at the feel of her hand on his arm, that day in the pub. Now her touch seems to be the only thing that's keeping him from completely losing it.

"She was outside my work, actually," Peter says. Malcolm brings Lady Governor into the kitchen and opens up a can of wet food for her. He can feel Peter's eyes on him—or maybe he's just looking at Lady Governor. He doesn't look to check. "I was closing up and I saw her in a bush near the front doors trying to hide from the rain. I took her inside the shop and tried to warm her up a bit before I saw that there was an address on her collar. I came as quickly as I could."

Malcolm swallows the lump in his throat, thinking of how scared Lady must have been. But Peter was there. He saw her, alone and terrified, and he came to her. He helped her, just like Malcolm did all those years ago. Malcolm looks up, and he catches Peter's eye. He looks away.

"Dude, come inside," Goby says, ushering Peter in. Peter stumbles along a little clumsily, eyes darting around the room like he shouldn't be there. "You must be freezing, take your coat off and warm up."

"Oh, no, that's alright," Peter says, tugging his jacket a little closer to himself. "I won't be here for long, I have somewhere to be."

"Well, wait until the rain lightens up a bit, at least," Jazz says.

Mona returns from where she had disappeared to apparently retrieve several towels. "I popped them in the dryer for a minute so they'd be a bit warmer." She hands one to Peter first, who accepts it with a smile.

Not even ten minutes after Lady was returned and the adrenaline of the night wore off, the others made flimsy excuses to head to their rooms. (Goby was the last to leave. Eventually they seemed to recognize Peter as the man who jogged around the neighborhood that Malcolm always stared at, and they quickly left the room with a wink and a bounce of their eyebrows at Malcolm. He prays that Peter didn't see.) And thus, Malcolm was alone with Peter.

Now Peter sits at the very corner of the couch and pets Lady Governor, who's been laying in his lap for the past several minutes. Malcolm isn't surprised that she's warmed up to him so quickly, he *did* save her from the storm and all. He still can't help but feel a little jealous.

He's just starting to wonder who exactly he's jealous of—Peter or Lady Governor.

Gaining feelings for his enemy is a colossally bad idea, Malcolm knows. Which is why it's a good thing he *hasn't* gained feelings. But he's starting to think it would be really, extremely easy to. The guy is playing with his cat, right after he had returned her to Malcolm after she had been lost in a terrible storm. Who would blame him for getting a fuzzy feeling or two at that?

So, no. He can't catch feelings. He could, however, try to build a more companionable relationship.

Malcolm slowly makes his way over to the couch, unsure whether he's trying to keep from startling the cat or the man who's petting her. Peter's eyes trail upwards until they finally meet Malcolm's, and he raises an eyebrow. Malcolm's vaguely aware that he's standing directly in front of Peter doing absolutely nothing, stiff as a board, like a sweaty British Guard. Peter watches him skeptically.

Malcolm finally gives himself a mental shove and sits down on the opposite end of the couch, his hands on his thighs. Peter looks away, one hand petting Lady while his other hand fidgets with something that Malcolm can't identify. It looks a little like a piece of a bike chain, barely the size of his thumb. Peter's fingers move with it continuously, flipping the chain around and around.

"What is that?" Malcolm asks, pointing at Peter's hand.

Peter stuffs it in his pocket quicker than Malcolm can blink. "Nothing." He doesn't withdraw his hand from his pocket after that. Malcolm's gaze falls to his lap.

Silence falls between them, heavy and uncomfortable. Peter must be still upset about Malcolm's outburst in the alleyway if he's being so icy. Or maybe he still considers Malcolm to be his enemy. Why should Peter try to be friendly just because Malcolm wants that now? He can't read Malcolm's mind. But the foot of space between their bodies feels infinitely vast, and all Malcolm wants to do is fill the void with *something*, so he does what he does worst and starts talking.

"I remember you being more chatty in college," Malcolm says, and Peter blinks at him.

"Sorry?"

"You just—you're pretty quiet right now," Malcolm says, turning to face Peter. He laughs a little bit, nervously, and says, "I mean, I know we never spoke in college, but from what I saw of you—I mean, not that I *watched* you, but— "

"We spoke in college," Peter interrupts, looking sideways at Malcolm as if he were making a joke that he didn't understand.

Malcolm pauses in his babbling, his hands mid-gesture. "We did?"

Peter nods. Before Malcolm can ask more, Peter rises from his seat, gently lifting up Lady Governor and placing her back on the couch. "I have to go. Thanks for, uh, letting me warm up. You've got a nice home."

"Oh, um. Sure. Of course. Thanks," Malcolm says.

Seconds after the door shuts behind Peter, the others emerge from their rooms. Mona seems to be dragging Jazz back at least, saying something about privacy. (Her grip is obviously lax, though, and she's looking at Malcolm with barely contained curiosity.) Goby smiles obnoxiously, their tongue playing at the gap in the side of their teeth.

"Did ya smooch?" Goby says, their arms crossed as they lean against the wall.

Jazz makes a few kissing noises, and Mona smiles in amusement. Malcolm raises both hands and flips them all off, rotating his arms in a half-circle to cover all his bases.

He forgets to call into the radio show that night.

11

Malcolm spends the entire week stressing about the radio show, pissed at himself for missing one of the few nights that Rebo is on. He forgot to even listen in that night, too busy thinking about assholes with pretty eyes who return people's lost cats in the middle of thunderstorms.

When he does get the chance to call in again on Friday, he doesn't waste any time. Rebo has barely even had the chance to introduce himself as the host before Malcolm is pulling up the show's contact on his phone and ringing in.

"I am *so* sorry I didn't call in last time," Malcolm says as soon as he knows he's made it through. "I lost my pet and it was this huge deal and I just—I completely forgot, I'm so sorry."

"Clark Kent, the one and only," Rebo says. He sounds relaxed, but Malcolm doesn't miss the hint of relief in his voice. "It's alright, man, you're not obligated to call in or anything. I have to admit, though, I was a little worried."

"You were worried about me?"

"Well, you are the most interesting part of this show. If you stopped coming I'd probably lose half my audience or something."

Malcolm's laughter comes easier to him now, and he closes his eyes. "So you're just using me for better ratings, huh?"

"Absolutely I am, yes."

Malcolm can hear his laughter verging on 'school girl with a crush' but he refuses to let himself feel an ounce of guilt about it. His chances with Rebo are non-existent. Rebo's just a voice on the radio. So what's the harm in playing around a little bit?

"What were you like in school?" Malcolm asks.

Rebo makes a curious sound. "Why do you ask?"

"Just trying to get to know this faceless stranger a little better."

"Oh, you know," Rebo says, and there's the squeak of a chair. Malcolm imagines him relaxing back against it, his arms locked behind his head. "Thousands of friends. Endlessly popular. Every morning kids would fall to my feet to offer me their lunch money."

"You were a loser, weren't you?"

"Big time."

Malcolm barks out a laugh, and Rebo follows with a string of low chuckles that settle like embers of a fire inside Malcolm's chest, warm and electric.

"Yeah, I definitely wasn't popular," Rebo continues, although his voice has gained a skittish edge to it. "Being the only, uh, openly gay Black kid in a small-minded school made me a pretty easy target."

Malcolm swallows, blinking up at his ceiling as he rests against his bed. He can tell that was big for Rebo to admit on the air. He shouldn't have to be brave alone.

"I get it," Malcolm says. He tacks on a little awkwardly, "I mean, I'm not Black, I can't really compare my experience to yours there, but—well, I was the only queer trans kid that I knew up until college, so. I get that part, at least. You're not totally alone."

There. He did it. He came out to Rebo. Not only that, but he came out to everyone listening to the show. Sure, they don't know who he is, but he *did it*. They both did.

"We're pretty fucking brave, huh?" Rebo says.

Malcolm smiles. "You think so?"

"Hell yes, dude. From the sounds of it, we both grew up in shitty little towns that constantly tried to beat us into the dirt. And yet, here we are. Still kickin'. Still being unapologetically ourselves because *why*?"

It's silent for a brief moment before Malcolm realizes he's waiting for a response.

"Because...we rule?" Malcolm ganders.

"Because we *fuckin'* rule!'

Malcolm shakes his head to himself. "You make me sound a lot cooler than I am."

"I think you're plenty cool, Clark."

Malcolm turns over on his bed, laying his cheek on the cool side of his pillow as he speaks. The new position squishes his lips together, so he sounds a bit funny when he talks. "It helps to surround myself with a bunch of other people like me. I have a total of three friends, and every single one of them is like me."

"They're all like you?"

"Well, not *exactly* like me," Malcolm corrects himself. "Out of the four of us, none of us are straight and only one of us is cis—as far as I'm aware, at least. We're a whole smorgasbord of different identities. We're a pretty eclectic bunch."

Malcolm ends up talking for a full ten minutes about his friends (in vague terms, leaving out names, of course), and Rebo listens intently to every second. He talks about Mona's love for skateboarding and her decadent cooking, Jazz's punk phase that never went away and her admiration of bumble bees, Goby's funky sunglasses collection and their habit of never wearing shoes if they can help it.

"Wow," Rebo says at the end, and he sounds a little dazed. "I haven't had a whole lot of friends that I can relate to before. That sounds...pretty damn amazing, honestly. I wish I could meet them all."

"Maybe you will one day," Malcolm says before he can fully think it through.

Rebo hums in thought. "Maybe I already have."

Malcolm's continuous fidgeting stops abruptly. It feels a bit like when Jazz hits the brakes just a little too hard, his stomach dropping quick as a stone. Rebo doesn't seem to notice anything wrong as he continues to speak.

"It's possible we've crossed paths already. Maybe we live in the same town and we've seen each other across the street, or in a store." Rebo lets out a breathy laugh. "We wouldn't even know. Wouldn't that be crazy?"

"Yeah," Malcolm says, and his voice sounds hollow to his ears. "So crazy."

Malcolm doesn't stay on the call for long after that.

• • • •

"Tell me again why you're freaking out about this?" Jazz says through a yawn. She's laying across Malcolm's bed on her stomach, kicking her feet in the air absentmindedly as she flips through the pages of one of his books. He thinks it's something from Neil Gaiman, the one about the angel and the demon. (Malcolm thinks the angel and demon are in love, but the characters are men-ish and it was the 90s when it came out, so it's all implication).

"I don't know!" Malcolm says, pacing the small length of his room. He picks up a Rubik's Cube from one of his shelves, gives it a few mindless twists and tosses it back, never breaking his stride. "It's not like he was saying he actually knows me in real life, he just said it's a possibility that we've seen each other before." Malcolm grunts in frustration. "I don't know why that freaked me out so bad, but here we are."

Malcolm runs his hand through his hair, his eyes burning. He hasn't slept a wink. He hasn't taken his morning shower yet either, he just called Jazz over as soon as it was a decently human hour to be awake. He would've called her right after the radio show, she's usually still awake at that time, but he didn't want to take that gamble. Jazz can be properly scary when you've interrupted what little sleep she decides to get.

He still ended up waking her at 7 in the morning. She had answered the FaceTime call still in her silk bonnet, her eyes half closed as she scowled at the bright screen. She'd threaten to hide his body where no one could find it if he didn't give her a good reason for waking her up.

"God isn't even awake right now," she'd said.

Malcolm had apologized profusely, but he couldn't explain his situation past a simple '*I'm freaking out, dude.*' She arrived at the apartment in less than an hour with coffees in hand for the both of them.

"Would it be so bad if you did know each other in real life?" Jazz asks, putting the book back on Malcolm's nightstand and sitting up, her eyes following him as he restlessly moves about the room.

"Yes!" Malcolm says, slapping his hand against his palm for emphasis.

"Why?"

"Because this isn't real!" He stops in the middle of the room, eyes wild. "None of it is supposed to be real, Jazz! Knowing him, *really* knowing him—that's not supposed to be a reality."

Jazz squints at him. "Knowing him is what bugs you?"

"Of course it is," Malcolm says. "If I know him, then this stupid fantasy crush would become a *real* crush, and then that real crush would turn into the deep shit, and then I'd fall for him for real, and that just—it cannot fucking happen!"

"Why the hell not?"

"Because I'm me! Jazmine!" Malcolm says. His chest rises and falls sharply, just once. He collapses into his desk chair, leaning his head back. "I am, without a doubt, the biggest fucking mess in this entire town. Possibly in the entire state."

"Well, that's bullshit."

"It's not."

"It is!"

"No, it's not!" He snaps, muscles tense as he tries to explain. "You know me, Jazz! You've seen me at every stage in my fucked up life, you *know* me. I can't do that to him."

"You act like you're some sort of fucking illness," Jazz says, and her face grows red with genuine anger. "Cut that shit out right now, you hear me? Don't talk about my best friend like that."

Malcolm huffs out a breath and closes his eyes. The fight drains out of him quickly, leaving him tired and raw. There's a dull throbbing in his right eyebrow. Do they have any ibuprofen left? No, they ran out last week. Damn.

"He's gay, Jazz," Malcolm says. "Like, fully. Only likes men."

"Okay? Isn't that a good thing? A point for Malcolm?"

"In theory."

"The fuck do you mean, 'in theory,'" Jazz says, making exaggerated air quotes with her fingers.

"Well," Malcolm stops, sighing as he gathers his words. "What if he has, like, a preference?"

Jazz stays silent for a moment, eyebrows furrowing. After a moment her face clears of its confusion, and her eyes grow dark. "Malcolm," she says.

"No, Jazz, it's a fair question," Malcolm says before she's finished. "What if I'm not, you know. Not enough like this?"

It's not an unreasonable question, he thinks. He knows there will be people he admires who don't see him as the man that he is—who won't be able to get past that part of him. It's why he never dated after he transitioned. It's part of the reason why he's so vehemently against the idea of falling for Rebo, or anyone else. It was hard enough getting to a place in his life where he was happy with who he was. He doesn't need anyone messing that up.

"That's horse shit," Jazz says. "That's your mom talking."

"Well, what if she's right?"

"She *isn't*," Jazz says. She stands from the bed and kneels in front of him, grabbing his hands a bit too forcefully before rubbing an apologetic thumb over his knuckles. "Anyone worth holding onto is not gonna care about how you were born. Do you think I care that Mona is trans?"

Malcolm shakes his head. "Of course not."

Jazz gives him a pointed look. "There you go, then. Proof. Anything your mom says is shit. You're gonna find someone who isn't an asshole, someone who loves you like crazy and would rather die than live the rest of their life without you."

"And what if that person doesn't exist? What if I can't find them?"

"Then you still have us, stupid," she says, swatting him upside the head a bit too hard. He yelps, and she smooths his hair back down in apology. "We fit all that criteria anyway, minus the smooching and the sexing."

"*Sexing*?"

"Although, from what I've heard about him, Rebo isn't the type of guy to give a shit about how you were born."

Malcolm shrugs, staring down at his feet.

"And if he is," Jazz continues, "we can always just kill him."

Malcolm finally laughs at that. Jazz smiles at him, her tongue between her teeth.

Jazz stands up and swiftly retrieves her phone out of her back pocket. Her thumbs fly across the screen in a blur, and a moment later Malcolm feels a buzz against his thigh.

"What was that?"

Jazz doesn't look away from her phone. "Just texted the group chat to let them know we'll be gone for the rest of the weekend."

Malcolm blinks. "We will?"

"Yes, we will," she says. "You need to get away from this shitty little town and live a little." She tucks her phone away before turning to Malcolm, her hand outstretched and a grin on her face. "Come on, dude. We're going on a road trip."

12

"You couldn't have waited, like, two more minutes for me to wake up?" Goby says, their voice whiny and grating over the phone speaker. "I wanted to go too!"

"Sorry, Goob!" Malcolm shouts over the wind. Jazz insisted on rolling all the windows down in the truck for maximum 'queer coming-of-age short-film' energy. "I would've waited for you!"

"No time!" Jazz says. "This is an official Malcolm emergency, we had to get on the road ASAP!"

"What kind of emergency?" Mona's voice crackles over the phone. "Is everyone alright?"

"We're fine!" Malcolm says.

"No, we are not," Jazz says dramatically. "Our dear Malcolm has forgotten his true self! We're on a mission to find it again!"

"Oh, a journey of self-discovery!" Goby says with excitement. "Good luck!"

"Thanks," Malcolm says blandly, before hanging up the call. "I'm pretty sure I already know my true self, man. I didn't grow that awful testosterone mustache my first year of college for nothing. Where are we even going?"

They're flying down the highway with seemingly no set destination in mind. The GPS is off, and Sex Pistols' "God Save the Queen" threatens to blow out the speakers.

"I dunno, you tell me," she says with a shrug.

"What?"

"This is your trip!" Jazz says. "You decide where to go."

"There's no plan," Malcolm says, more of an incredulous statement than a question.

"Don't need one. This is about doing what makes you happy in the moment," she says. She digs into the glove department and pulls out a sucker, shoving it into Malcolm's chest, all while keeping her eyes on the road. "Don't think, dude. Just *do*."

Malcolm hesitantly unwraps the sucker and sticks it in his mouth. Strawberry.

"I've always wanted to go to New York."

Jazz whoops and bangs on the ceiling of her truck. It's covered in years worth of doodles and writings from their group, marking their places in her life. He can see where he wrote his name in big block lettering the day she bought this truck, right at the front for all to see.

Malcolm laughs and hollers, his shouts drowned out by the fury of the wind.

• • • •

Malcolm feels younger with every minute that passes inside the truck. He feels 18 again—newly adult and unstoppable. He feels 16—sneaking into abandoned parks with Jazz after curfew. He feels 12—just on the brink of learning about the cruelty of the world, but not yet crossing that boundary. The world is good here, singing along too loudly to The Cure with his best friend. The world is kind.

The sun is high above the horizon, blinding white in a canvas of clear blue. Malcolm forgot how beautiful the sky can be when it's not painted in the gray of storms. What few clouds there are in the sky are sculpted to perfection, not a single wisp to be found, only flawless cotton candy mounds.

Malcolm's stomach growls and he remembers quite suddenly that the only thing he's had for breakfast is a coffee. He makes Jazz pull into a McDonald's before they go any further, and they make it just before breakfast ends.

"So," Jazz says, gulping down a bite of hash brown. "What's in New York?"

"Hrrm?"

"You said you wanted to go to New York," Jazz explains. "What do you wanna do there?"

Malcolm thinks for a moment, pulling off a stray corner of cheese from his McMuffin and sticking it in his mouth. He sucks the grease remnants off of his thumb with a shrug. "I dunno. Just seems crazy that we live a few hours from there and yet I've never been."

"Fair point."

"D'you ever think about that, Jazz?" Malcolm says, turning to stare out the car window. "There's a whole world out there to see, and we just decide on one place to stay forever. Why don't we go out and see things? We have feet. We have cars, we have bikes. You don't even have to go that far to see something new."

There's a pair of siblings in the minivan next to them who seem to be arguing over an iPad. The older one sticks their finger in the younger one's ear, and the younger one's mouth opens in what Malcolm assumes is an ear-splitting screech. Malcolm turns back to Jazz, only to see her staring at him with an odd look on her face.

"What?" Malcolm says.

Jazz shakes her head, her eyes returning to the road. "Nothing, man. I've just missed you."

He's not entirely sure what she means by that. They see each other practically every day. But she's turning up the music before he can ask her, and his thoughts are drowned out by the thrum of the bass.

When he reclines his seat to take a nap, Jazz smacks him on the arm and switches the music to 'Wake up sleepyheads' by the Modern Lovers, blasting it to max volume so every inch of the car is vibrating. He glares at her and gives her the finger, and she laughs as she shouts along to the lyrics.

They're halfway to New York when Jazz finally turns down the music.

"Hey," she says, poking him as if there was anyone else in the car she could've been talking to. "Do you remember that field trip in sixth grade? To the aquarium?"

Malcolm blinks up at the ceiling, searching his brain. He finds the memory and his eyebrows shoot up in surprise. "Holy shit, yeah. Yeah! With Ms. Duran?"

"Yes! Ms. Duran!" Jazz starts laughing, and he can't help but join her. "We got into so much trouble that day."

"I would've been fine if it weren't for you!" Malcolm says, beaming at Jazz with an open smile. "You're the one who dragged me into shit!"

"Oh, come off it, you liked our adventures more than I did."

"'*Adventures*' she says. Sneaking into the otter exhibit is not an adventure, that's a crime."

"A misdemeanor, at most," she says dismissively.

Malcolm throws his head back and laughs. It fills up his body, into the tips of his fingers and the top of his head. When he settles again, his body relaxing back into his seat, he feels as if he's had a drink. His cheeks are warm and he can't seem to stop smiling, even when he accidentally makes eye contact with the motorcyclist passing by. He likes to think they smiled back underneath their helmet. (They probably didn't.)

Jazz is thankfully not a complete sadist and does let him drift off for a short nap. He remains in that state of half asleep and half awake, the music and the sun bleeding through his eyelids preventing him from fully going under. He imagines himself in scenarios to match the music playing; a passtime he's sure that everyone does but hardly anyone admits to. When the song is loud and brash, he imagines himself running along the edges of buildings, leaping through the air like a vigilante. When the song is slower, he allows himself to indulge in something a little sweeter. Something like holding someone's hand where no one else can see them, a badly kept secret that makes their cheeks flame and their stomachs flutter with exhilaration.

He's grateful that Jazz thinks he's sleeping. If she were to look at him right now he's sure she'd read his mind and call him out on his disgustingly romantic imagination. He's embarrassed enough that she knows about his radio show crush, she can't know that he starts having domestic daydreams as soon as he gets warm and sleepy like Lady Governor in a sunbeam.

What was left of his pleasant daydream is interrupted when the car jostles violently over a pothole in the road, sending Malcolm's head crashing into the door with a painful *thunk*. Jazz dissolves into a fit of laughter as he rubs at his skull with a mumbled curse. He starts to lean back in his seat again to try a second attempt at sleep, but Jazz stops him.

"It's good you're awake, actually," Jazz says. "I need you to tell me where the fuck we're going."

"I told you already."

Jazz rolls her eyes. "New York isn't exactly specific. We're not just gonna trek the entire state, are we?"

Malcolm pouts, but stays silent. He hadn't actually thought about that.

Jazz continues, "Do you wanna see Times Square? That statue lady? What?"

"Did you just call the Statue of Liberty 'that statue lady'?"

"I don't know her personally."

They make the vague decision to drive to New York City; if there's anything worth seeing in the state of New York, it will be there.

"My uncle's been there," Jazz says. "He said after a few days in the smog you'll start blowing black snot out your nose."

Malcolm makes a face. "Yum."

• • • •

Malcolm doesn't believe in Hell. However, if he were to guess what it felt like, he thinks it would be similar to the act of trying to drive into New York City.

"The hotel is literally *right there*," Jazz growls, gesturing to the building in the distance. They could probably get out of their car and walk to it.

Everyone who has ever endured the traffic in NYC deserves a personalized gift basket, Malcolm thinks. Chocolate covered fruit. Baguettes. Maybe a Xanax.

He's pretty sure they've driven eight feet in the past twenty minutes. It takes an additional fifteen to finally get to the hotel, and Jazz nearly bursts Malcolm's eardrums when she screams in triumph at the sight of an open parking space.

They haul their shared suitcase out of the trunk, and Malcolm falters when he sees Jazz bring something else out along with the luggage. The portable radio from his room.

Malcolm squeaks. "When did you take that?" Jazz simply winks at him and marches towards the hotel lobby, radio in hand. He shouts at her back, "Stop trying to be aloof! You're not aloof!"

Malcolm follows her into the building, grumbling all the while. She's already checked them in at the desk and starts to lead him toward the elevators, so he gives his eyes time to wander. His eyebrows raise up, up, and even further up his forehead as he takes it all in. It's well decorated—and *clean*. He's never stayed in a hotel so spotless. There's always at least one questionable stain on the browning carpet. This place doesn't even *have* carpets. It's all sparkling white tiles that he can see his reflection in.

"Can we afford this?" Malcolm says. "I'm fine with booking something cheaper. I saw a building that looked haunted a few miles back, maybe they'll take us."

"Shut your hole," Jazz says. "I'm using my heapings of beekeeper money to land us this schmoozy place. This is your time to have fun, dude, don't worry about anything else."

Malcolm wants to argue further, but Jazz has stopped in the middle of the hall, pointing through a wall made of clear glass which allows them to see into the back of the hotel.

"Mal, look," she says excitedly. "*Pool.*"

Malcolm glances outside, where there is, in fact, a decently sized swimming pool. There's a family of four out there already, laughing and splashing at each other's faces. "Jazz. We didn't pack swimsuits."

"So?"

"*No*, Jazmine," he says, dragging her to the elevators.

They don't spend much time in their room near the top of the building. Jazz shrugs off her jacket and takes a minute to bounce on their single bed, touching her hand to the white popcorn ceilings, and Malcolm winces when she doesn't take her shoes off. Nearly everything in the room is some shade of white. He feels a bit out of place, with his unwashed hoodie and Jazz's sleeveless Nirvana t-shirt. He has to remind himself that they bought this room; they're not the intruders he feels like they are.

He heads over to the large window, looking out and down at the vast city. He doesn't think he'd be able to live here. It would be pretty shit to have one of his episodes in such a busy place where there's almost nowhere quiet to hide and calm down. '*Overwhelming*' is New York's entire aesthetic. But he can't deny that it's a breathtaking view.

They leave the room, and Malcolm has to drag Jazz away from the sight of the swimming pool once again. It's a weird shift, stepping out into the city after being in that hotel. The hotel smells of citrus, the sharp scent of disinfectant and something else that's supposed to disguise the chemical smell but does a poor job of it. The air outside the building is stark in contrast. It smells of sweat and dirt and gas. It's pretty gross, but it smells like life.

Malcolm decides he prefers it outside.

13

The similarities between Bugswick and New York begin and end with the fact that Malcolm has now been in both of them. If you count Jazz's presence, that's two similarities. Other than that, not a single inch of the bustling city feels like his home. Malcolm's surprised to find that it's not necessarily a bad thing. It's just *new*.

Walking through New York was a bit like when Malcolm went to see the Queen Mary with his parents as a child. There was a room in which you could look down into the water and see the ship's propeller; and he's not sure if it was the dim lighting, or the way the ocean remained unnaturally still in that dark selected space, but when he looked down into the sickly green water, his breath caught in his chest. He wasn't sure what he was expecting. Of course a large ship would have a large propeller to match, but something about the machinery's size was incomprehensible in Malcolm's young brain. It could rip someone to shreds if it wanted to. It was gorgeous. It was terrifying.

He got that same feeling as he craned his neck up towards the sky now. He'd never seen buildings so tall. He felt infinitesimally small within their shadows, but he found that he didn't mind very much. There were thousands of people living their lives around him, going to work, driving through infuriating New York traffic. They were ants to the city, just like him.

Jazz manages to snap him out of his thoughts when she shoves a hot dog into his hands, the bun warm and soft.

"I thought you were vegetarian again," Malcolm says as Jazz takes a massive bite of her own hot dog. He chuckles when she pants and wheezes through the steaming mouthful, trying to cool it down without losing her bite.

"We're in New York," she says, fanning her mouth.

"So?" He squints at her. The silver rings adorning her fingers flash against the sun, blinding him every time they hit a certain angle.

"So, it doesn't count."

"That's not how it works," he laughs, taking another bite.

"It's how mine works."

"You can't just change the rules of vegetarianism!"

Jazz shoves him halfheartedly and he stumbles, cackling. He's sure it's a disgusting site, his mouth wide open to show the world what he had for lunch, but he's too happy to really care. From what he's observed in the dark corners of New York, a man laughing with his mouth full is the least disgusting thing people see around here.

"You think we'll see the rats?" Jazz says. They've started walking with no particular destination in mind, bumping their shoulders together every few steps.

"The what?"

"The rats! The New York rats!" Jazz says, crumpling up her hot dog wrapper and stuffing it into Malcolm's shirt pocket. He takes it out and throws it away. "People from New York always talk about, like, rats stealing their pizza and shit."

"They do?" Malcolm wrinkles his nose.

"Yeah, dude! I wanna see them."

"Of course you would," he says. Jazz spots a large crack in the sidewalk and makes a giant leap, stomping onto the crack with both feet. Malcolm does the same. (Neither of them are very fond of their mothers.)

After several minutes of debating what they should do next, they make the decision to go to a museum; although it takes much longer to decide which one. Apparently, there are a lot of museums in New York City. Like, a lot. They found out that there's a Museum of Sex, which apparently has a *'boob themed bounce room,'* according to what Jazz found online. (She wanted to go. Malcolm said no.)

They end up flipping a coin that Jazz found on the ground (he makes her wash her hands before she touches him again) and they end up at one of the many visual art museums of New York. There's a large statue of a mythical creature of some sort at the front that Jazz valiantly tries to climb, but Malcolm forces her down before the guards can see.

The air is chill and clean inside the building, similar to that of the hotel but not as stiflingly barren of life. There are marks on the floor where people have tracked in the dirt from outside, and a certain kind of earthy smell that feels familiar and comforting. It reminds Malcolm of the library at school that he used to visit during lunch.

"Hmm," Jazz hums as she stands in front of an abstract painting. There's a collection of harsh slashes and splatters where Malcolm can see the painter dashed their brush across the canvas. There's the beginnings of a rectangle painted in the corner, but one line is absent. "Yup. I see."

"See what? What do you see?" Malcolm says, looking at her curiously.

Jazz nods her head solemnly, stroking her chin. "Absolutely fuck-all."

Malcolm has to slap his hand over his mouth to keep from snorting in this incredibly silent art exhibit, although the slap makes a disturbing noise all on its own.

"They're just fuckin' shapes and colors, dude, I'm not an art critic," Jazz says in a quiet voice, although her shoulders shake from her effort to keep her composure.

"Didn't you make a shit ton of abstract art a few years ago?" Malcolm says. She wanted to be a professional painter at the time, before she moved on to glass blowing for a good six months.

"That doesn't mean I knew what I was doing!"

Malcolm's cheeks hurt, his stomach cramping in his effort to keep his laughter contained. He doubles over, holding onto Jazz's arm for support. They fold inward towards each other, like wilting flowers. Their energy is far too high for such a classy place, but they can't seem to stop it. He can feel Jazz shaking now, her lips pursed as quick puffs of air escape from her nostrils, desperately trying to keep her laughter down.

They settle down eventually, thank god, and make their way to the room adjacent to them. Then Jazz points her thumb towards a statue with a decently sized package and makes a *'not bad'* sort of face, and Malcolm loses it all over again. He has to leave the room for a minute before they can continue.

He never thought he would enjoy himself so much at a museum. Being here with Jazz was just like that field trip to the aquarium; they weren't breaking into any otter exhibits this time, but they were having so much *fun*. Even as they left the museum, the sky a warm pink with the setting sun, Malcolm was clutching his stomach as giggles leaked out of him. He felt air-light, like he could float up into the atmosphere at any moment.

The pizza they ate for dinner was greasy and heavy and the most delicious thing he had ever eaten. He almost blotted the top of the pizza with his napkin, something his mother had always taught him to do, before he saw Jazz's raised eyebrow. He knew what she was silently asking. *Is that what you want to do, or what you think you should do?*

He threw the napkin to the side and let grease drip down to his chin with each heaving bite. He smiled at Jazz with his cheeks full of cheese and pepperoni.

• • • •

It's near 11pm when Jazz says they have to get back to the hotel.

"What?" Malcolm says. He puts back the black cowboy hat he had been trying on. They were in some sort of country-themed shop with more cowboy paraphernalia than he thought existed. "Why? It's not that late."

"Yeah, but *you*," she sticks a finger into his chest, "have a date. Why do you think I brought the radio, stupid?"

Malcolm blanches, his cheeks burning. "You want me to call him tonight? In the hotel?"

That's exactly what she wanted him to do. She drags him back to the hotel, promising on the way that she'd be on her best behavior while he was on the call.

"Tell me why you're forcing me to do this again," Malcolm groans as he sets up the radio on their bed. Jazz sits across from him, her legs crossed patiently. He made her take her shoes off this time.

"Because you need to learn to let yourself have good things, Malcolm," she says. "Now shut up and put the boy on!"

Malcolm groans and switches on the radio, although all that comes out is a rumbling static. After a moment he can hear the faint whisper of music, but it cuts out frequently.

"Oh noooo," he says with little feeling. "We're a bit out of range. So sad. Better luck next time."

He turns to set the radio aside on their nightstand. When he turns back, Jazz is holding his phone out to him.

"Good thing you don't need the radio to call in, then," she says with a devilish smile.

"I don't know the number," Malcolm lies.

"Yes you do," she says, thrusting the phone at him. "It's in your contacts."

"How do you know that?" he gapes, clutching the phone to his chest.

"Your password wasn't hard to figure out. What four letter name have you been obsessed with lately?" She asks rhetorically.

He flushes up to the tips of his ears. "Shut up."

"Malcolm, dude," Jazz says as she leans in towards him. Her eyes are soft, and he thinks for a moment that this will be another one of her kinder moments, where she'll reassure him that things will be okay. She gives him a smile. "Don't be a pussy."

Malcolm gives her his most unamused look before pulling up the contact. He clicks the call button and lifts it to his ear, but Jazz quickly snatches the phone and puts it on speakerphone instead. He's about to make what was probably going to be a very embarrassing whining sound, but the screener picks up and tells them to hold, so he stays silent. The hold lasts longer than usual—he might've called right in the middle of a song.

He's more nervous now than he's ever been about calling into the show. He's not sure if it's because Jazz is listening this time, or because the last time he called he ended up having a mental breakdown over his love life and fucked off to New York. Whatever it is, it's making his palms sweat an irritating amount.

"Hey," Jazz whispers. They're facing each other, their knees bumping together, and she nudges his shin with her toe. "It's just Rebo."

Malcolm lets all the air he's been holding escape through his nose. Somehow, that's exactly what he needed to hear.

"It's just Rebo," Malcolm repeats.

"Indeed it is!" Rebo says over the phone. It startles Malcolm terribly and he jumps, and Jazz covers her mouth to keep her laughter from being heard, but she fails miserably.

"Uh, hey, Rebo," Malcolm says. "It's Clark."

A dramatic gasp. "Clark Kent! Love of my life!"

Jazz raises an eyebrow at Malcolm, and Malcolm waves a dismissive hand at her despite the redness blossoming on his cheeks. Rebo's like that with all of his callers. Probably.

Jazz continues to wiggle her eyebrows suggestively, and Malcolm hisses a sharp, "*Shut up!*"

"Okay, not a fan of the pet names, got it," Rebo says.

"No, no, those were—uh—fine," Malcolm stutters.

Jazz whispers incredulously, "*Fine?*"

"Good! They were good," Malcolm corrects.

There's a beat of silence before Rebo says in an amused rumble, "Clark, have you brought a guest with you tonight?"

Malcolm sighs, dragging a hand over his eyes. That barely lasted a minute. Jazz gives him a questioning look, and Malcolm's shoulders sag in defeat.

"Yes, I have," Malcolm says. "Rebo, this is—"

"Oh, oh, let me pick my secret name," Jazz interrupts. "Let me pick it dude, your secret name sucks."

There's quiet laughter over the line from Rebo, and Malcolm sighs again, louder this time to make sure the phone picks it up.

"Fine. What's your pick?"

Jazz debates her choice for a moment. "Call me," —she throws her hands out and squints her eyes dramatically— "*Ludo.*"

"Like, the big hairy thing from the Labyrinth?" Rebo says.

"Exactly like that!" Jazz says, smacking her hand down into her palm. "He was my favorite character as a kid."

Rebo pauses. "You were a strange kid, weren't you, Ludo?"

"I was cool as hell," she says. She lays back on the bed, leaning her weight on a propped elbow. "Can't say the same about you, though, *Max Rebo.*"

"Don't say where it's from!" Rebo shouts quickly.

"I won't, I won't," Jazz assures him. "I know all about the weird little bet you have going on with M—uh, with Clark, here. Your secret's safe with me."

"Can't believe you guys are already ganging up on me," Malcolm says sourly.

"I've gotta get the approval of your friends, Clark. Don't you know that's the best way to a man's heart?" Rebo says, and Malcolm shuts up very quickly.

After a moment, Rebo asks, "Is he blushing? Please tell me he's blushing."

"He's gone full lobster," Jazz answers.

"Oh my *god*, I hate you both," Malcolm whines. He grabs the nearest pillow and shoves it at Jazz, who takes it with a cackle.

Rebo clears his throat. "Speaking of, like, hatred," he starts. Malcolm sobers up at the change in tone. "I need to ask you guys for some advice."

"We are possibly the worst people to ask for advice," Malcolm says. Jazz gives a nod in agreement despite Rebo's inability to see it.

"Well, I'm pretty desperate, and I trust you guys," he says.

"You just met me," Jazz points out.

"True," he says. "But I know Clark, and I trust him. If he says you're trustworthy, then I'll believe him."

"She's not," Malcolm says.

Rebo barks a laugh, light and pleased. "Well, it's the best I've got at the moment, so we'll have to make due."

Malcolm asks what he needs advice with, and Rebo goes quiet for a moment. Then Rebo laughs something short and nervous.

"It's kind of embarrassing...but I'm trying to figure out how to be someone's friend."

"Like, anyone?" Jazz asks.

"No, uh, someone specific," he laughs. "But this dude kind of hates me. Like, a lot. He's hated me for a while for no reason, as far as I can tell."

Jazz leans up straighter on her elbow, eyeing the phone. Malcolm's eyebrows furrow.

"This guy sounds kind of shit if he hates you for no reason," Malcolm says.

Jazz's eyes flicker up to him, and Malcolm looks away. He knows it's a bit hypocritical, but what can he say? What kind of person could hate Rebo?

Rebo laughs and says, "Yeah, he kinda is. But I feel like maybe we could be friends if we tried. It's not just him that's been a bit of a dick. He has a habit of bringing out the worst in me."

"I'm sure he's deserved it every time."

Rebo chuckles again, and Malcolm feels the force of his smile pushing at his cheeks. He draws up his knees, wrapping his arms around them so he can rest his chin in the crook of his elbow. He can feel Jazz staring at him intently.

"Why do you want to be friends with him if he's such a twat?" Jazz says.

"*There is a line to how much you should curse on air,*" a voice says.

"Sorry Kit!" Rebo shouts, his voice farther from the mic for half a moment before he returns closer than before. "It's not that simple. Sure, he's a…jerk, sometimes, but I don't think he means to be. I see him with his friends, even with strangers, and he's always like a completely different person. I think we just got off on the wrong foot."

"Have you tried talking to him about that?" Malcolm asks. "Maybe he'll understand." Malcolm certainly does. That's exactly how he feels with Peter. He wants nothing more than to just go up to him and say, *Please, can we start over?*

Rebo exhales, the air blowing through the mic like the low rumbling of a train. "It's hard," he says, his voice more tired than it was a moment ago. "This is our routine, I guess. Every time I think I'm going to start acting differently, I close up again. He'll say something shitty, I'll say something shitty back, and the cycle continues."

They're all quiet for several moments. Malcolm stares down hard at the bed comforter, dragging his nails over its soft fabric. He looks up, and Jazz is staring hard at the phone, contemplative.

"Is he really worth it?" She says. She looks up at Malcolm, and there's a meaning to her gaze that he can't quite understand. "It sounds like being his friend would take a lot of work."

"Yeah," Rebo says immediately. "I think so, at least. I'm just—*so* sick and tired of this animosity."

Jazz is looking at Malcolm still, and he tilts his head in question. She stays silent.

"Try talking to him the next time you see him," he says, turning away from Jazz's burning stare. "*Really* talking to him. Tell him everything you just told us—that you're tired of fighting."

Rebo makes a noise, thinking. "I guess it wouldn't hurt."

"Say, you've got a crush on this guy, or something?" Jazz says suddenly, and Malcolm's eyes grow wide in alarm. He shoots a murderous look at her, but she keeps cool, merely smiling back at him.

Rebo's amused answer is directed at Malcolm despite Jazz being the one who asked. "Don't worry, Clark, you're still my number one guy."

Jazz laughs, and Malcolm buries his burning face in his arm.

14

After the call ended they turned the radio back on despite the bad signal, and they let the faint staticy music fill the room like a white noise machine. Jazz and Malcolm lay on their bed facing each other, their bodies mirrored in a fetal curl.

"Do you remember when I wanted to be a tattoo artist?" Jazz says. Her voice comes out in a whisper. Malcolm understands the desire to keep this quiet atmosphere in place, and he nods his head against his pillow, strands of black hair falling into his eyes.

"Of course I remember," Malcolm whispers back with a smile. "I have two stick 'n pokes to make sure I never forget it." A tooth on his calf and a goby fish on his right shoulder blade. (Goby—the human one—obviously requested the latter.) His skin aches at the memory.

Jazz laughs, the sound softer under the blanket of night. "You've always supported me and my ideas, even though I change my mind about what I want to do every two months."

"You say that like it's a bad thing," Malcolm argues. He continues when Jazz stays silent. "I think it's amazing. You chase after what you want, even if you know it won't last forever. No—*because* you know it won't last forever." Malcolm reaches out and clasps Jazz's hand with his own, pulling it towards him with a determined shake. "That's cool as shit."

"You don't think I should've just—" she shrugs, "I dunno, played things safe? It's dumb to go after whatever I want, isn't it?"

Her voice sounds almost insecure. Jazz is never insecure. He rises up until he's looking down at her with a determined frown. "You have experienced so many amazing things in this world, and you deserve every single moment that ever has and ever will bring you happiness, Jazmine. You go after what makes you happy in the moment," he continues. "That's what life is supposed to be, isn't it?"

There's a moment where they say nothing, just staring at each other as the words sink in. Then, Jazz grins. "You know what I'm about to say?"

Malcolm blinks.

She blinks back.

Then he groans, flopping down onto his back. "You tricked me."

"This is not a trick, you said all that shit yourself," Jazz says, poking at his arm. All the false insecurity in her voice has evaporated, replaced with cocky satisfaction. "I'm just saying, if *I* deserve the things that bring me happiness, then you sure as hell do, too. If you take *anything* away from this trip, it should at least be that."

"I know I deserve happiness," Malcolm grumbles, his cheek squished.

"Do you?"

Malcolm says nothing, looking down at their joined hands. Jazz has taken off her rings for the night, and her fingers look bare without them. He picks at the dark gray paint on her middle fingernail. It's been chipping for the past week anyway, so she lets him.

"What do you think of Peter nowadays?" Jazz says suddenly.

Malcolm looks at her, bewildered. "Peter? I thought we were focusing on Rebo now!" Malcolm says, dropping her hand. "You can't be bugging me about Rebo *and* Peter!"

She presses anyway. "Just humor me, man. I won't even make any jokes, swear to god."

Malcolm rolls his eyes to the ceiling. If he's going to talk about this, he's not going to be facing her.

"No jokes?" He double checks.

"No jokes."

Malcolm blows a gust of air up at the hair in his eyes. (It flutters once, then falls right back where it was). He clasps his hands together on top of his chest, rubbing a thumb over his forefinger, back and forth and back again.

"He saved my cat," he says.

"Yes, he did."

"He brought her home in a thunderstorm."

"Yes, he did."

"That was...kinda hot."

Jazz snorts. "Yeah, it was, wasn't it?"

Malcolm groans and covers his face with his hands. "I really did have a crush on him in college, didn't I?"

He doesn't have to look to know she's smiling at him. "Yup."

He groans again, a little louder. His hands fall back to the mattress, bracketing his head. Jazz leans up to mirror the position he was in before, hovering over him with an eyebrow lifted in amusement.

"This is the worst," he says.

"Why?"

"Because I can't like him!"

"We've literally *just* been over this."

"This is different from the Rebo thing!"

"How?"

"I'm not—I'm not upset about it for the same reasons, I swear I'm not," he assures her. "The possibility of me and Peter being a *thing* is so low that I'm not even spiraling in a puddle of self doubt this time."

"Then what is it?"

Malcolm turns to look at the painting hung up on their hotel wall. It's blank, with a single stripe of gray down the middle. He wonders if it was expensive, or if the owner's kid just painted it during their break at school.

"I don't know," he says softly. "I just want to be his friend. I can't fuck that up."

"You don't want to be more?"

"Even if that were possible, I don't know if it would be a good idea."

Jazz shakes her head and says, "That's not what I asked. Your heart doesn't give a shit about good ideas and bad ideas. What does it *want*?"

Malcolm makes a distraught noise. "I don't *know*. Is it okay for me to like him and Rebo at the same time?"

Jazz turns to lay back on the mattress, facing the ceiling like Malcolm. "I don't think you have to worry about that."

"Yeah. Yeah, I guess you're right. It's not like I'll have to actually choose between them. One of them can't even stand the sight of me."

Jazz's head turns sharply to stare at him, and he looks back calmly. "You still think Peter hates you?"

Malcolm gives her a look. "Uh, yeah? Of course he does."

"You're an idiot," she says bluntly, then turns on her side and clicks the nightstand lamp off before Malcolm can ask what she means. The room is left in total darkness except for the city lights streaming in through the small crack in the curtains. Malcolm can still hear Rebo's voice valiantly trying to make it through the radio static.

"Goodni—slee—well, everybo—" Malcolm hears from the radio, and he knows his segment has ended.

Malcolm draws the blankets up to his chin and turns on his side. He shuffles backward until his back is against Jazz's, and she makes a happy noise, pressing back against him.

"Goodnight, Jazz."

"Goodnight, dummy."

He closes his eyes and thinks of Rebo and Peter both. Maybe having feelings for them wouldn't be the worst thing. It won't kill him to admit it to himself. As long as he doesn't act on anything, he's still safe.

15

Admitting his feelings to himself was a terrible idea. It's like it opened up a dam, all of his stupid emotions rushing to the surface in a flood, and now he can't *stop it*.

He can't get shit done. His thoughts have gone haywire. It's always Rebo's voice, or Peter's face, and it's getting annoying. At least with Rebo he can just *not* listen to the radio; with Peter, it's not that easy. Ever since Malcolm returned from New York, Peter seems to be everywhere Malcolm goes. Malcolm goes to the grocery, and there he is. He goes to the bank, and there he is. He looks out his window, and there the bastard is, jogging around the neighborhood in those stupid jogging shorts. It's a nightmare.

To make matters worse, he's starting to imagine Peter's face at the worst of times. Just the other night Rebo had laughed at something Malcolm said during their call, and suddenly Malcolm was imagining that it was Peter in a fancy leather chair in some studio far away, humoring Malcolm's playfully mean jokes with a fond smile on his face.

The guy definitely still hated him though. He rarely acknowledged Malcolm's presence, and on the few times they made eye contact he always looked away before Malcolm could get a word in.

Maybe Malcolm's desperation for the guy to notice him is the reason why he finds himself in the position that he's in now: standing precariously on the middle of a skateboard while Mona holds him steady. Goby's on a bench recording him, waiting for him to wipe out.

Mona had offered to teach him a million times before, and he always declined. But after New York, he got a sudden vision of him skating coolly past Roisin Records, sunglasses over his eyes and his hair wind-swept, with Peter staring at him from the entryway with his mouth agape and his eyes filled with hearts, Looney Tunes style. He accepted Mona's offer the very next time she brought it up.

She wasted no time dragging him to the skatepark, one hand around her board and one gripping his collar to make sure he didn't change his mind at the last minute and make a run for it. Goby was quick to follow. If Jazz weren't busy with work, she would have loved to join for the chance to see him eat shit.

Mona is a surprisingly good teacher, so he hasn't completely wiped out—yet. She didn't put him on the board and immediately shove him down the bowl like he feared she would; she helped him first figure out what stance is most comfortable for him, then got him used to the feeling of the board beneath his feet. He panicked when she told him to bounce a couple of times to test out the feel of it, but she promised to keep her hands at his sides. He knew she'd catch him if he needed it (which he did, a few times).

The worst part is learning how to fall, which is what they're doing now. He was hesitant when Mona said he *had* to fall, but he reluctantly agreed when she said it'll get the anxiety of it out of the way. He's going to fall no matter what; might as well learn how to do it properly so he doesn't hurt himself.

"Alright," Mona says. "Just keep your body loose and try to roll into it when you can."

They've been doing it on the ground so far, dramatic reenactments of falling off of a skateboard. He does a sort of somersault on the concrete, wincing as his back twinges where it rolls over a pebble.

"I can't even imagine how stupid I must look right now," Malcolm says.

"Would you like to see?" Goby shouts from the bench, holding up their phone. Malcolm glares into the camera lens.

"Are you ready to try it on the board?" Mona asks.

He's not, but he can't avoid it the whole day. He gets on the board, steadying his feet. He's not nearly as graceful as Mona always is. His arms are spread outward, pinwheeling every couple of seconds to keep him from toppling over.

"Now, I can't be holding you for this part, but you'll be fine. Just do what we've been practicing," Mona says.

He stands on the board, taking a few deep breaths to prepare himself. He puts one foot down, ready to take the fall; but then he gets the feeling of a new pair of eyes on him. He looks up, and there's Peter jogging past the park, watching them.

His foot pushes too hard. The board shoots out beneath him, and he goes tumbling into the concrete. He tries to roll into it like Mona taught him to, but his knee still ends up scraping hard against the ground. He lands on his shoulder with a loud curse.

He starts swearing up a storm; not because it's the worst pain he's ever experienced, but to cover up his embarrassment and his flaming hot face.

"Nice one, Mal!" Goby cheers. "Baby's first fall!"

"You okay, love?" Mona says, kneeling down next to him. She doesn't seem too concerned, but she winces when she sees the blood on his shin.

Unfortunately for Malcolm, Peter's jogging route goes right past them, and he gets close enough for Malcolm to see the sweat dripping down his temples, his chest heaving. Malcolm's suddenly glad he has his skating screw up to blame for the burn in his cheeks.

"Way to go, dumbass!" Peter calls out.

Malcolm glares at him and flips him the bird. Peter returns the gesture and turns away to continue his jog, but not before Malcolm catches the amused smirk on his face.

"Dude," Goby says, who's suddenly much closer to Malcolm than they were before. They're standing next to Mona, staring down at him. "Was he just flirting with you?"

"What?" Malcolm says. "He insulted me! He called me a dumbass!"

"Practically a marriage proposal," Goby says.

Peter's almost out of sight now, but Malcolm can still catch a glimpse of his muscular legs as they carry him out of the park.

"You starin' at his butt?" Goby says, who's now an inch away from Malcolm's cheek. Malcolm groans and pushes their face away with his hand.

"I was not!"

"I dunno, hun," Mona says, smiling. "It definitely looked like you were."

Malcolm huffs and stands up, turning to leave.

"Aw, no, come on, we were just teasing!" Goby says, and Malcolm flicks them on the temple.

"I'm not leaving because of you idiots, I've gotta get my knee patched up and check on Lady Governor anyway." He's also a little embarrassed, but he really can't remember if he fed Lady Governor that morning or not, so...not a complete lie.

"Do you need any help?" Mona asks.

"Nah, really, I've got it. I'll see you guys later, yeah?"

"Later, gator!" Goby calls out as he walks away.

"Text us if you need us!" Mona says, and he waves his hand to let her know he heard her.

He waits until he's fully out of sight from the others to really let himself wince at the twinge in his shoulder and the burn of his shin. He wishes he had worn jeans instead of shorts—or actual protective padding. That would've been smart. Hindsight, and all that.

Luck finally seems to be on his side for once, because he makes it to the apartment without a hitch. (He'd been on the lookout for Peter the entire walk back. The last thing he needed was for Peter to see him pathetically limping home after his first fall on a skateboard.)

Lady Governor greets him as usual as he enters, meowing excitedly and weaving in and out of his legs.

"Make way for the King, my good Lady," he says as he awkwardly side steps her, trying not to trip over her.

He's checking her food bowl for evidence of that morning's breakfast when his phone rings.

16

He stops. Lady continues to circle him, oblivious to the beckoning call. He can feel his blood as it drains from his face, sickly slow. He slips the phone out of his pocket. He doesn't need to check the screen. He knows who it is, of course. Normally Goby would be tossing his phone into the fridge by now, or Jazz would be stuffing it into her shirt to hide it from him. Mona would let him choose, but she'd remind him of all the reasons why it's a *bad idea to answer.*

None of them are here to stop him from answering her. It's not like he wants to answer. He really, really doesn't. But she's still his mom.

He answers the call.

"Sweetheart!" Her voice always sort of sounds like she's trying to bribe someone; overly, unauthentically sweet. "I've been calling for ages! Is your phone not working?"

"Sorry, Mama," he says. He sits down on the couch, tucking his free hand between his thighs, shoulders hunched. "I should probably buy a new one."

"Do you need me to take care of it?"

He closes his eyes. "No, Mama. I can do it myself. Thank you, though."

"Of course. You know I'm still here for you, even if you moved away to get away from me." She says it like a joke, her words dripping with cheery venom.

Malcolm bites his tongue before the apology can slip from his mouth on instinct. Lady Governor seems to sense his distress and hops up next to him, nudging at his arm until he lets her onto his lap. His hand falls limply to her spine.

"How are you?" Malcolm says. His voice doesn't sound like his own. He's pitched it up on instinct—trying to recreate the voice of his past, the voice he had before his transition. The voice his mother will love more.

"I'm quite well, actually! Dorris has been stopping by to help me water the plants, isn't that sweet? Sometimes she'll bring her dog with her—Kroger, you remember Kroger?"

Malcolm smiles. Closes his eyes. "Of course. The corgi?"

"Yes, the corgi!" She chuckles, her voice light and fluttering through the phone like a moth. "What a precious dog. He's grown rather fond of my marigolds, though."

He makes an amused noise, just to let her know he's still listening. It's quiet for a beat before he hears her sharp inhale, gearing up to say something. He tenses and prepares for the worst.

"I've missed you, Malcolm."

His breath leaves him in a painful exhale, stuttering and weak. He clenches his jaw, teeth bared like a wounded dog. It's not the first time she's called him by his true name, but it never fails to bring an ache to his chest. Like hot apple cider that's too close to boiling, burning your insides even as you crave more of its sweet taste.

Maybe things are different this time.

"I've missed you too, Mama."

She sighs. "You know all those things I said before, all those years ago...you know I was just grieving, right?"

He remembers her using this voice with him as a kid. He remembers her holding him in his bed as he cried into her chest, and she'd cradle his head and pet his hair until he wore himself out. He remembers her whispering to him until he fell asleep in her arms. *You can always come to me. You're safe. I'm here, I'm here, I'm here.* He doesn't remember what he was crying about back then. He's not sure if it matters.

He wraps his arms around himself and feels a tear drip down his cheek. He doesn't bother to wipe it away. "I know, Mama."

"I missed my husband. I missed my daughter."

Malcolm hiccups. "I'm sorry."

"Don't apologize. You've made your choice. But I love you no matter what, dear. You know that, right?"

"I know."

Lady Governor licks his knuckle. He doesn't quite feel it like he should, the sandpaper roughness of her tongue, but he latches onto the feeling as best as he can anyway.

She takes a breath and lets it out slowly, crackling over the phone. It reminds him, for the briefest of moments, of the radio. Then she says, "It hurts me too, you know."

Malcolm stays quiet. She continues talking as if he had answered.

"I know it's not easy for you, with your condition." That's what she always calls it. A condition—a problem. A decision. "But it's hard on everyone around you as well. You have to understand that."

Malcolm stares down at his fingers, still resting on Lady Governor's back. He can feel her fur, but it's almost like someone else is petting her.

"I'll always love you," she says. "I just wish you were a little less selfish, that's all."

He's waiting for the tears to start falling again, but his eyes are dry.

He's not here.

"Oh, dammit, the rabbits have gotten into my garden again," she says, like a switch being flipped. "Listen, sweetheart, I have to go, but call me more please! I miss you so much."

"I miss you too." There's that voice again, the one that doesn't feel like his own. It isn't his own. *Who's talking?* He thinks. *It can't be me. I'm not here.*

"I love you!"

"I love you too, Mama." *I'm not here. I'm not here. Have I ever been here?*

She ends the call. He realizes he still has his phone up to his ear after several moments of silence, and he lets it fall to his side. Lady Governor stands and pushes her paws up against his collarbone, sniffing at the salt on his cheeks. He lifts her up and carries her, dropping her at the kitchen counter before making his way into the bathroom connected to his room. He closes the door behind him so she can't follow.

Looking into the mirror feels like looking at a painting. Whoever's staring back at him, that isn't him. But it is. He blinks, and the man in the mirror blinks. He moves his arm, and the other man does the same. But it doesn't feel true. His eyes are too blank. His face is too unfeeling. There's nothing underneath all that skin and bone. He can't feel it. He can't feel a thing.

He peels his shirt off his chest, slowly, methodically. He looks at the thin surgical scars framing his pecs, pink and faded. He remembers the day he told his mother he would be getting top surgery, and her voice rings in his mind.

"*You can be so cruel, sometimes.*"

The chill of the bathroom hits his skin, and it's enough to snap him out of his numbness. He shivers once, and his face crumbles. A noise rips out of his throat, guttural and pained. He bares his weight down on the bathroom sink, his knuckles white and his wrists aching as he grips the counter.

His shin throbs dully, the wound left untreated. A trail of blood has made it into his sock. He rips off his shoes and socks mindlessly, opens the bathroom door and hurls them into his bedroom. They hit the bedframe with an unsatisfying *thump*. He bites at his cheek, clenching and unclenching his fingers as he stares into his room.

"*Mrrp*," Lady Governor chirps from the doorframe. She's a fair distance away, startled from the loud noises. He deflates.

"'M sorry, Lady," he whispers. "Don't mean to scare you. I never want to scare you."

He steps towards her, but she darts away.

"No, no," he mutters, stumbling after her, but he stops himself. He doesn't want to scare her any more than he already has. "'M sorry. Fuck, I'm sorry."

He leaves the apartment quickly, double checking the lock before rushing down the steps. It takes him longer than it should to realize that he left his shoes behind. The ground is uncomfortable, cracks and pebbles diggin into the sensitive underside of his feet, but he can't go back. He can't stop moving. He feels like a shark; if he stops moving forward, he'll sink. He'll die.

The world is brighter than it was before. Too fucking bright. The sun is blinding. He can hear the engines of the cars that pass by, and the idle conversations of people passing by, and it's too much.

"No, not now," Malcolm breathes. "Not another one, *please*."

He keeps walking, hoping the cool air and momentum will help him calm down, but it only seems to make things worse. A car horn blares, and he shoves his hands against his ears to block out the noise. He walks faster.

"Stop, stop, stop," he whines. "Stop it, please, just *stop*."

His eyes are nearly closed shut in his effort to block out the overwhelming sunlight. He doesn't see the body in front of him until it's too late.

"Shit!" Peter shouts as Malcolm tumbles into him. "Dude, what are you—"

Malcolm sucks in a gasp at the sudden contact, and it's too much, *too much*. He shoves Peter, stumbling over his own feet to get away.

"Hey, what—Malcolm!" Peter shouts as Malcolm turns away.

"I can't—I can't," Malcolm repeats. He can't get a proper sentence out, his ragged breaths getting in the way. This is a bad one.

He's several feet away when Peter catches up to him and latches onto his arm. The contact is almost painful, and Malcolm rips his arm out of his grip.

"*Stop!*" Malcolm cries out. "Please, please, just stop—I can't—I can't *breathe*, I can't—"

"Malcolm," Peter says sharply, and his voice is lower now, like he's speaking to an animal in a cage. His arms are raised, palms up. "Come with me. Please."

Malcolm stares at him, his tears blurring his vision. He can see Peter well enough to see the sincerity on his face. It feels foreign. He's never seen Peter look so kind. Not when he's looking at Malcolm, at least.

"Okay," Malcolm breathes. He hiccups. Nods his head. "Okay. Okay."

17

Peter doesn't try to touch him again, but he does lead him to the door of the record shop just a few feet away. Malcolm hadn't even realized he'd gone in this direction. Peter must have been opening up the store when Malcolm ran into him. The keys are already in his hand, and he opens the door to let Malcolm in. Peter makes sure the sign is still flipped to the side that reads CLOSED before leading Malcolm further inside.

Peter takes him into the very back, where he opens a door to a small room. There's a couch inside, more worn out than Malcolm's old hand-me-down. Malcolm glances at it, shifting on his feet. Peter nods, and Malcolm sits down. His muscles stay tensed, his shoulders raised to his ears.

He looks up and finds Peter staring at him, his arms crossed and his eyebrows furrowed— analyzing him.

"What?" Malcolm snaps, his voice hoarse and biting. "I'm not a lab rat, quit fucking staring."

Peter squints at him for a moment longer, then nods his head. He leaves the room without another word, and Malcolm feels his stomach drop. He did it again. He hurt someone, *again*, and now he's *leaving he's leaving he's leaving—*

Then, suddenly, the room changes. The lights have dimmed, almost off but not completely, leaving the room in shadows that bounce away from the soft glow of the lava lamp in the corner desk. The buzzing noise that was accompanying the overhead lights is gone, and he sighs. He hadn't even realized the noise was there, but he's relieved as soon as it's gone. The harsh drumming from the music playing throughout the store cuts out, and it's quiet. He curls his toes, bare feet against the purple rug.

Peter comes back into the room, and Malcolm's sure the relief is visible on his face. Peter holds out his hands, and Malcolm finally notices what he's holding. Headphones. The big clunky kinds that cover your ears completely. He walks up to Malcolm and kneels down in front of him, lifting the headphones slowly, then pauses. His eyes are on Malcolm, asking a silent question as his hands hover between them. Malcolm blinks once, and stays still. Peter places the headphones over Malcolm's ears, careful not to touch him anywhere else.

Malcolm lets out a trembling breath, his heart pounding. He's not sure whether it's due to his panic or Peter's proximity now.

A moment later, sound begins to filter through the headphones. He looks down and sees Peter placing his phone next to Malcolm on the couch, the plug to the headphones connected to the phone's headphone jack. The phone's open, displaying the title of the song that's playing. "Cosmic Dancer" by T. Rex. It's a slower song, but not exactly the meditation music he was expecting from someone trying to calm him down from what he thinks was a panic attack. It helps, though. It's something to focus on.

When he glances back at Peter, he's sitting on the floor, still looking at Malcolm. Then, slowly, Peter brings one hand up to his own chest, his palm flat over his sternum. He starts patting his hand against his chest, and it takes a moment for Malcolm to figure out what the hell he's doing. The music is leaking through the headphones, and Peter's hand is moving to the beat of the song.

Peter nods his head at Malcolm, flicking his gaze down to Malcolm's own hand before returning to his face. Malcolm brings up his hand and mirrors Peter's motions, weakly tapping the rhythm of the music against his chest. The corner of Peter's lip quirks up in a small, pleased smile. He nods again, this time in approval.

They sit like that for the entirety of the song, and once again as the song repeats. At the end of the second play, Malcolm lets his hand drop from his chest.

"How did you do that?" Malcolm says quietly, hesitant to break the silence in the room as he removes the headphones. The music still leaks out, muffled and calming.

"Do what?"

"You calmed me down. Like, super easily," he says. He takes a deep, steady breath. He still sounds weak and rattled, but it's better than before. Much better. "It usually takes me ages to do that. How did you know what to do?"

Peter bites at his bottom lip, thinking over his answer. It's not exactly a *sexy* lip bite; he's more gnawing at it than anything. Malcolm still stares.

"You know, I used to think you were an asshole," Peter says, and Malcolm makes an affronted noise. Peter laughs. "I thought you were such a jerk for the longest time. The first time we met, back in college, you said some...pretty shitty things to me. You looked all frenzied and I tried to help, but when I reached out for you, you shoved me and told me to fuck off. Sound familiar?"

Malcolm's eyes flit down in shame. He's sure that was during one of his episodes. "I...I don't remember that. I'm sorry." All this time, he thought Peter hated him for no reason. Apparently he had a pretty good one.

Peter leans down to catch Malcolm's eyes again. He gives him a reassuring smile. "I think I misunderstood you, Malcolm. I thought you just had major anger issues that you didn't bother to fix."

Malcolm twirls the cord of the headphones around his finger. Anger issues sound about right, but it seems like Peter has a different idea. "You don't think that anymore?"

"No," he says. "I don't think you have anger issues, Malcolm. I think you have sensory issues."

Malcolm's nose scrunches up. "I have what?"

"Sensory issues," Peter repeats. He readjusts his position on the floor until his feet are planted firmly on the ground, his elbows resting on his bent knees. "Do you know if you have PTSD, ADHD, autism, anything like that?"

Malcolm shifts in his seat. "Uh...yeah. ADHD."

"Nothing else?"

Malcolm glares. "Careful."

Peter lifts his hands in surrender. "Sorry. I'm not trying to mock you, I swear. I just..." He thinks for a moment. "Have you done much research on it? Your ADHD?"

"Why would I need to?" Malcolm asks. "I know I have it, and I know what it means; I can't sit still and I can't focus for shit."

Peter gives him a smile that looks a little sadder than the ones before. "That's definitely not all there is to it. These episodes you're having are likely part of your ADHD."

"How is an anger management problem a symptom of ADHD?"

"It's not about the anger, it's about what causes it," he says. "Sometimes your brain can't process all the shit that's happening fast enough, and it gets overloaded. Everything is fine, and then *bam*. All at once, it's too much."

"Too much," Malcolm repeats.

Peter smiles. "Sound familiar?"

Malcolm nods.

"And it hurts, right?" Peter continues. "When you experience it, it's almost painful. No wonder you're lashing out, Malcolm. Anyone would if it felt like all their senses were suddenly turning against them."

Malcolm's eyes begin to burn again, and he turns his face away. No one's been able to understand what it feels like for him. Not really. It's overwhelming to hear someone else talk about it like they know, like they *really* understand.

"How did you know the music would help?" Malcolm asks, swiping a hand across his eyes. Peter's kind enough not to mention it. "Usually people play, like, forest sounds and shit like that when they're calming people down. How did you know it would work?"

"Actually, uh, that was a bit of a gamble," Peter says, scratching at his neck. "Different things work for different people."

"So how'd you know that would work for me?"

Peter looks away. "The first time you came to the store. You looked, I don't know...peaceful. I figured you just thought the decor was cool or something, but you weren't looking at the records or the posters. You were just listening to the music. You just closed your eyes and—and breathed it in. Like the music was oxygen."

"You make me sound a lot more poetic than I actually am."

Peter tilts his head, thoughtful. "I think you've got more poetry inside you than either of us realize."

He's wrong. Malcolm's sure of it. If he had an ounce of poeticism in him then he'd be able to come up with an eloquent response, but instead he just stares at his feet and hopes that Peter doesn't notice his red cheeks.

"How do you know all this stuff?" Malcolm asks. "About ADHD, I mean."

"I've done my research," Peter says. "People tend to think ADHD is just about the hyperactivity and the lack of focus. They never bother to learn about the other shit, the sensory overloads and the shutdowns and all that."

"Shutdowns?"

"Yeah, they're like—" Peter brings his thumb up to his lip, rubbing the scar there. Malcolm doesn't think he realizes he's doing it. "Like, when you have sensory overload, you lash out, right? You get angry, you explode. Sometimes it's the opposite. Sometimes you just—stop. You shut down. It's hard to move, it's hard to talk. You just turn off."

Malcolm hums. "I wish I could do that."

"You say that now, but it's not as fun as it sounds," Peter says.

"You know, I think my friend goes through that. They have these moments sometimes where they just kinda...shut off."

Peter nods. "That could be what it is. Overstimulation."

"You know, you're gonna have to write some of these terms down for me, dude," Malcolm says, and Peter laughs.

"Sorry, sorry. I like to talk about this kind of stuff."

"What got you interested in it anyway?" Malcolm asks. "Do you have ADHD too?"

Peter shrugs. "Probably. Either that or autism. Or both." He scratches the corner of his nose with the flat of his fingernail, thinking to himself. "Actually, it's probably both."

"You don't know for sure?"

Peter smiles kindly. "A diagnosis is crazy expensive, dude. I need to save my money to tend to other things, so I've never been able to get one. That's why I do so much research, so I can help myself if I need it."

Malcolm feels hot shame drip down his spine. He had the privilege of getting a diagnosis at a young age, and yet never even bothered to learn how to help himself with his issues past a basic Adderall prescription. He just lashed out at the people he cared about and chalked it up to being a shit human.

"Hey, quit it," Peter says, standing up from the floor and plopping himself down next to Malcolm on the couch. He leans in, poking Malcolm on the bridge of his nose. "Stop that."

Malcolm flusters, going crosseyed to look at Peter's finger. "What?"

"I can smell the cogs in your brain burning with overuse. Stop thinking so hard." Peter leans back, and Malcolm prays for his heart to settle. "I'll help you, you know."

"Help me with what?"

"Your sensory overload shit," Peter says. "I've done my research, and you obviously haven't—" Malcolm gives him an offended look, but Peter pushes on, "so I'll help you find ways to cope. We've already got one down." He holds up the headphones, giving them a triumphant little shake.

"Thank you," Malcolm says, a little stilted and awkward, but nonetheless genuine. "For helping me. I really appreciate it, Peter."

"Of course, Malcolm." Peter says. He draws his feet up until he's sitting cross legged on the couch, his hands in his lap. "I know what it's like, being afraid of the things you don't understand about yourself. The least I can do is help these things seem a little less scary."

The ache Malcolm feels when his mother speaks to him is always empty and painful, like when you don't eat for far too long and the force of your hunger leaves your stomach gnawing at your insides, desperate for something to fill it. The ache he feels now, deep in his chest, is nothing like that. It's like the vast nothingness inside him has suddenly been filled to the brim, all at once, and it takes his breath away. It's so much. But it's not *too much*.

He knows if he tries to express his thanks again he'll just fall apart, and Peter's already seen him crying too much today. Luckily, Peter chooses that moment to slap his hands down onto his knees and rise from the couch.

"You wanna get food?" Peter says.

"God, yes."

18

Peter digs out a spare pair of flip flops from the back for Malcolm (he's afraid to question where or who they came from), and Malcolm's infinitely grateful that Peter doesn't mention how the flip flops dwarf Malcolm's small feet. They wait until Peter's coworker comes in before leaving. Malcolm finally gets a good look at Travis; messy blond hair, sunken eyes, pale as a roll of toilet paper. He looks like a Travis.

"Trav owes me one, so I can take a bit longer on my break if we need it," Peter explains as they walk down the sidewalk. Malcolm has no idea where they're headed, but Peter seems to know what he's doing at least.

Malcolm kicks at a pebble, watching it skitter down the sidewalk a few feet in front of them. Once they reach it again, Peter kicks it. They take turns like that, kicking the pebble like a little soccer ball. Once Peter kicks it out of their path, Malcolm says, "I wish I had known about you." Peter gives him a curious look. "About you being like me. ADHD, or autistic, or whatever. If I had known we were more similar than I realized, maybe we could've bonded and...I dunno, become friends a bit earlier."

"You think we're friends?" Peter says. Malcolm shoves his shoulder, and Peter laughs. "Nah, I don't fault you for never knowing about me. I'm not surprised. I've had, like, years of practice when it comes to blending in with neurotypicals. It's fucking exhausting, but it means survival when you're in a town as closed-minded as ours."

"Tell me about it," Malcolm says. He takes a breath, steeling himself. "Being queer doesn't help either."

Peter makes an understanding noise. "Yeah, I get that. I'm gay."

They keep walking, as if Peter hadn't just thrown Malcolm's world off its axis. Malcolm clenches and unclenches his fist, keeping his eyes ahead of him and trying to remember how to walk like a normal person.

"Anyway, I probably should've caught on to what you were going through earlier," Peter says. They walk beneath the shade of a tree, and he flicks at a leaf absently. "I'd seen how kind you were to your friends, and I always wondered what it was about me that made you hate me so much." He clicks his tongue. "I never considered it was just some real shit timing when we met. We could've skipped years of animosity if I had clocked onto it sooner."

Malcolm's shaking his head before Peter's even finished. "It wasn't your job to do that. Just because there's a *reason* for why I acted like that doesn't mean I get a pass for never trying to fix things with you. The hurt I caused during my episodes is my responsibility, not yours."

Peter shrugs. He stuffs his hands into his pockets and says, "I'm not saying it's necessarily my fault, but I still wish I had noticed. At least you wouldn't have been alone."

Malcolm looks away, flustered by Peter's kindness once again. He thinks, *You're not gonna make it easy to get over you, huh?*

• • • •

Peter leads them to a small burger joint that Malcolm has only been to a couple of times. It's covered wall to wall in windows, so he can see the worn leather booths on the inside, and the open grill where an older man flips patties. There's a sign out front, handwritten in chalk:

HOW DO THEY PREVENT CRIME IN HAMBURGER CITY? WITH BURGER ALARMS!

Malcolm breathes out a laugh through his nose, even though it's not a particularly funny joke. Peter notices the sign and groans. "They always do this," he says. "This one doesn't even make sense. Burger alarm?"

"I think it's a play on the word 'burglar,'" Malcolm says. "Like a burglar alarm? But, you know. Burger."

Peter falters. "Oh. That makes sense. Still terrible, though," he says. "They write a new one every week, and I'm pretty sure they get worse each time."

"I can't imagine it could get worse than that," Malcolm laughs.

"Oh, trust me. Next time, you'll see."

Peter opens the door, and Malcolm forces himself to focus on the chill of the interior of the diner instead of the exciting promise of *next time*. Peter didn't exactly say there would be a next time *together*, but—you know. He's pretty sure it was implied.

The host tells them to take a seat wherever they like, and Peter leads them to a table in the corner.

"I hope you don't mind," he says. "This is where I always sit."

"You come here a lot, then?"

Peter nods. "One of my favorite places. Whenever my sister's in town, this is where we go."

"I didn't know you had a sister."

"There's a lot of things you don't know about me, Malcolm."

There was a short time where Malcolm had wondered if he had chosen the right name. He had picked it quickly, and he worried that he was too hasty with his decision. But after hearing Peter say it so many times today, he knows he made the right choice.

The waiter comes by with a cheerful "Welcome to Mr. B's!" and writes down their drink orders; a Sprite for Malcolm, and a lemonade for Peter, who complains about soda having too many bubbles. (Malcolm argues that that's the best part.) The drinks are given to them in little styrofoam cups and lids with the pushable buttons on top. Malcolm dents them all inward with his fingernail, and when he looks across the table he sees that Peter has already done the same.

Malcolm orders a bacon cheeseburger with fries, and Peter orders a double burger with no tomatoes. When they get their burgers, Peter immediately opens the top bun and removes the lettuce, pickles, and onions with his fork.

"Why didn't you just order it without all that stuff if you're gonna take it off anyway?" Malcolm asks, tearing off a piece of bacon that was falling off the side of his burger and popping it into his mouth.

Peter smiles down at his burger as he continues to dissect it. "It's gonna sound silly."

"It won't."

"It will."

"Okay. Tell me anyway."

Peter gives him a look, but Malcolm presses on. Peter's lips purse for a moment, then he says, "I feel weird asking for a burger without all of the vegetables, but the tomato juice stays on the burger if I leave it, so I order without tomatoes at the very least."

"You don't like the veggies?"

Peter shakes his head. "Not on my burgers, at least. The mixed up textures kinda—" he gestures at his head, "make my brain freak out a little. Doesn't feel good."

"You know no one actually cares if you order your burger without greens, right?" Malcolm says. "There's no burger police."

"That's not what the sign out front implies." Malcolm rolls his eyes, and Peter says, "I know it sounds weird. And you're right that no one gives a shit about my order, I know that logically, but...I don't know. That's just how I do it."

Malcolm sips at his soda, looking at Peter consideringly. "Is that part of how you—what did you say, blend in? Ordering a burger with shit on it you don't like just so people won't look at you weird?"

Peter shrugs. "That's probably more of a weird anxiety thing than a blending in thing, but yeah, I guess that's part of it too. It's just less stress and effort to say 'no tomatoes' and pick off the rest."

"That seems like *more* effort to me."

"Yeah, to you."

Malcolm tries to imagine it for a moment—calculating every single move you make, just to make sure that no one ever notices you being out of place. It's not that hard to imagine, considering he spent years paying attention to the way he walked and asking Jazz if it was obvious he didn't have a penis. Jazz had to remind him fairly often that most people won't be looking at his crotch for evidence of his crown jewels.

"That must be draining," Malcolm says after a beat.

Peter looks at him consideringly. "Most people just call me picky."

"What else do you do? To, y'know, blend in," Malcolm asks.

"It's called masking. And, uh, for example," Peter reaches over the table and brings his thumb up to the area right in between Malcolm's eyebrows, then smooths it over the arch. "I can make eye contact with people usually, but it doesn't come naturally, so it can be kinda draining to put in the effort. If I need a break, I'll look right here. Most of the time people won't notice that I'm not looking at their eyes if I just look right above them, or in between them."

Peter's hand still rests along Malcolm's brow, and Malcolm swallows. Peter's eyes flicker downward—just once, too fast for Malcolm to track—and he removes his hand.

"Do you do that with me?" Malcolm asks. Not offended, only curious. "The eyebrow trick?"

"Not a lot, no. It's easier when I know the person. Even easier if we're friends."

"And we're friends now, yeah?"

Peter makes a considering face. "I think we're getting there."

Malcolm looks down at his fries and pops one into his mouth, smiling. "Cool."

"You know, I think if we had known each other in our grade school years, we might've been friends," Peter says. He nudges at Malcolm's ankle with his foot, and Malcolm feels his spirit leave his body for a moment.

Malcolm scoffs. "I was still just as much of an asshole back then as I was in college. Also, I was a complete loser. You were probably Mr. Cool."

"*Mr. Cool?*"

"Yeah!" Malcolm smiles and Peter barks out a laugh, leaning back in his booth. Malcolm leans forward, as if his body can't help but gravitate towards the other. "You're all *cool* and *chill*, y'know? I bet you were super popular in high school."

Peter's laugh fades naturally, and his smile goes soft at the edges. "I have a friend who said the same thing."

And Malcolm begins to feel a sense of deja vu.

Peter continues, "I'm surprised none of my teachers ever insisted on me getting a diagnosis of some sort. I was a poster child for ADHD back then. Bouncing off the walls in the middle of class, your typical hyperactive kid."

"Really? I wouldn't have guessed," Malcolm says genuinely. "You've always seemed so down to earth."

"I told you, I've had years of practice toning down my '*muchness*,' as my friends used to say."

"Your friends said that?" Malcolm asks, his mouth agape in surprise and offense for Peter.

"Yes! They did! '*You're too much, Peter, tone down the muchness,*'" Peter puts on a voice to mock his old peers, rocking his head left to right.

"Well, that's just rude as hell, isn't it?"

"That's what I said!" They've started laughing now, and neither of them can find a good reason to stop. "God, teenagers are such twerps."

"*Twerps?* What are you, 80 years old?"

"That's what they are!" Peter insists, spreading his fingers wide across the table in emphasis. "They're fucking twerps!"

Malcolm doubles over and lets his head fall to the table, his whole body shaking with laughter. He can hear Peter laughing as well, and their legs are bumping together, and Peter is slapping his hand against Malcolm's arm as if he can push the joy into him through skin contact alone. Malcolm bites down on his lip.

The silence that falls after their laughter dies out isn't awkward. They continue to eat, comfortable in the quiet between them. Every now and then, Peter's foot will nudge against Malcolm, and Malcolm will go a little insane trying to decide if it was a deliberate action or just a twitch of a muscle.

"Hey."

Peter looks up, the corner of his mouth lifting. "Hey."

"I like this better than fighting." Malcolm sips at his drink, and it makes that slurping noise that happens when you've hit the bottom. He hadn't realized how long they'd been here already.

Peter makes a noise in agreement, nodding his head serenely. He's fully relaxed into his seat, his arms crossed, hands loosely cupping his elbows. "Me too."

Malcolm squints at Peter's shirt, noticing the faded graphic displayed on his chest. "Hey, what is that?"

Peter unfolds his arms, looking down at his shirt. It's an image of Han Solo, pointing his blaster. Malcolm feels a grin split across his lips.

"Oh my god," Malcolm says.

"Don't you dare make fun," Peter says, faux-threateningly.

"I would never!" Malcolm says. "Good choice, man. Han Solo was literally the catalyst for my bisexual awakening."

"I'm pretty sure he's a part of everyone's sexual awakening."

"As he should be," Malcolm says. "So you're a Star Wars fan?"

Peter nods, eyebrows raised and a fond smile on his face. "You could say that. My sister and I, we've loved the movies since we were old enough to watch them. Even the prequels."

Malcolm makes a face. "God, the *prequels?*"

"Hey! I won't have some—uncultured *troglodyte* diss the charm of the Star Wars prequels."

"*Troglodyte?*"

"Yeah!"

"I feel like I need a dictionary just to speak to you," Malcolm says.

"I think that says more about your intellect than anything else."

Malcolm snatches a fry from his plate and throws it in Peter's direction, who tries to catch it in his mouth but ends up getting a salty fry to the nose instead. He wipes off the grease with a crumpled napkin, laughing.

"We used to watch the movies every Christmas," Peter continues. "My sister and I. We'd fall asleep before we could get through them all, but we'd try our best."

Malcolm crosses his arms on the table and rests his chin on his arm, looking up at Peter through his eyelashes. Peter isn't paying attention to him, too lost in the memory. His eyes are fixed on some spot on the table, unfocused. The smallest of smiles quirks the corners of his lips upward. Malcolm can't seem to look away from it.

"I used to call her Jabba," he says. He laughs, and it's light and airy, and Malcolm can't help but laugh with him. "God, she hated that name. There's this character in the show that works for Jabba the Hutt, or entertains him or whatever, so she called me that as revenge. Not a very good comeback, though, since the name is sort of catchy."

"What was the name?" Malcolm asks, his voice still breathy with laughter.

"Rebo," Peter says. "That's what she called me. After the Max Rebo Band."

Peter's too caught up in his own happy memories of his sister to notice Malcolm's laughter fade away. Malcolm stops smiling, frozen in place, and thinks:

Oh.

Oh, fuck.

19

Malcolm, as far as he's aware, met Peter for the first time on their first day of college courses. They shared one course: Intro to Stats. Malcolm was barely poking his toe into adulthood, just turned 18 and going through a second puberty thanks to his new hormone therapy. (He started testosterone as soon as he became a legal adult. He was prepared for the voice cracks and the increased libido—he was *not* prepared for all the hair he expected to grow on his face to migrate to his ass instead.)

He was tapping his pen on his notebook, eyes darting around the room. Someone with bright red hair and short shorts was jiggling their leg in the front row. He looked around and counted: seven other people were doing the same thing. When did it become a common activity, bouncing your leg in class? How many of them were bouncing their legs because they were bored? How many were doing it because they were anxious? And how many were like him and did it because they needed the extra stimulation to pay attention? Fuck, he should be paying attention.

Someone caught his eye before he could tune back into the lecture. Luckily it was the first day and the professor was only going over basic formulas that Malcolm already knew by heart, so he allowed himself to peek at the stranger from beneath the hair falling over his eyes.

This was the first impression Malcolm ever had of Peter. Just a boy, roughly his age, sitting across the room from him, staring not very subtly at Malcolm. His hair was longer back then, done up in a twist out style that fell over his face when he angled his head downward. The cut of his jaw adorned a reasonable amount of scruff that Malcolm was intensely jealous of. His eyes were roughly the same color as his hair, a deep brown that was nearly black. He was, quite frankly, beautiful.

As soon as the boy realized that Malcolm had seen his staring, his eyebrows lowered into a harsh glare, and he turned away. Not a single word spoken, and Malcolm had already managed to piss someone off, it seemed. That was the first time Malcolm met Peter.

Except, it wasn't. Not really.

The true first meeting between Malcolm and Peter happened precisely one week prior. Malcolm doesn't remember this. He remembers everything before it.

He remembers his phone volume not being loud enough for his alarm to wake him up that morning, which made him late. Waking up late when he has somewhere to be is always a surefire way to throw Malcolm into an episode, the adrenaline hurling his heart into an anxious frenzy before he's even had breakfast.

He remembers rushing to campus, Jazz having been kind enough to lend him her truck since his mom wasn't home yet from the hospital to drive him herself. He remembers calling his mom on the way to school only for her to say that his father was too tired to speak to anyone, and he remembers wondering if that was the truth. He remembers thinking, *He's getting worse. He's getting worse, and she might not let me see him before it's too late.*

He remembers running, looking periodically between the buildings and his phone, desperately searching for the auditorium where he should be for freshman orientation. At that point, his hands had begun to shake, and the familiar too-muchness of the world began to rush at him in waves; from the shrieking voices of incoming freshmen, to the blinding sun, to the sweat-damp shirt sticking to his back.

Around this point, Malcolm forgets. He doesn't remember running, and running, and running until a body stopped him from going any further, two firm hands on his shoulders.

"Hey, hey, what's up? Are you alright?" A voice said to Malcolm. It was kind, and deep, and warm, and still too much. Too much, too much.

"Don't fucking touch me," Malcolm said. He shoved at the boy, the boy with the kindest eyes he'd ever seen, the boy who just wanted to *help him*. He shoved him and staggered backward. "Do not fucking touch me, I swear to god. Who the fuck even are you, *fuck*."

"I'm—I'm sorry, I didn't—" the boy said, stepping back.

"You what? You didn't think? You didn't *mean* to?" Malcolm spat. His chest heaved and burned. "Fuck *off*."

There was more said—more ugly words thrown in the face of a boy who just wanted to be kind. The memory of this altercation was lost amongst the chaos of freshman orientation week and Malcolm's own miserable mind. He doesn't remember it, but Peter does.

(Peter remembers, quite vividly, trying to help the scared kid with the olive skin and the pretty moles on his face: one above the arch of his eyebrow, one below his eye, one near the corner of his lip. He remembers wondering how he messed up so badly, so quickly. He remembers deciding that Malcolm was just one of those guys who were shits for the sake of being shits. He remembers deciding that if Malcolm was going to hate him for no good reason, then he'd do just the same.)

(He does not remember when, exactly, that decision changed. Or if he had ever really hated Malcolm to begin with.)

20

Malcolm stares unblinking at the popcorn texture of his bedroom ceiling, fingers rubbing against the soft fabric of his bed. There's a notepad abandoned on the floor next to him containing two lists. The first is titled "Things I Know About Rebo," and the second, "Things I Know About Peter." He brought the two together in a Venn diagram and eventually came to the conclusion that he is the biggest fucking idiot alive.

Of course they're the same person.

His brain feels appropriately melted. He hasn't even begun to touch on the whole "having a crush on two people who are actually the same person" mess. If he thinks about it for longer than a second he might scream.

He turns his head. The clock tells him it's only been an hour since he's been home after his lunch with Peter. Peter, thank god, had to go back to work soon after Malcolm's realization, so he didn't notice Malcolm's odd behavior. Malcolm's never been great at lying on the spot. Now, it seems, he might have to.

Because what the actual *fuck* will he do if Peter finds out who he is?

• • • •

By the time Rebo's voice filters through Malcolm's radio, Malcolm hasn't moved an inch from his bed. He startles at the sound, turning to stare at the old radio as if Rebo himself would pop out of it at any moment. Now he knows what he'd see if he did. Dark brown eyes, long legs, a scar on his top lip. It's how he'd started imagining Rebo anyway, but now he knows it's the truth.

He sits for a long while, just listening to the voice on the radio. Rebo. Peter. Shit. He's not sure what to call him now.

The longer he listens, the more he realizes why he was so oblivious to Rebo's identity this whole time. It's Peter's voice, he can hear that now, but it's different on the air. Calmer. More sure of itself. Is this what Peter sounds like when he has nothing to hide? No one to try and blend in with—just him and a microphone? Is this what the *real* Peter sounds like? Or is it another act? Another mask?

Does he even know Rebo at all like he thought he did?

It doesn't matter now. Rebo and Peter are undeniably the same person, and all Malcolm can focus on is how foolish he feels for never noticing it before.

"Hey," Malcolm breathes out when he's patched through. There's a pulse in his ears. He swallows. "It's Clark."

"Clark Kent!" Rebo says, like he always does. He sounds relieved to hear Malcolm's voice. "You had me scared for a minute, buddy, I thought you'd gone ahead and fallen in love with another handsome radio host."

Despite everything he knows now, Malcolm is hopeless to fight the smile that grows onto his face. He's scared shitless, but he really can't help it. It's still Rebo. It's just that it's also fucking *Peter Tollemache*.

"You know you're the only one for me, Rebo," Malcolm says, a little weakly. He's more aware of his voice than he's ever been before. He wonders what Rebo hears on his end—if he has an image in his head of what Clark looks like. He wonders if it looks anything like him.

How has Peter not figured him out yet? If Rebo sounds this different from Peter, how different does Clark sound compared to Malcolm? And if Peter and Malcolm are getting closer—which he hopes is what's happening—does that mean Peter is going to figure him out eventually?

Is there a time limit on how long Malcolm can have all of this?

"Clark?"

Malcolm blinks at Rebo's voice. "Hm?"

"Are you alright?" he asks kindly. "You sound kind of off."

Shit. Malcolm needs to get better at hiding his feelings if he's going to keep this up. He doesn't want to lose whatever he has with Rebo—*or* with Peter. Not any sooner than he has to.

"Yeah," Malcolm says, clearing his throat. He's shit at lying, but this is a truth he can tell. "Sorry, I just had a call with my mom earlier today. It didn't go great. They never really do."

"Oh, man," Rebo says, "I'm sorry to hear that. What happened?"

"Oh, you know, the usual," Malcolm sighs. "She accepts me being trans, but it hurts her and everyone else around me. Being myself is an act of selfishness. Yada yada yada."

It's silent, and Malcolm realizes with a twist in his gut that he probably said too much depressing stuff. In a fit of nervousness, he starts talking even more.

"I mean, it could have been worse," he says when Rebo fails to respond. "At least she didn't say I was never gonna find real love cause I'm only 'sort of a boy.' She saves those talks for special occasions." He laughs, but it's a weak sound, and Rebo doesn't laugh back. Malcolm gulps, waiting and waiting for Rebo to say something.

The voice that returns over the phone is Rebo, but it's darker than Malcolm has ever heard it before. "She says that shit to you?"

"Uh, yeah...yeah, sometimes." All the time.

"Clark," Rebo says, and Malcolm shivers. "Listen to me. Not a thing that woman says is true, you hear me?"

"Yeah, I know," Malcolm says, an automatic response, but Rebo cuts in before he's even finished.

"No, no, you don't. I can tell, man, I can hear it in your voice, her words are in your head. And I'm telling you, they're bullshit. Complete and utter bullshit. The people who really care about you don't care that you're trans. They don't just love you in spite of it, they love you *including* it, yeah? You and all your queer fuckin' glory, that shit's amazing, you hear me?"

Rebo's kind of rambling now, but Malcolm doesn't care. His cheeks are hurting at the force of his smile, and his eyes are stinging; he's about to cry on air, but he really, truly doesn't give a shit.

"And all that shit about you not finding real love because of who you are, that's ultra bullshit!" Rebo goes on. Malcolm laughs a bit giddily into the phone, but Rebo doesn't stop. "I can tell you right now, with absolute fuckin' certainty, that you won't have a single problem finding someone to love you for exactly who you are, Clark, 'cause I—"

He stops abruptly, as if the call had been cut short. Malcolm pulls the phone away from his face to double check that he hadn't accidentally hung up.

"You...?" Malcolm prods.

There's a breath over the line, and Rebo says, "Anyone would be lucky to have you, Clark. Anyone would be goddamn lucky."

Malcolm's heart might just beat out of his chest.

"Ah," Rebo says, "looks like my supervisor's had enough of my cursing for the night. I'm gonna have to let you go. But you're coming back, right?"

Malcolm nods and says, a little shakily, "Yeah. Yeah, of course."

After the call, Malcolm turns over onto his belly, letting the cold side of the pillow cool down his burning face. His stomach is raging with butterflies, toeing the line between pleasant and uncomfortable. He can already tell they'll be keeping him awake tonight.

"Well," Malcolm says into his empty room, cheek squished against the pillow. "I'm fucked."

21

Jazz shows up at the apartment the next morning, takes one look at him sitting at the kitchen island as he stares into his increasingly soggy bowl of Frosted Flakes, and says, "You figured it out, didn't you?"

He drops his spoon into his bowl. "You *knew*?"

"Of course I did," she says, leaning over the island. "Doesn't take a genius to connect the dots, dude."

"How did you figure it out before I did?"

"You kidding me?" She snorts. "Remember all that shit he said back in New York? *'There's this guy I want to be friends with, but he kind of hates me,'* blah blah blah. Sound familiar?"

Malcolm blinks, his eyebrows raising up into his hairline. "Oh my god."

"Yup."

"Oh my *god*."

"Take your time."

"He was talking about *me*."

"There we go."

"And you didn't say anything!" Malcolm shouts, smacking Jazz's arm. She jumps back with a yelp, rubbing at the skin.

"You would've freaked out, dude! Just like you're doing right now," she argues. She leans back against the fridge, arms crossed, and smiles. "Also, it was funny."

"You're a mischievous little bastard, you know that?"

She shrugs, shifting some of the magnet letters on the fridge to form an inappropriate word. "So are you gonna ask him out now?"

"And why would I do that?" Malcolm says, stirring his dissolved cereal. "Peter still doesn't know that I'm Clark. Plus we only stopped being enemies, like, a day ago."

"Wait, really? You finally don't think he hates you anymore?" She shuffles closer to him, leaning her hip against the kitchen island. "What changed?"

Malcolm blows out a long raspberry, leaning back. "He saw me during an episode."

Jazz whistles a low note. "Damn."

"Apparently, that wasn't the first time."

"No shit?"

He hums in confirmation. "In fact, he caught me during an episode the first time we met, according to him. I just...don't remember it."

There's a quiet pause before she says, "Things are starting to make a lot of sense."

Malcolm nods. He knows what she's feeling, that sudden clarity, everything clicking into place like magnets. "Yeah."

"Wait, so, how did you two make up after all this time?"

"Well, like I said, he caught me during an episode yesterday. But this time, he—" Malcolm clears his throat, remembering everything Peter did. "Well, he helped me."

At Jazz's confused look, Malcolm tells her the whole story. How Peter found him in front of the shop, took one look at his frantic state and immediately insisted he come inside. How Peter sat him down, turned off the lights and gave him one thing to focus on: the music. How he sat with Malcolm until he calmed down, patting the rhythm of the song against their chests.

He refuses to blush as he recounts everything to Jazz, who sits silently through it all. He feels like he's telling her something far more intimate than just how Peter helped him recover from a bad episode. It feels like something more. He wants to hold parts of it close to his chest, keep the details just for him, but he tells her as much as he can bear.

(He doesn't tell her what song they listened to. As strange as it probably is to deliberately withhold such a minor part of the story, he wants that for himself. That song is his to keep. His and Peter's.)

He tells her about Peter's explanation for it all, this new phrase he never knew of. Sensory overload. An explanation for why he feels this way sometimes, why the world suddenly becomes too much to handle.

"He says different coping mechanisms work for different people, but he'll help me figure out what works for me," Malcolm explains. "I really should've done more research on this before, but...shit, it just feels good to know that there's, like, an *answer*, you know?"

Jazz is silent when he looks at her. She's looking down at the floor, her arms hugging her torso. Finally, she mutters to her shoes, "All this time, we could've been helping you."

Malcolm deflates. "Jazz..."

"Just a simple Google search and we could've found some answers, and we didn't even do that much," she says. "God, I'm so sorry—"

"Jazmine," Malcolm says, standing from his seat to hold her by the shoulders. "Don't say that shit, dude, this is on me, too. I could've done a lot more to better myself, but I didn't. None of us ever considered it was a part of my ADHD because none of us knew that was even an option. It's not your fault, okay? If anything, it's mine."

"You didn't know."

"No, but I could've tried harder. I could've tried *something* other than just shutting myself out or hurting the people around me." He says, pulling her hand towards him until she wraps her arms around his middle and slumps into the hug. "We know now, yeah? Better late than never. Now that we have some answers, things will start getting better. I'll be better."

"Quit saying that like you're something that needs to be fixed."

"Quit blaming yourself for all my problems then, doofus."

Jazz pinches his ear and he snorts a laugh into her hair. She sighs, and he feels her breath on his shoulder. "You know, this doesn't have to be a bad thing," she says. "The whole Rebo-being-Peter thing. It could be good."

"Forgive me for failing to see how this could possibly be anything other than a huge fucking mess."

"Oh, it'll be a mess, for sure," she says. "That doesn't mean it's bad, though. It could be a good mess. Like that time Mona tried her hand at cake decorating."

Malcolm makes a noise in agreement. "The ugliest, most delicious lemon cake I've ever had."

"Exactly. This whole thing with Peter is just an ugly lemon cake. Messy and kinda scary looking, but delicious when you get to the insides."

"Are you gonna...dissect Peter?"

"If he hurts you, then yes."

They move over to the couch, shifting together until Jazz is reclined with her legs propped up on the coffee table, and Malcolm has his feet resting in Jazz's lap. Lady Governor has curled up into a ball on the couch in the gap between Malcolm's knee and Jazz's thigh, and Malcolm's leg twitches when her fur tickles his skin.

"You don't have to tell him yet," Jazz says. Malcolm looks at her.

"I don't?"

She shakes her head. "I don't think so. You should probably tell him *eventually*, but I don't see why it needs to be an urgent matter. Just, you know, try to be friends first."

"*Friends*," he says, a little disbelievingly.

She gives him an unimpressed look. "Yes, *friends*. You literally said yourself that you want to be friends with him."

"I know, I know! It's just—" he makes a defeated noise. "How do I do that?"

"My dude," she says, reaching over to place a hand on his leg. "You're already doing it. You've already had a bonding moment, and he basically took you on a date, so—"

"It was *not* a date, it was pity food after he caught me having a breakdown right in front of his store—"

"My *point is*, you're already golden, man. Just, I dunno, do some normal friend shit with him to let him know you're serious about ending all the enemy BS."

"Normal friend shit?"

"Normal friend shit."

"Right," Malcolm says, determined. "Okay. I can do that."

22

Malcolm tries to be kind to everyone. It's kind of a principle of his, especially after a particularly nasty episode back in high school that led to him nearly losing every friend he had. After that, he vowed to be a genuinely nice dude. When people think about him, they'll think, *yeah, that guy was pretty swell.*

The thing is, Malcolm hasn't really made a *new friend* since his current friend group was established. So he's not entirely sure how to go about this whole "being friends with Peter" thing. He might be a bit rusty at the process of it all.

He decides to go to the record shop. That's a good start, right? Step one: be in the general vicinity of the person you're trying to be friends with.

He stands outside of Roisin Records for a solid three minutes before finally forcing himself to go inside. It feels different now, just slightly. The last time he was here, he was in the middle of a full blown panic attack. But then again, it was also the place where Peter really *saw* him for the first time. Where he turned off the lights without a word, and put his headphones on Malcolm's ears so gently, careful not to touch him without a warning. Malcolm thinks about that moment most nights.

"Hey, you made it inside," Peter says when Malcolm enters the store. "I thought you were gonna stand out there forever."

"Shut up," Malcolm says, grateful that Peter doesn't ask further questions, but embarrassed that he saw him standing outside like a dolt in the first place.

Peter laughs and leans over the counter, resting his weight on his arms. He brings a hand up to rub against his shoulder as his eyes flick around the store. "What, uh, what brings you by?"

Okay, so Peter's feeling awkward too. Strangely enough, that makes Malcolm feel better about his own anxiety. It was easier to be friendly when the circumstances kind of forced it out of them, but when it's just two dudes in their twenties trying to turn years-long hostility into friendship...well, it's harder than it sounds to act normal about it.

"I'm looking for a record," Malcolm answers after a too-long pause.

"Obviously, dumbass."

The insult makes Malcolm smile. That's something he's more familiar with.

"Asshole," Malcolm says. "I'm...looking for something for my friend. They want to get into more, uh...'70s punk. Yeah."

"Good choice," he says. He hops up onto the counter and swings his legs over, jumping down with a dramatic roll of his torso. Malcolm rolls his eyes.

"You could've just walked around."

"Yeah, but I looked cool, didn't I?"

He did, but Malcolm refuses to give him the satisfaction.

"Which friend is this?" Peter asks.

"Goby," Malcolm says, throwing out the first name that comes to mind.

"Goby. That's the lanky one with the pumpkin hair, yeah? Your roommate?" Peter asks, walking towards the punk section.

Malcolm nods. "One of them, yeah."

"What kind of music are they into?"

Malcolm considers this for a moment, trying to think of the few times that Jazz let Goby control the aux in the truck. "Mostly dad-rock...some Britney Spears...the Mamma Mia soundtrack..."

"Interesting," Peter says, nodding his head. "I think I'd like this Goby person."

"You know what, I have a feeling they'd like you too."

"Hm. They single?"

Malcolm trips at the question, almost knocking down a stack of CDs in the process. "What? No. I mean—yes, they are, but," he clears his throat, "I mean, they're not really your type."

Peter turns around to look at him, walking backwards as he brushes his hand over a row of records. He gives Malcolm a look. "And you know my type?"

Malcolm's mouth feels dry. "Maybe?"

"Relax, dude. I'm teasing you," he says, and turns back around.

Malcolm lets out a relieved breath as soon as Peter's eyes leave him, and he scrubs a hand down his face. He's not quite sure how he's going to survive this.

"You said your friend listens to dad-rock, yeah?" Peter says, flipping through a few records. "'70s punk isn't too big of a departure from that. The two can definitely overlap. Well…I guess it depends on the dad."

Peter looks at Malcolm, and Malcolm blinks. "Right."

Peter makes a thoughtful noise, turning back around to thumb at a different row of records. He stops and slides out a record, eyes flitting over it before sliding it back in.

"Is the Dictators too dad-rock, you think?"

"Uh. Maybe?" *I have no idea.*

Peter says nothing, continuing his search. Malcolm watches his back, his shoulders shifting underneath the fabric of his white shirt. He almost doesn't catch it when Peter speaks again.

"So, Goby's your roommate, as you've said," Peter says, still turned away from Malcolm. "Why don't you just let them listen to the '70s punk albums you already have? I've been to your apartment now, I know you have a few."

Malcolm falters. "Not enough, I guess." *C'mon, dude, work on your lying skills.* "We play that stuff all the time. I figured they'd like something new, that's all."

Peter nods. "Fair enough. It was a pretty sad collection."

"Wh—fuck you, it's not that bad!"

"It could definitely be better, dude," Peter laughs, pulling out another record. He hands it to Malcolm. "I guess you'll just have to come by here more often."

Malcolm looks at Peter. He wonders if Peter's looking into his eyes or in between his eyebrows this time. "I guess so."

Peter's eyes flick down, and Malcolm goes a little dizzy before he realizes Peter's staring at the record that Malcolm hasn't done anything with yet. Malcolm looks at the album.

"The Dictators," Malcolm reads. "Not too dad-rock after all?"

"It's their debut album," Peter says, heading back towards the front counter. Malcolm follows him dumbly. "Could probably fall under the dad-rock umbrella, but it's definitely a good place to start if your friend's wanting to get more into punk."

"Right, yeah, totally."

He's running out of time. Peter's at the counter now, ringing up his item, bagging it, holding it out to Malcolm. Malcolm takes it, gears up to say *something*. Anything. This is his moment.

"Have a good day, man," Peter says.

"You too," Malcolm says.

And he turns to leave.

He makes it all the way to the door before stopping. He has to force his heels into the ground to keep himself from bolting right out the door. After a few customers frown at him for blocking the exit, he turns around and marches back to the counter. Peter eyes him curiously the whole way.

"Back so soon?"

Malcolm takes a breath. "You don't have to pretend around me, you know."

"Oh," Peter pauses, his expression unreadable. He blinks at Malcolm. "What?"

It wasn't what he had been planning to say, but it's out there now. Can't stop now. "You just—you never have to pretend to be someone you're not when it's just me. Or—or my friends, Goby and Mona and Jazz. You can always be yourself with us, you know? You don't have to, um, mask. I don't know if I'm saying that right, but, uh…yeah."

Peter, for the first time since Malcolm's known him, seems to be at a loss for words. He shakes his head a bit. "I appreciate that. Really, but…I mean, as long as I'm working in the shop or getting groceries or whatever, I'm probably gonna mask just to avoid the stares. It's just…easier. Safer, sometimes, too."

"No, yeah, I get that, yeah," Malcolm says, "but, I mean, if you ever need a break from doing all that, we can always just hang out at my place or something."

That…was not what he wanted to say. Peter's eyebrows shoot upward, and Malcolm feels his ears go hot. He just invited Peter Tollemache to his house. To *hang out*.

"The whole gang will be there!" Malcolm rushes to say. "We have game nights all the time, so like—you can totally come to the next one, if you want? I mean, you'll be free to be yourself there. None of us will judge you; I mean, you've seen us."

Peter finally smiles. "Game nights? Now who's 80?"

"Shut up," he laughs. "It's still you."

Peter breathes out a laugh and shrugs. Then he sticks out his hand. "Okay. Gimme your phone."

"Why?" Malcolm says as he hands it over.

"So you can text me your address, stupid."

"Oh," Malcolm flushes. "Right."

Peter's fingers fly across Malcolm's phone screen in a flurry, and Peter's phone screen lights up with a buzz on the counter. Peter picks his phone up and tosses Malcolm's back to him. Malcolm's phone has barely reached his hand before it buzzes with a reply.

hey sexy

omg malcolm not at work

"You ass!" Malcolm shouts, and Peter dodges his hand with a delighted laugh. "That's so not funny." Malcolm grabs his bag and stalks out of the store, grumbling to himself as Peter's laughter fades with distance. He texts Peter his address before he can forget, along with a slew of middle finger emojis, then stuffs his phone into his pocket.

(It isn't until he's nearly home that he remembers, quite suddenly, that Peter's been to his apartment. He already knew the address.)

23

It's easier to talk to Peter after that. Peter loves to text, apparently, and sends him nonsensical memes in the middle of his workday that Malcolm has to hide from Mona so she doesn't start interrogating him. Mona catches him, of course, because he's about as subtle as a brick. She manages to steal his phone during their slow hours and text Peter a myriad of pictures—a photo of Terrance the stick bug in his terrarium, a selfie of Mona smiling next to Terrance, another selfie of Mona with Malcolm shouting at her back, a semi-blurred picture of Mona running as Malcolm chases her down, an extremely blurred picture of the pub after Malcolm briefly knocked the phone out of her hand. Peter responds with an audio message of him wheeze-laughing for seven seconds straight.

"So you two are friends now?" Mona asks him once she finally relinquishes the phone.

Malcolm shrugs, smiling sheepishly as he pockets the phone. "I guess."

"'*I guess*,' he says," Mona mocks, cuffing his shoulder. "He's sending you memes! You're besties now. That's, like, the law."

"You never went to law school."

"You don't know everything about me! I could've been doing law shit before we met. Maybe I ditched law school to pursue my dream of bartending. Like Nick Miller, but girlboss."

"I think Nick Miller should qualify as a girlboss."

"You're avoiding the subject."

"And you're harshing my vibes," Malcolm says, and Mona kicks at his leg.

When Malcolm tells Mona he's going out for his lunch break, she gives him a knowing look that he pretends not to see as he ducks out of the pub. He pauses outside Roisin Records when he sees Peter at the counter looking down at his magazine, unaware. Malcolm pulls out his phone and snaps a photo.

A well-defined curl falls over Peter's eyes in the photo, and his hand is half raised to push it away. Malcolm tries not to stare at it for too long before he sends it to Peter. Peter's phone lights up from where it sits on the counter, and he opens the message. Malcolm can hear Peter's bark of laughter from outside.

"And you called me a stalker," Peter says when Malcolm enters the store. "What're you doing here?"

"Taking my lunch break," Malcolm says.

"You don't have any lunch," Peter says, looking down at Malcolm's empty hands.

"Very observant. You do detective work?"

Peter rolls his eyes, then disappears behind the counter. Malcolm peeks over the edge to see him maneuvering through a cramped drawer filled with pens and jars and boxes. Peter makes a satisfied sound and pops back up, tossing something in the air that Malcolm has to scramble to catch.

"Eat that," Peter says. "I already took my break, I can't leave again."

Malcolm looks down at the package of cherry Pop-Tarts. "Dude, I don't—"

"*Eat it,*" he repeats sternly, and Malcolm frowns.

"Okay, Mom," he answers dramatically. Malcolm chews at the Pop-Tart but refuses to let Peter see how much he enjoys it. Cherry is his favorite.

"You're a grown ass adult now, you better not make it a habit to skip your lunches," Peter says, returning to his magazine as if he doesn't care as much as his words imply. "And get out of the way, you're gonna block customer traffic."

Malcolm makes an unattractive squawking sound around his mouthful of Pop-Tart. "Where else am I supposed to go? This store is eight feet wide!"

"Come here, stupid," Peter says, waving Malcolm over.

"Is that allowed?" Malcolm says. "Am I gonna get arrested?"

"Yes, I've already called the police. This was a setup."

"I knew the Pop-Tarts were a trap," Malcolm says as he hops up onto the counter, and Peter shakes his head at him, but Malcolm can see his lips pulling up into a smile.

"You're stupid."

"And yet, you're the one letting me behind the counter."

"Already regretting it."

"Tell me to go back, then," Malcolm says, and he doesn't mean for it to come out like that—like he's teasing, *flirting*—but it does, and when Peter turns to look at him, Malcolm doesn't look away. He's taller than Peter this way, sitting up on the counter, and he likes that Peter has to tilt his head up to look him straight on. Peter's eyes narrow for a moment, and he hums.

"No. I think I'll keep you here," he says. Malcolm holds his breath. Then Peter says, "It'll be funny to watch you try to get back to work on time."

"Shit, what—" Malcolm jumps from the counter, turning on his phone to check the time, only to see that he still has ten minutes left of his break. Peter has already doubled over with laughter. "Oh, fuck you, dude."

"I'm sorry, I'm sorry," he says through giggles. "God, your face. Wow."

"So not funny, man," Malcolm says, fighting a smile.

"It's a little funny."

"I could've had a heart attack! What would you have done then, huh? What would you have done with a heart attack victim on your hands?"

"Save your life, obviously," Peter says, "I'm CPR certified."

Malcolm scoffs and turns away, very deliberately *not* thinking about Peter giving him mouth to mouth. "Yeah, right. You and your string bean arms?"

"*String bean?*" Peter exclaims. "I'm muscle-bound, motherfucker."

Malcolm makes a disbelieving noise, and Peter knocks against his shoulder but luckily does nothing else. Malcolm had feared for one mortifying moment that Peter was going to rip off his hoodie to prove he's as "muscle-bound" as he claims to be. He can't promise he would've been able to look away if he had.

The next day, around noon, he gets a text from Peter that just says, lunch break? and suddenly, it's part of their routine. (If Malcolm thinks too hard about the fact that they seem to have a *routine* now, he'll combust.) Malcolm goes to Roisin Records during his lunch, and Peter lets him sit behind the counter (or on top of it, if they're having a slow day), and he makes sure Malcolm eats, and they talk. It's good. It's really good.

"Why don't I come to the pub next time?" Peter says one day. "You always come here for your breaks, maybe I wanna bug you for once."

"You already bug me enough," Malcolm says, snagging a chip from the open bag of barbeque Lays Peter has under the counter and popping it into his mouth. "And if you come to the pub I can't guarantee Mona will leave us alone."

"I like Mona," Peter says, cramming a handful into his own mouth. Malcolm grimaces and shakes his head. "She's got pizazz."

"Oh, she definitely won't shut up if she hears you say that."

"Let the woman speak!" Peter says, throwing his arm into the air, brandishing a large barbeque chip the way Shakespear might hold a skull before devouring it with a flourish. Malcolm bites down on a smile.

"You're dumb."

"I fight for women's rights to speak and you call me dumb. Wow."

Malcolm steals the bag of chips after that, and Peter just laughs. It's strange, when he stops and looks at Peter, head thrown back and shoulders shaking with unrestrained joy. It's strange to see this side of Peter up close, just for him. He feels like he was never meant to see it. It feels like a privilege, or maybe a gift. He never wants to look away—but of course, when Peter's laughter dies down, he does.

Malcolm's wiping at the bar counter next to Mona the following day when he looks up and sees Peter approaching the pub, a smug grin on his face.

"Oh, that prick," Malcolm mutters under his breath. He turns to Mona and says, "I don't suppose I can convince you to take your break, now, right this second?"

"What in the world—" she starts, then cuts off as Peter enters the store. Her confused expression dissolves into a look of pure glee. "Peter, my darling!"

"Mona! Aren't you a sight for sore eyes," Peter greets her, and she leans over the counter to give Peter a kiss on the cheek. "You should start giving Malcolm fashion tips, he's in the same pair of jeans every time I see him."

"Since when are you two so close?" Malcolm says, scrubbing a little harder at a nonexistent stain. Mona raises an eyebrow at him, unimpressed.

"Since when did you stop hiding behind the counter when Peter comes into the pub?" Mona asks, and Peter chokes on a laugh, eyebrows raised.

"Dude," Peter says.

"Shut up," Malcolm says. "Don't say a word."

"I can't just *not* say something about that."

"You absolutely can. See, you're doing it right now. Good job."

Peter's smile is incredulous and unrelenting. "You *hid*? Like, full on, soldier in the trenches, duck and cover—"

"Shut up!"

"He dropped like Andy's toys in *Toy Story*," Mona says, and Peter wheezes, his eyes squinting shut.

"Yes, thank you for your input, Mona," Malcolm grumbles. Mona slaps Peter on the back as he struggles to get his breath back through the force of his laughter. Malcolm points an accusing finger at Peter and says, "This is why I didn't want you coming here. I don't trust you two together."

"Well, this would've happened eventually since I'm coming over for game night," Peter supplies. Malcolm closes his eyes, regretting everything he'd done in his life to bring him to this moment. When he opens his eyes, Mona is leaning towards him, looking for all intents and purposes like the cat who caught the canary.

"Malcolm, my love," Mona says, voice sickly sweet. "Peter's coming to game night?"

"You didn't tell her I'm coming?" Peter asks.

"He did not," Mona confirms. Peter can't see the devilish grin on her face, but Malcolm most certainly can. Malcolm tries not to squirm. He can feel the heat of a blush creeping up his neck. "It probably just escaped his mind. Excuse me, boys."

Mona starts to leave, but not before Malcolm catches her pulling her phone out of her pocket. She escapes into the back room, and not a second later Malcolm feels a vibration in his own pocket that he's sure is from the group chat. He pulls it out to confirm his suspicions.

Malcolm's bringing a date to game night, Mona has texted.

NOT a date. just a friend.

you have friends? Jazz replies. Malcolm starts to form a retort before she adds, **other than us i mean.**

yes, asshole

Guess who it is, Mona says. **Guess guess guess.**

IS IT CUTE BUTT, Goby finally chimes in. **PLS TELL ME ITS CUTE BUTT. IF ITS NOT CUTE BUTT IM SUING FOR EMOTIONAL DISTRESS**

pls learn how to turn off caps lock ur giving me a migraine

but yes its peter

Jazz replies, **i love that you didn't need a better descriptor to know who goby was talking about**, and Malcolm shoves his phone back into his pocket.

"I'm guessing they all know I'm coming now?" Peter says from his seat at the bar.

Malcolm nods. "Mona definitely took care of that."

Peter looks down at the counter, tapping his nail against the wood. "They don't mind, right? I'm not intruding?"

"What? No, of course not." Peter doesn't look up, so Malcolm moves in closer to get his attention. "Hey, seriously, dude. They're stoked that you're coming. Jazz is just glad I'm finally making other friends, honestly. She's a bit sick of seeing me all the time."

Peter squints. "Liar."

Malcolm smiles, shrugging as he turns around to busy himself with useless tasks. Looking at Peter feels like looking into the sun, sometimes. "If you're not comfortable at game night, you can always leave. And I'm not saying that in a guilt-trippy way or anything. I wouldn't want you to stick around if you were just miserable the whole time. You're not obligated to stay, but I think you'll have a good time if you do. And, uh," Malcolm clears his throat. "I'd like to have you there, or whatever."

Malcolm chances a look up into the mirror along the shelves of alcohol and sees Peter looking down at the bar counter again. He's trailing his thumbnail along his cupid's bow, an absentminded action. He looks ever so slightly pleased. Malcolm averts his eyes.

Like the damn sun.

24

He convinces the gang to hold game night on a weekday, after a fair bit of complaining from both Goby and Mona. They *always* have game nights on the weekend; that's what they argue as they lay strewn across the living room and kitchen, wondering why Malcolm wants to switch up game nights for the first time in years.

But Rebo works on weekend nights, which means Peter wouldn't be able to stay long.

Jazz seems to sense Malcolm's train of thought. "I think a weekday works better for my schedule," she chimes in from the couch, having a staring contest with Lady Governor as she sits on Jazz's chest. "Got lots of, y'know, beekeeper shit to do this weekend. Can't keep the bees waiting."

"Aren't you in the research department?" Goby asks. A soggy bite of Nutri-Grain bar sits in their open mouth, and Malcolm cringes.

"Yeah, and I've got lots of important bee information to write about. Did you know male bees' dicks explode when they ejaculate?"

"Whoa. Punk."

That seems to convince Mona (about game night, not the bee sex), and Goby's outnumbered 3 to 1 once Mona is on board, so game night gets moved to Wednesday. Malcolm mouths a 'thank you' to Jazz, and she throws him a wink.

Peter sends a text that night that just says, **show me the baby**. Lady Governor is comfortably asleep on Malcolm's chest, purring loudly. He smiles and adjusts the camera until she's within view and presses record. He brings a hand up to brush down her back, and she makes a soft *mrrp* noise, burrowing further into his chest. The collar of his shirt pulls down with her, but he doesn't dare fix it and disrupt her peace. He huffs out a quiet laugh, not wanting to wake her up, and kisses her on the head before ending the recording.

When he sends it to Peter, the three dots that indicate he's typing pop up about four times before he finally sends a simple, **cute**. Malcolm spends more time debating whether Peter was referring to him or the cat than he cares to admit.

•   •   •   •

The night before game night, Malcolm spends hours in his bed trying to fall asleep. He was half tempted to lay out his clothes for the morning, like he would for the first day of school when he was little. He tries every method of falling asleep that he knows of: counting down, counting up, counting sheep. A lot of counting. He played YouTube clips of rain, thunderstorms, something titled "Wind Chimes and Flutes for Meditation," but nothing did the trick. He was stuck thinking of how tomorrow could possibly go; but even when he went through every scenario—from best case to worst—his body still failed to let him calm down and drift off.

Malcolm grabs his phone, hissing when the light hits his eyes. He blindly lowers the brightness, blinking a few times until the burst of color behind his eyelids goes away. He pulls up his messages, debating. Goby's definitely asleep, and so is Mona. Jazz might be awake, but he doesn't want to risk her wrath if he accidentally wakes her up...

He's just making excuses. He knows who he wants to text.

hey.
sorry i know its late.
or early. whatever.
are you up?
wait this is dumb.
ignore this.

hey i'm awake.
are you alright?

i'm fine.

WELCOME, CALLER

just can't sleep.

neither can i.
wanna call?

Malcolm imagines it, for just a moment. Calling Peter, talking to him, just the two of them without an audience of who-knows-how-many people listening in. Slowly hearing Peter's voice grow tired since he wouldn't have the radio show to keep him awake. Speaking in hushed tones and sleepy laughter. Staying on call even when the phone goes silent except for their quiet snores, connected through a single line of communication even in their sleep.

i can't.

don't wanna wake the others, y'know?

gotcha. we can just text.
what's keeping you awake?

You, Malcolm thinks vehemently, desperately. He wants to say it. He even types it into the message box. But he can't. He can't.

just. thoughts.
ya know.
thinking too much.

i get that.
honestly, i'm kinda nervous about tomorrow.

what? why?

i don't have a whole lot of friends, dude.
like, seriously. i have a roommate who's
pretty cool, but we don't talk much. i have a
sister but calling her one of my closest
friends just sounds kinda sad, even if it's
true. but anyway.

i guess i'm just. nervous to be myself.
you said i could be myself in front of your
friends. unmask.
but the thing is, i've been hiding myself for
so long, man. i'm kinda wondering if i even
know how to stop.

Malcolm stares at his phone. He didn't know any of that. Peter's been teaching him so much, and the guy's done all this research to help himself and others; Malcolm just assumed Peter had everything figured out about himself.

His thumbs hover over the keyboard. How does Peter do this so easily? How does he always know the right thing to say? Malcolm's not like that. His words are jumbled and clumsy and sometimes do more harm than good.

But he can try. He owes Peter that much. He *wants* to do that much.

goby sometimes takes stimming breaks
when they've had a long day.

just, you know, sits in the living room
and rocks back and forth, or spins in
circles to get all their energy out.

mona puts reminders on the fridge for
me to eat breakfast, cause i forget a lot.
especially if i haven't taken my meds yet.

i used to read jazz the study guides for
our finals out loud cause letters can get
real mixed up for her sometimes.

why are you telling me this?

i'm saying i'll help. we all will.

*you'll learn how to be yourself again,
peter. and while you figure it out, you
won't be alone.*

i promise.

The read receipt appears under Malcolm's texts, but it takes longer for the typing bubble on Peter's side to pop up again. It takes so long for Peter to respond that Malcolm falls asleep before it's sent, the buzz of his phone only a distant sensation in his drowsy state. When he wakes, he checks his phone to see only two messages from Peter, much shorter than he anticipated from the amount of time it took him to respond. Malcolm looks at the time stamps and sees that there's a twenty-minute gap between the first text and the next.

**thank you malcolm
sweet dreams**

25

"Beige or orange?" Malcolm says.

Goby frowns. "Why is it you only have, like, three colors in your entire wardrobe?"

"This is why Peter asked me to give you fashion tips, darling," Mona quips.

They've all gathered together in Malcolm's bedroom an hour before game night is set to start, and Malcolm still hasn't decided on what to wear. He stands in front of his mirror in only a black tank top and a pair of red boxers, holding two slightly different colored t-shirts in front of his chest. Several pairs of ironed pants lay flat on his bed. Goby sits on the floor next to him, looking bored and amused at the same time, while Mona sits delicately on the edge of his bed to avoid wrinkling the trousers. Jazz has cleared a spot on his desk and made herself comfortable on its surface, her legs bent and propped up on a chair.

"This is dumb," Jazz says. "We always end up in our pajamas anyway, what's the use in getting all dressed up?"

"Let him dress up for Peter, it's cute!" Mona says.

Malcolm throws the shirts down, ears red. "I am *not* dressing up for Peter."

The group looks collectively unconvinced, which is enough to get Malcolm to aggressively shove his clothes back into their drawers and settle with his usual game night attire: a worn out Street Fighter II t-shirt and sweatpants. The sweatpants hang low on his hips, and he has a brief moment of weakness where he imagines himself reaching up for something in the kitchen, and Peter not being able to help but look at the strip of skin that reveals itself as he stretches his arms upward...

Malcolm groans and runs a hand down his face, pulling the sweatpants up to his belly button.

"I saw that," Goby says, and pokes Malcolm's ankle.

"You saw nothing," Malcolm says. "You know nothing."

"I know everything," they say. "My mom's a psychic, it's only a matter of time until I inherit her abilities."

Goby's mom is one of those so-called psychics that do palm readings and tell people their future in small off-brand-Las-Vegas cities. Malcolm's never quite figured out if Goby really means it when they say they're bound to inherit these so-called abilities, or if they're just really committed to the joke. He calls bullshit either way.

"Alright, tell me how tonight's gonna go then," Malcolm says, turning to Goby with his hands on his hips.

Goby groans as they stand up, their knees cracking far too loudly for someone their age, and faces Malcolm. They bring their hands forward, then promptly slaps them onto Malcolm's cheeks, smooshing them together. He blinks up at them as they close their eyes.

"Hmmm," Goby says mysteriously. "I'm seeing laughter. Smiles. A chance to connect."

"How inshighful," Malcolm says through puckered lips.

"I'm sensing warmth," they continue, "and...truth. A moment of honesty." They open their eyes and look squarely into Malcolm's. "Don't be afraid to be honest, Mal."

Malcolm blanches, and his eyes flit over to where Mona and Jazz are fiddling with the radio on his nightstand. Jazz glances over at him, an eyebrow raised, and Malcolm looks away.

"Um—"

A violent ringing sounds from his bed, and everyone jumps.

"Christ on a bike," Jazz swears passionately, her hand to her chest. "Why is your phone so fuckin' loud?" Mona looks to be in a similarly startled state, while Goby remains relatively cool.

"I knew that was gonna happen," Goby says.

"Oh, shut the fuck up," Jazz says as Malcolm moves toward the bed.

It takes a bit of shoveling around the mess of sheets before he finds the ringing phone. His heart sinks when he sees the caller ID.

Peter's laughing face flashes on his screen, the smiling poop emoji next to his contact name staring back at Malcolm. He can't answer this. The only other time he's talked to Peter on the phone is when he's Clark. What if he recognizes his voice? He can't find out like this, not now.

Malcolm looks at Jazz, eyes wide, and their years of sibling-level bonding comes in clutch. She seems to read his mind, nodding her head once before grabbing the phone out of his hand.

She puts the phone on speaker and says, "Hello, Malcolm speaking."

"Hello, Jazz," Peter says. It's surreal, hearing him like this. Like Rebo, but not quite. "Where's Malcolm?"

Jazz looks at Malcolm and says, "Takin' a shit."

Malcolm drops his head into his hands as Goby struggles to keep their laughter quiet. When he looks back up, Mona is shaking her head at Jazz, stifling a smile.

"Oh, okay," Peter says. "If he stinks up the place before I get there I'm never coming to game night again."

Malcolm feels a piece of him die a little. Goby has to hold onto the edge of a chair to keep themselves from falling to the floor, their face red from the effort to keep quiet. They're failing spectacularly.

"Whatcha need, boss man?" Jazz asks.

"Just wanted to ask Malcolm if I should be bringing anything to game night. Foods, drinks...?"

"I mean, we're just gonna order some pizza, but I wouldn't object to a bag of Doritos if you're passing by the store anyway."

"What kind?"

"Nacho," Jazz says.

WELCOME, CALLER

At the same time, Goby says, "Cool Ranch."

Peter laughs. "I'll grab both."

"Good man," Goby says.

As soon as the call ends, Goby cackles openly at Malcolm's distraught expression, and Mona gives him a sympathetic pat on the arm.

"I know you're having an internal crisis, love," Mona says, "but I just have to say, I like that boy. I hope he sticks around."

Malcolm sighs. "Yeah. Me too."

Time passes very slowly as Malcolm waits for Peter to arrive. When the doorbell finally rings, Malcolm forces himself to stay in his seat and pretend that he hadn't just been watching the entrance for the past twenty minutes with the intensity of every neighborhood crime watch combined.

Goby doesn't have the same restraint. They bolt towards the door before the vibrations of the bell have even settled, laughing at Malcolm's visible struggle to remain even a little bit chill.

Goby throws open the door and bows dramatically, "St. Peter."

"My Lord Gobias," Peter responds with an identical bow. "I've brought gifts." He raises the two Party Size bags of Doritos, clutching them in his fist like a trophy.

"Great Scott! How marvelous!" Goby shouts.

"'Great Scott' isn't Medieval, dumbass, you're messing up the bit," Jazz says as she enters the room, shoving a giant green hoodie over her head. She pulls her dreads out of the hoodie, and they fall over her back in a wave. "Hey, Pete."

Malcolm gags. "*Pete?*"

"Yeah, sorry, I'm with him," Peter says, setting down the Doritos on the kitchen island. "Not a fan."

"You're right, it sounded wrong as I said it," Jazz says. She makes for the Doritos, then pauses, blinking down at Peter's outfit. "You're overdressed."

Peter looks down at his button-up and jeans. "How am I overdressed?"

"You're wearing a *belt*, dude. Goby's not even wearing pants." She gestures to Goby's KFC themed boxers.

"I like the breeze," Goby says.

Jazz heads over to a large cardboard box sitting by the jacket closet. It's covered in Sharpie doodles and patterned tape. "I'll go through the Pit and find you something."

"The...Pit?" Peter says carefully.

Malcolm stands, finally, hoping he can forget the fluttering in his heart once Peter takes off his clothes. Not like that. Peter just looks too *good* right now, so maybe if he can get him into some ratty t-shirt he might stop imagining Peter kissing his nose real soft.

"The Clothes Pit," Malcolm explains. "Whenever someone finds a piece of clothing in their laundry that belongs to someone else, it goes in the Pit. If you're missing clothes, check the Pit. We just always forget to look through it, so it's constantly filled with random stuff." He joins Jazz in the rummaging, tossing the smaller clothing items on the floor haphazardly. He'll clean it up later.

They reemerge together, Jazz holding a pair of Grinch pajama pants and Malcolm holding a t-shirt that says "arson" in glittery letters, stamped above a picture of Michael Cera. He can't remember if the shirt belongs to Jazz or Goby.

"Your outfit for the night, good sir," Jazz says.

"Oh, Jesus," Peter mutters, grabbing the clothes and making his way to the bathroom to change.

"Wait!" Malcolm calls before Peter can leave. Peter pauses just in time for Malcolm to bolt into his room and return with a pair of scissors in hand. He motions for Peter to hold the shirt out, then snips the tag from its neckline. He steps back, holding the removed tag, then looks up to find Peter staring at him curiously. "Sorry, um. Those always bother me, so..."

"No, yeah, uh. They bother me too," he says. "Thanks."

Malcolm nods, giving an awkward half-smile before Peter turns away and locks the bathroom door to change. When Malcolm turns around, everyone is staring. Mona had been in her room before, but now she's leaning against her door, smiling. He doesn't like it.

"What?" He says, a bit too defensively.

"That was cute," Mona says.

"Are you gonna start cutting the crusts off his sandwiches, too?" Jazz says. Mona *tsks* and cuffs her upside the head.

"Man, I wish I had someone to cut the tags off my shirts for me," Goby says, sighing dramatically. "How romantic is that?"

"You're all vile little creatures," Malcolm says, stalking back to the couch and flopping down next to Lady.

Peter emerges from the restroom with his old clothes folded up neatly in his hands. "Sorry, could I use a plastic bag or something to put these in?"

Goby grabs a bag from the kitchen, but Malcolm barely notices. Peter looks...soft. So, terribly soft. The pajama pants hang loosely from his hips, pooling at his feet. He's wearing fuzzy purple socks. (Those weren't from the Pit—he must've already been wearing them. God.) The shirt is too large for anyone in the house, much less Peter, so it dips around his neck, exposing the hollow of his throat and the curves of his collar bones. Peter tugs at the hem of the shirt, inspecting it, then turns to Malcolm and gives him an amused smile, as if they're sharing an inside joke. It's very Jim-and-Pam, and it makes Malcolm want to crawl under the couch and live there forever.

"Fuck," Malcolm mouths to himself, and Lady Governor meows in agreement. He turns away from Peter, too painfully enamored by the outfit to handle looking at it for a moment longer, and finds Goby staring right at him, their full eyebrows bouncing up and down on their forehead suggestively. Malcolm rolls his eyes and subtly gives them the finger, and they blow him a kiss.

"Alright," Mona claps her hands together. "Pizza will be here momentarily. Shall we begin the games?"

Goby slaps their hands down into the kitchen counter and shouts, "Uno!"

"Fuck no! You cheat!" Jazz protests.

"I *win*."

"We're not playing Uno," she turns to Malcolm, a challenge in her eyes. "Mario Kart?"

"Nuh-uh," Mona shakes her head. "Last time you two played together, Goby got a black eye."

"Worth it," Goby says.

"Do you guys have Sushi Go?" Peter pipes up, a little hesitantly.

"Oh *hell* yeah, I love that game. Wait here," Goby says, and dashes into their bedroom. Malcolm turns to Peter and gives him what he hopes is an encouraging smile. Peter looks away with a shy grin.

After several moments of loud crashing noises and unnecessary shouting, Goby finally pops out of their black hole of a room with an exclamation of triumph and the card game held firmly in their grasp. "Let's get our sush' on."

"Only if you never say that fake ass word again," Jazz says.

The thing about game night is that they very rarely make it through a full game. This time, Mona makes it all the way through the instructions before the doorbell rings for the pizza, and while Mona gets up to retrieve it, Jazz and Goby begin to discuss the complexities of time travel. Any hope for continuation of the game is lost from there.

"Sorry," Malcolm mutters towards Peter. Jazz and Mona had sat together on the couch while Goby took up the chair, leaving Peter and Malcolm to sit next to each other on the floor. "This kinda happens a lot. Half of us have a shit attention span and the other half have no impulse control. Mona's the best at keeping us on track but she can't resist good food."

"Oh, look at this *beauty*," Mona moans from the kitchen as she opens the lid to one of their three pizzas. She takes a long sniff and moans again, lewder than a pizza probably deserves. "The only decent pizza place in Bugswick. Peter, your balls are gonna fall off the moment you take a bite of this."

Peter chuckles and leans into Malcolm's space, and Malcolm holds his breath. "Nothing to apologize for. Your friends are pretty cool."

Malcolm smiles, watching Jazz slap one of her hands onto the other as she emphasizes her point about paradoxes not existing because 'whatever changed has already happened'. "Yeah," Malcolm says. "They are."

Malcolm notices something moving in the corner of his eye, and looks down to see Peter's hand braced against the floor, fidgeting discreetly with something. His fingers flip the small object around over and over, soothingly repetitive. It looks like the same thing he had been holding the first time he came to the apartment, after he rescued Lady. Malcolm was never able to identify it. Peter's movements falter, and he starts to put his hand back into his pocket.

Malcolm almost makes a comment about it. Peter doesn't need to hide like that. He can do whatever he wants, move as much as he wants. He wants Peter to know that he's safe to be himself here. Then, Malcolm notices Peter's hand pause, hovering over his pocket. Malcolm tries to look as subtly as he can to see what's caught Peter's attention.

Goby's still talking to Jazz about time travel, and they've started to flap their hands in between them excitedly, bouncing on their folded knees. Peter looks at Goby, stimming out in the open, and brings his hand away from his pocket. He fidgets with the small toy;

hesitant, but no longer hiding. Malcolm turns away, his chest tight and warm.

It's a start.

26

Peter unwinds slowly throughout the night. Mona offers him a slice of pizza, and he accepts it with a smile. Jazz pokes fun at his outfit, and he pokes fun at hers right back. Malcolm knows one night of hanging out isn't going to undo years of hiding his natural self, but he hopes the laughter bubbling out of Peter's mouth is real.

The most unsurprising turn of the night is Goby and Peter taking a liking to each other. While Peter had made a joke about being interested in Goby, Malcolm can see there's no romantic connection between the two. They've molded together like long lost siblings, once again discussing the logistics of time travel after Jazz had given up on entertaining Goby's fixation on the subject any longer. Malcolm learns that Peter fully believes in time travel, and thinks it's completely possible he's met his future self already.

"How would I even know if it was me? I wouldn't, if it was some old wrinkly version of me," Peter says as Goby nods along intensely. "He could just walk up to me and say hey, you dropped some cash, and I'd go all my life never knowing that was me until eventually it'd be my turn to go back in time and give my past self the cash he dropped."

"*Exactly*," Goby says. "You get me, P. You get me."

"Hey, Peter," Jazz says, flopping onto the couch with a new plate of pizza. Mona follows, two slices in hand, and throws Malcolm an orange soda. "Did you know Goby used to be a problem kid at school?"

"Why does that not surprise me?" Peter says.

"I feel like I should be offended, but I don't blame you," Goby says with a laugh. "I used to get into all sorts of fights. Not that they were all my fault! But, uh, some of them were. You see this gap right here?" They lift up their lip and point to the empty space in their teeth in the top row, poking their tongue at the gum there.

"Got knocked out back in high school by some transphobe. It's fine, though, he got it worse."

"That's actually pretty badass, Goby," Peter says. Then he points to his own lip, to the scar that Malcolm has become so familiar with over the past few months. "I got this from someone's ring. Lousy punch, but some damn sharp jewelry. Dude must've thought he was a mafia boss or something. Honestly, it's kind of an embarrassing scar 'cause the guy who gave it to me was, like, 90 pounds soaking wet."

"Look out for the small ones, they're feisty," Goby says. "Take Malcolm, for instance."

"Oi, watch it," Malcolm says sharply.

"See?" Goby whispers to Peter conspiratorially. "Feisty."

Mona finally interrupts, always the diffuser in the group. "Do you have any siblings, Peter?" She leans forward, her interest genuine. She always knows how to make people feel special.

"Yeah, actually, my sister," Peter says. He pulls out his phone, scrolling for a few seconds before turning it around to show the rest of them. "She does roller derby. There she is, on the left side."

They all marvel at the picture. Her braids whip behind her as she slams into the girl next to her, speeding around the track. She looks—

"Fucking badass," Goby says, eyes wide. "Is she single?"

"Filter, Goob, remember your filter," Mona says.

"I'd sell my brain-to-mouth filter for a bag of Takis."

"Clearly," Jazz says.

"How did you all meet?" Peter asks suddenly, and they all look at him. He shrinks just the smallest bit, tugging at his pant leg.

"That's a very long and interesting story," Jazz says, popping a chip into her mouth. "In the beginning, God created the heavens and the earth. Some unimportant shit happened for a few years until eventually we got to the birth of me, Jazmine Chikondi, the leader of our pack."

"You are *so* not the leader," Goby argues. "If anything, it's Mona. She's like our mom."

"Gross," Jazz says, "that's my girlfriend you're talking about."

"Darling, please continue," Mona says, stroking a hand down Jazz back.

Jazz gives Mona a quick love-struck grin before turning back to Peter, hands outstretched. "Right, so, it started with me and Malcolm. We've known each other for, like, always. We met in elementary school—I think I shoved him over and he bit my arm and we've been friends ever since. Mona and Goby didn't come around until college."

Mona nods, picking off a slice of pepperoni from her pizza. "I met Malcolm in a trans and gender non-conforming support group. We both ditched after the first couple of sessions, but decided to stick together." She leans forward and whispers loudly, "Malcolm had a bit of a crush on me in the beginning."

"I didn't know you were a lesbian!" Malcolm shouts.

Peter looks between Malcolm and Mona with a delighted, shit-eating grin. "You liked *Mona*?"

"Hey, it's not *that* surprising," Mona says. She leans back, putting on an air of mock arrogance. "I am pretty spectacular. You want to know what he said when he found out I was a lesbian, though?"

"Oh, god," Malcolm mutters, letting his head fall into his hands.

"He said, 'Oh, my best friend's a lesbian! Maybe you know her!'"

They break into a fit of giggles, except for Malcolm, who has decided he'll be jumping out of his bedroom window tonight. Peter falls toward Malcolm in his laughter, leaning his weight onto Malcolm's shoulder.

"Dude. That's the straightest thing I've ever heard come out of a gay person's mouth," he says. "That's, like...*so* bad."

"Shut up! I know!" Malcolm whines. "I just panicked! And if I *hadn't* introduced Mona to Jazz then they wouldn't be together right now, so, you're welcome."

"Yeah, it only took them eight hundred years of pining first," Goby says.

"You two weren't together right away?" Peter asks, eyebrows raised high.

"I know, it's surprising, right?" Mona says, climbing onto her knees on the couch and leaning forward until her arms drape over Jazz's shoulders. She kisses Jazz's cheek, and Jazz suppresses a grin. "You'd think we've been together for years, but that's just all the pent up romantic tension finally bubbling to the surface."

Goby makes a retching sound, and Peter laughs. "How about you, Goby?" Peter asks, turning to them. "How'd you end up with this circus?"

"Malcolm found me via clown to clown communication," Goby says. "Like echolocation."

"You're a moron," Malcolm says.

"That's *basically* what happened."

"Malcolm found Goby vandalizing shit in a junkyard," Jazz finally says.

"It's not vandalism if the stuff was garbage anyway!" Goby argues. "No one's gonna care if I spray paint a couple of dicks on a broken car."

"What were you doing in a junkyard?" Peter asks Malcolm, a half-smile quirking up into his cheek.

"Oh, I was gonna smash stuff," Malcolm explains.

"Bad day?"

"Bad day," he says. He reaches over to Goby and ruffles their hair, ignoring their grunt of protest. "Goob and I still go out there to wreck shit sometimes. It's pretty cathartic, actually."

"Hell yeah! To catharting!" Goby says, raising their red SOLO cup like a glass of wine.

"To catharting!" they all chorus, raising their drinks. They tap their cups together, careful not to let anything spill onto the remarkably unstained carpet. Peter raises his cup and playfully dips his head to Malcolm, like a 19th century gentleman greeting a friend from across the ballroom. Malcolm nods back stiffly, cursing his affinity for period romances.

He spends a majority of the night pretending he isn't staring at Peter. This is convincing only to Peter (thank fuck for small mercies and oblivious hot boys). His dipshit friends, however, aren't kind enough to act like they haven't noticed.

"Touched his bum yet?" Goby asks as he passes them on the way to the bathroom.

"One day you're gonna wake up with a finger missing and no one will be able to trace it back to me," Malcolm says. "I'll make Lady eat all the evidence."

"So you haven't touched it."

"*No,* I have *not.*"

Mona and Jazz at least don't mention it with words, but the knowing glances are almost worse. Three times now he's caught them making inappropriate gestures at him while Peter's back is turned. Mona turns around and rubs her arms up and down her back to feign a makeout session, exaggerated head movements and all. Jazz just pokes her two index fingers together and wiggles her eyebrows. Yeah, he definitely regrets introducing them.

Despite this, Malcolm can't help but feel like this is how things are supposed to be. This is what his home is supposed to look like, all five of them together. He looks at Peter, who's been waving his hands back and forth ever since he noticed Goby rocking side to side to the beat of the record Jazz had put on. Peter's smile widens the more he moves, his eyes closing, head bobbing.

Malcolm finds every last ounce of courage he has left in his body and crosses the room to Peter. He waits until Peter opens his eyes before he holds out his hand. Peter blinks once at the offered hand before grabbing hold and using Malcolm's weight to haul himself onto his feet.

Malcolm doesn't dance very much, and he has no idea if Peter does, but he's come this far. So he looks at Peter, deathly serious, and starts doing the only dance that comes to mind—the Bully Maguire dance from Sam Raimi's Spider-Man 3. Peter watches him, expression uncracked. He nods a few times to the beat before finally starting to move.

It's not exactly majestic by any means. Peter moves his body slowly at first before it suddenly ramps up. It's like he's wiggling the energy out of his fingers, shaking his hands out like he's trying to wake them up, and he's beaming ear to ear. He jumps up and down a few times, head turning side to side, and at this point the others have noticed. Goby's jumping like their legs fell asleep, and Jazz and Mona have sauntered in, hand in hand, to join the commotion.

They jump and shake and wiggle, matching Peter's energy beat for beat, and Malcolm finally realizes that Peter *isn't* dancing. He's stimming. No wonder he looked so damn happy when the song came on; stimming with music probably just looks like dancing to anyone who isn't paying attention. To Peter, music is a sign that he can unmask without fear of judgment.

Warren Zevon howls on the record player, and Malcolm joins in. "*Ah-hooo, werewolves of London!*"

They shout and laugh and sing together, dancing like this moment will never end. Peter howls long and loud, his hands cupping his mouth and his eyes clenched shut. He's smiling harder than Malcolm's ever seen him smile, and Malcolm realizes that this might be the first time he's really seeing Peter. Not just the boy who he thought hated him since they met; not just the boy who's helping him with his issues. Just Peter. He likes stimming to rambunctious music and smiling with all his teeth. He's a little bit of a dork and fully embraces it. He likes Malcolm's friends, and, against all odds, Malcolm.

He looks at Peter and thinks of Rebo. *Don't be afraid to be honest, Mal*, Goby had said. Do they know he's lying about himself to Peter? Is it really lying, or just sort of...omitting the truth? Those are different things, right? Fuck. In every movie and TV show ever, the ones who say those are different things are usually the ones in the wrong.

Malcolm turns up the volume and howls, and it blends with the shouts of the others until he forgets whose voice is whose.

27

Peter falls asleep on the couch twenty minutes into *Alien*, the light of the screen flickering against his relaxed face, his mouth open wide. His head is thrown back as he snores, one leg propped up on the coffee table and the other tucked beneath him. Goby's strewn their feet on top of his lap in their sleep, and his hand curls protectively over their ankle. Malcolm seems to be the only one left awake apart from Mona, who's tracing Jazz's hand with the tips of her fingers as she sleeps against Mona's chest.

He should be asleep. It's late, and he has work in the morning. Every time he considers heading to his room for the night, though, two things hold him back:

1. His mind swarms with thoughts of Rebo every time he closes his eyes. The guilt of not telling Peter that he's Clark is only overpowered by the fear of him knowing. Rebo knows so much about Clark, more than Malcolm would have ever said if Rebo hadn't just been a faceless voice on the radio. It's easy to be vulnerable to a stranger. He's a coward like that. He knows that, and he doesn't want to think about it more than he absolutely has to.

And 2. He doesn't want to stop looking at Peter.

Peter's sleeping in borrowed pajamas on Malcolm's old raggedy couch right now. This might be the last chance he gets to see it. So he sits on the floor against the wall and watches.

After a while, it feels more creepy than romantic. Peter lets out a particularly violent snore and burrows his face into the couch, his lips squished against the cushions. Malcolm decides to stand up and look away before the drooling begins. He leans against the kitchen counter, facing away from the group. Looking at the scene for too long, with Peter fit into the picture so perfectly, just reminds him that he can't have this forever. Good things don't last, in his experience. And Peter Tollemache is a damn good thing.

He jumps when something brushes against his arm, and Mona chuckles softly. "Sorry," she whispers, "Didn't mean to startle you."

"Shut up, you totally did," he whispers back.

"Maybe a little. It's funny." She leans against the fridge, slipping her hands into her pockets. She glances out towards the living room, then back at Malcolm. He avoids her gaze, but he can hear her gearing up to speak. She exhales once, barely even a sound, before she says, "You really do like him, don't you?"

She says it in that honey sweet voice of hers that always makes him feel like a child again—but not like he's being talked down to. More like he's being given the comfort he always needed when he was younger. That voice cracks him open like an egg.

"I think—" he stops. Swallows. "I think I like him quite a lot, Mo."

As much as she adores giving nicknames to others, Mona doesn't allow them very often for herself. It's telling she doesn't say anything about it this time.

"Are you gonna tell him?"

He shakes his head once and hugs his torso.

"What's stopping you?" She asks. It's not an accusation. Just a gentle nudge.

"He thought I hated him for *years,* Mona. That doesn't just go away." Malcolm scuffs his foot against the tiled kitchen flooring. "And there are some things I haven't told him...about myself."

"Are you talking about you being trans?" Mona asks, lowering her voice even further, just in case.

Well, yes, there is that. That's been on his mind too, of course it has. With a mother like his, it's impossible not to think about it. Years of being told you'll never find true love because of who you are...well, that tends to stick with you.

"Malcolm, stop," Mona says. She places a hand on Malcolm's head, and he blinks up at her. "I can see you thinking, and whatever it is, it's not true. That's your mom talking."

"No, yeah, I know," he assures her, bringing her hand down to hold it in his. "I promise, that's not it. I mean, yeah, all the shit she's said is always gonna fuck with my head a bit, but I'm not worried about that with Peter. Honest."

He knows Peter isn't like that. He heard it himself through Rebo. Peter would never hate him for who he is, and he'd never say all of the cruel things Malcolm's mother has said.

"I just—" Malcolm sighs. "Should I tell him?"

"Do you *want* to tell him?" Mona asks. "It's not about whether you should or shouldn't. It's your choice. You always have a choice, Mal."

Malcolm squeezes Mona's hand once, and nods. "Yeah. I think I do."

Mona's eyes flick behind him, and she quickly whispers, "Well, take all the time you need, doll, but if you were thinking of doing that soon then here's your chance."

Malcolm turns to watch her as she leaves the kitchen, and sees the reason for her quick escape. Peter shuffles sluggishly across the floor toward Malcolm, giving Mona a sleepy smile as she passes. Behind Peter's back, Mona gives Malcolm a pointed look and a wink. Malcolm turns away.

"Hey, man," Peter says, his voice lacking in its usual intonation from his exhaustion. He yawns, scratching at his stomach, and Malcolm lets out a shaky exhale. "Sorry, I didn't mean to fall asleep. As ugly as that couch is, it's damn comfortable. I can head back now, just gotta change."

"Hey, no, it's fine," Malcolm hurries to say. "You don't have to head back at all. It's late, you're beat. Just stay the night."

Peter doesn't even pretend to argue, which Malcolm takes as a testament to how truly drained he is. "Yeah, okay. I was hoping you'd say that, actually."

Malcolm laughs, more of a breath than a sound, and Peter smiles. It feels different this time, somehow, compared to all of the other times Malcolm has seen Peter smile. It's not a smile just for smiling's sake. It's quiet and vulnerable, barely even there but there nonetheless, and it's entirely directed at Malcolm. Like Malcolm's the sole reason for Peter's happiness in this quiet moment. Malcolm can't help but give a small smile back.

For a split second, Malcolm imagines a world where sharing sleepy smiles in the kitchen at 3am is a common occurrence for them. He wishes there were music playing, so maybe he could find that courage from earlier and take Peter's hand once again. They'd sway together, their socked feet shuffling against the tile, leaning heavier and heavier against each other as their exhaustion takes over.

Christ. He needs to sleep.

"Thank you for inviting me," Peter says, looking down at his fingers. He's fiddling with the small fidget toy from before. "It means more to me than you probably realize. Being around people like me. Being able to be myself, or at least, being able to try."

Malcolm blinks. Everything feels delicate. Goby's soft snoring echoes throughout the room. Jazz and Mona have migrated to Mona's bedroom already, so in a way, it's just them.

"It's been a while since I've been able to just...*be*, y'know?" Peter continues. "Without anyone staring at me for how much I move or how loud I get when I start to talk about Star Wars. It's...really nice. So, yeah. Thanks."

Malcolm's shaking his head before Peter's even finished. "You have nothing to thank me for, dude. You're always welcome to be yourself with us. Always. And, to tell you the truth," he leans forward, and Peter ducks his head, like they're sharing a secret, "the Peter I met tonight is probably my favorite Peter so far."

Peter smiles again, and fuck, does it feel dangerous. Malcolm can barely breathe, too scared to break whatever he *hopes* is happening right now. Peter hasn't moved away, leaving their faces only inches apart, and for a moment Malcolm thinks he catches Peter's eyes moving downward.

A sharp snore cuts through the air like a whip, and they split apart, Malcolm hissing when his back hits the edge of the counter hard. Peter reaches out as if to make sure he's okay, before returning his hands to his pockets. They look at each other for a brief second, and within that second Malcolm realizes he's been given a second chance not to fuck everything up. He laughs awkwardly, and Peter laughs in return, although it seems more like one of those "what the hell is going on" laughs. Malcolm ignores it and gestures to the couch.

"C'mon, we can get you set...up." He pauses when he sees that the entirety of the couch has been taken up by Goby, who's gone full starfish since Peter left his space unoccupied.

"They're just all limbs, huh?" Peter says.

"They almost named themself Gumby."

"No shit?"

Malcolm nods, and Peter lets out a laugh that sounds a bit more true this time. "It was a close call, honestly. It was between Gumby, Goby, or Cheese. Our world could have been very different."

"That's an interesting array of choices," Peter says, and Malcolm snorts.

"You can probably take Goby's room if you'd like, I'm sure they wouldn't mind," Malcolm says, heading towards Goby's door. When he opens the door, though, the foulest smell ever to have been born on this earth escapes from their room, and Peter and Malcolm look at each other with scrunched noses and squinted eyes.

"Oh, that's fucking rank," Peter says.

"I think I can *see* the smell coming out of this room. Is that onions? They don't even eat onions."

Peter leans over Malcolm to close the door with a determined *shunk*. Malcolm looks down at where their palms overlap on the door handle and slides his hand away. Peter doesn't say anything about it.

"Alright. Looks like I'm headed home then," Peter says.

Despite the guard inside Malcolm's chest shouting '*No! No! Are you dense? Do you have beans for brains? No!*' Malcolm finds the words already spilling out of his mouth, "You can take mine, if you want." Peter raises an eyebrow, and Malcolm continues, "It doesn't smell, promise. Well, actually, it kinda smells like peanut butter, but only because Jazz was eating some out of the jar in there. Hopefully you're not allergic. Oh, god, are you allergic?"

"I'm not allergic to peanut butter," Peter says.

"Okay. Right. Good."

"Yeah. Good."

So, Malcolm leads Peter into his room for the first time. This wasn't exactly how he imagined it to go, but he's not complaining. Well, he's kind of complaining. He can't feel his fingers and he's so sweaty that his shirt is sticking to his back. Peter, thank god, doesn't seem to notice.

Peter's eyes move around the room quickly, taking in everything that they can, and Malcolm presses his hand against his chest to calm his nerves. Peter touches the plant on Malcolm's desk and says, "You need to water this poor thing."

"Yeah, I'm kind of shit with plants," Malcolm says.

Peter looks left to right before his eyes land on a half-empty water bottle on Malcolm's floor. He picks it up, opens the lid, gives it a whiff, then once he's deemed it to be actual water and not vodka in a water bottle, he pours some into the plant's soil.

"Yeah, sure, go ahead," Malcolm waves his hand. "Make yourself at home."

"She's thirsty," Peter explains.

"You're weird."

"A corner of your wall is dedicated to paintings of memes. You're one to judge."

"I'm not judging, just observing," Malcolm says. "'Weird' isn't even an insult anymore—they started turning that shit into a compliment years ago. Get with the times, old man."

"So, you're complimenting me?" Peter asks.

"That's to be determined."

Peter *tsks* and shakes his head. "You are a strange, strange person, Malcolm."

"I think I'm cute," Malcolm says with a cheeky smile, just to be annoying.

Peter hums. "That too."

Malcolm's smile drops, his eyebrows raising, but Peter has already moved on before he can say another word.

"Which side of the bed do you prefer?" Peter asks.

"Oh, um, no preference."

"Good, cause I was gonna take the right side anyway," he says, burrowing into the blankets.

Malcolm shakes his head and turns away, making for the bathroom.

"Oh, shit, you got your own bathroom in here? Faaan-cy!" Peter says, eyeing Malcolm from the strip of light that the bathroom casts along the bed.

"Yeah, and an extra toothbrush, too, so get your ass in here. I'm not putting up with your morning breath," Malcolm says.

Peter kicks his way out of the bedsheets. "Bossy."

"Hygienic," Malcolm argues.

Peter kicks out at Malcolm's leg and Malcolm throws him the spare toothbrush, which hits Peter's forehead before landing in his hands. Malcolm slaps a hand over his mouth to keep from bursting into noisy laughter. Everything is funnier at night, when you aren't supposed to be making too much noise. Peter snorts and his mouth opens in a noiseless wheeze, eyes squeezed shut. Malcolm shushes him and swats at his arm.

"Shut up, shut up, brush your damn teeth," Malcolm says.

"Yes, Mother," Peter says.

Malcolm tries not to let that get to him. It's just a phrase people use—he's not actually being called a woman. Malcolm swallows down the itchy feeling underneath his skin and brushes his teeth.

He probably should've made them brush their teeth at different times. Catching Peter's eyes in the mirror and looking away when he looks back, it all feels far too domestic for Malcolm's suffering heart. The next time Malcolm catches Peter's eye, Peter makes a face, the foam of the toothpaste spilling out of his mouth, and Malcolm is so startled that he splutters a laugh and toothpaste goes spraying all over the mirror. They can't stop themselves from dissolving into a fit of giggles at that point.

By the time they've cleaned up the mirror (and themselves), Malcolm's eyes are burning, which is when he promptly remembers the contacts he's been wearing all day. He hisses a curse and takes the contact container out of the mirror cabinet, hidden behind his bottle of Concerta.

"Since when do you wear contacts?" Peter asks as Malcolm puts a careful finger to his eye.

"Since always," Malcolm says, his mouth open in an 'O' shape like it always does when he's messing with his face.

"I didn't know you wore contacts."

Malcolm blinks rapidly once the contacts are out, the world slightly more blurry than before. Peter's just close enough to be somewhat in focus, but he still has to squint a bit. "I don't like how I look in glasses."

Malcolm turns for the bed, and Peter says, "I bet you look good."

It's stupid how easily Peter's compliments get to Malcolm. He's sure Peter says that kind of thing to everyone. He's nice like that.

They shuffle into bed together, facing each other. At first Malcolm debated whether or not he should sleep on his back to make things as non-romantic as they can possibly be, but he never sleeps easily like that and he knows Peter would be able to tell he's acting weird. The best thing to do is just act like it's any other night. Nothing special at all about this. Not one bit.

It's an awful plan. As soon as he lays down and sees Peter looking at him, he feels like his heart is gonna fall out of his ass. It's dark, and the blanket is soft, and Peter is so close that Malcolm doesn't even need his contacts to bring him into focus. It's the same feeling from the kitchen increased tenfold: they're alone, properly now, and everything is delicate. It feels like one of those nights where something magical happens. Where everything changes. Nothing about this night is normal.

"If I were to change my name, I think I'd pick 'Luke,'" Peter says.

Malcolm blinks. "What?"

"You were just talking about how Goby almost picked a different name, and it got me thinking. What would my name be if it weren't Peter?"

Malcolm feels his smile returning, and he bites his lip. "Luke. Of course you'd pick that."

"I'd pick Han, but it seems a bit out of style."

"Oh, and 'Goby' is in style?"

"I'm gonna tell them you said that."

Malcolm grabs a free pillow from his side and whacks it against Peter's face, who laughs brightly before holding the pillow against his chest, curling against it like a middle schooler telling stories at a sleepover.

"What would you pick? If you wanted to change your name?"

Malcolm doesn't feel nearly as scared as he thought he would when he says, "I already have."

"You've changed your name?" Peter says curiously. Malcolm nods. "Why?"

"Cause I'm trans, Peter," Malcolm laughs.

"Ooooh, okay. Gotcha."

"Mhm."

"That doesn't answer my question, though. If you could change it *again*, what would you change it to?"

Malcolm looks at Peter, wishing he could just reach over and touch his hand. He thinks Peter would even let him. "Peter?"

"You can't take my name."

"No, I'm saying something to you, dumbass."

"Oh. Yeah?"

Malcolm sighs, his fists curling up in the sheets and wishing it were Peter's shirt instead. "I'm just really glad you came."

Peter's face softens, and he looks down. If it were lighter in the room, Malcolm's sure he would see a blush. "Me too, Malcolm," he says quietly. He licks his bottom lip, and Malcolm can hear his fingers fidgeting against the sheets. Then Peter looks up and says, "Still haven't answered the question, though. What name would you pick?"

Malcolm pretends to think for a moment. "Han."

Peter takes the pillow out from where it was trapped under his arms and slams it against Malcolm's face.

28

Work the next day is a nightmare. He relies on muscle memory alone to get him through orders while his head floats off into the clouds, running the interactions of that morning through his mind like a rock tumbler.

Just a few short hours ago, Malcolm woke up in bed next to Peter Tollemache.

He woke before his alarm, the gap in the blinds allowing a strip of sunlight to bleed through his closed eyes, dyeing the world a glowing red. He felt a weight on his chest, and for a split second before he opened his eyes, he had thought it was Peter. He thought about it a bit the night before, waking up to Peter cuddling him in his sleep, his soft snores in his ear. But no, a quick glimpse and he saw that it was just Lady purring happily on top of him, her eyes squinted closed. He wiggled a bit until she finally slunk down into the gap between him and Peter, curling up into a ball.

The clock told him he still had several minutes until his alarm. That's the only reason he felt safe enough to look at Peter longer than he probably should've.

It was strange seeing him like this—calm without intention. He looked relaxed, and not just because he was *trying* to look relaxed. He wasn't pretending for anyone, he wasn't hiding. He was beautiful.

There was a spot of sunlight that fell along Peter's cheek due to a broken spot in Malcolm's blinds. His skin was glowing. He looked warm. Malcolm wanted to know if he felt as warm as he looked. In his sleep-addled state, he didn't think it was such a bad idea to see for himself.

He raised his hand slowly and brushed his knuckles against his skin. It was soft, with the exception of a few acne scars near his jaw that Malcolm ran his thumb over, his fingers trailing along Peter's neck. That's when Peter opened his eyes.

Malcolm froze, eyes wide and hand stuck hovering above Peter's face. Peter reached his own hand up and placed it on top of Malcolm's. He pressed Malcolm's palm against his jaw again, harder than Malcolm had been doing before. He blinked, and it had taken a moment for his eyes to open back up again.

"Light touches don't always feel good for me. It's like..." he blinks again, slowly. Not fully awake. "Like ants on my skin. You have to be firm."

Malcolm swallowed, not daring to move an inch. "Got it."

Peter closed his eyes again. He breathed in deep through his nose and let it out in a sleepy exhale. His hand was still holding Malcolm's hand down. Malcolm thought he may have been dreaming.

The moment only ended when they smelt something burning, and Malcolm had to run into the kitchen to keep Goby from catching a piece of toast on fire. Mona was already yelling at them for making toast when she had already said she was making omelets. Mona had tried to catch Malcolm's eye, but he kept his eyes to the ground.

She's doing the same thing now at the bar, but this time he won't be able to run to the bathroom to hide from her stare.

"You seem a bit lost in thought today, love," she says. "Is this about last night? With Peter?"

"What?" Malcolm blinks, startled. "What do you mean? Nothing happened. What?"

"Well, he did come out of *your room* this morning," she says with a sly smile.

"Because Goby is a couch hog and *their* room is uninhabitable. Would you have liked me to stick him with you and Jazz?"

"That would've been fun," Mona says. "We could've painted his nails."

Malcolm promptly swats away the image of Peter with painted nails and says, "He's already enough of a pain in my ass without Jazz's influence."

"You *wish* he was a pain in your ass."

"Mona!" Malcolm yelps, ears burning.

She chuckles, but thankfully doesn't continue with the innuendo. "If nothing scandalous happened, then did you at least mention what we talked about in the kitchen?"

"Yeah," Malcolm says with a shrug. "He knows now."

She pauses, an expectant look on her face. "And? I need to know if I should bring out the party poppers or the battle axes."

"*Neither*. He was cool about it, but there's no need to celebrate," Malcolm says. "Of course he was cool about it, Mona, we knew he would be."

Mona smiles as she leans her hip against the bar, tapping a finger against its surface. "Still. I'm happy for you, hun. Coming out is a hard thing to do, no matter how many times you've done it before." Malcolm shrugs, and Mona's brows furrow. "Okay. Obviously there's something else, then."

Malcolm lowers his head, eyes fixed on his shoelaces.

"Malcolm, sweetheart, what's going on?" Mona says, placing a hand on his elbow. He looks up and gnaws at his cheek, eyes stinging.

"Mona—" he cuts himself off, swallowing down the lump in his throat. "Mona, I'm going to fuck up. Probably soon."

"How are you going to fuck up?" Mona asks. Malcolm blinks a few times and sniffs, his mouth twisted to the side. "Can't say yet?" she asks. Malcolm nods. "Okay. That's okay. Are you absolutely sure you're going to fuck up? Nothing we can do to keep that from happening?"

"It's like—actively happening. I am actively fucking up."

Mona nods slowly. "Okay. Well...I can't say for sure that I won't be pissed since I don't know what it is. If you're, like, poisoning Terrance or something I definitely won't forgive you."

Malcolm lets out a wet chuckle and says, "Don't give me any ideas."

Mona smiles. "How about this, then. Just...try to be better tomorrow. Or next week, or next month, or however long until you're done with your current fuck up. Just try to be better next time, yeah?"

Malcolm nods, then ducks his head when he feels his lips beginning to wobble with force. "Yeah. Yeah, I'll try, Mona."

"That's my boy," she says, patting his head. "Now go grab us some fruit snacks from the back."

He swipes his wrist across his nose and gives another sharp nod. Before he turns to leave, he feels a vibration in his pocket and pulls out his phone. The screen is lit up with a single message from Peter, asking him if he's free for lunch break.

He makes a decision. It's not a good one.

Malcolm swipes at the message until it's gone from the screen and tucks his phone away. When he looks up, Mona's eyeing his phone curiously. Her mouth flattens into a line, and he can't tell if it's a look of sympathy or disappointment. He hurries to the back room before he can find out.

29

Woke up this morning to my roommate giving his dog a mohawk
he's kind of an ugly thing so the mohawk is a step up at least
the dog, not my roommate
hey are you getting these?

Malcolm scrolls through Peter's texts, smiling at the remarks about his roommate's dog, then cursing himself for finding happiness in Peter's texts when he doesn't even have the guts to respond to them.

He knows he's being ridiculous. He's already received a barrage of texts and voicemails from Jazz about how much of an idiot he's being. It's been days. Everyone knows he's avoiding Peter. They just don't know why.

He shoves his phone into his pocket with force, returning to the video game he's playing with Goby. Goby's kicking his ass more than usual, and they keep glancing over at him every time he falls off the edge of the floating stage where their characters are battling. Goby's stylish princess sweeps the legs of Malcolm's little gnome for the third time, and the gnome goes tumbling off the edge once again. Goby huffs and grabs Malcolm's controller from him.

"Hey!" Malcolm starts to protest as Goby pauses the game.

"Shut up," Goby says, and turns to face him. Malcolm refuses to move, pouting down at his hands where his controller would be. "What the hell are you doing, dude?" Malcolm opens his mouth, but Goby cuts him off before he can even try to lie. "Nope, nuh-uh, don't try to pretend you don't know what I'm talking about. Why are you avoiding Peter?"

Malcolm sighs, more in annoyance than anything else. He slumps back against the pillows they had propped up on the floor against the couch. "It's nothing you need to worry about, Goob."

"Don't 'Goob' me right now, Malcolm, I'm peeved," Goby says sternly, and Malcolm shrinks back. "If you're avoiding Peter, it's not just gonna affect you; we're *all* friends with Peter now, so we *all* have to deal with it. But that's not why I'm mad."

"It's not?" Malcolm asks.

"No, dude," they say. "I'm mad because you *very obviously* want to talk to him. So why the hell aren't you?"

Malcolm tries to bring the words to his mouth, but he can't seem to find them. He has his reasons, but it's not that simple. "You wouldn't get it."

Goby throws their head back and groans. "Fuck, I forgot how dramatic you can be."

Malcolm pouts and grumbles, "I forgot how harsh you can be."

"It's what you need," Goby says. "Mona's the nice one, Jazz is the mean one, and I'm whatever the hell I gotta be to get through your thick skull."

"Take it down a notch, I'm still a bit fragile right now."

"Tough!" Goby shouts, then lowers their voice, gently plopping their hand on Malcolm's head. "Sorry, I was on a roll. I'll cool it. But seriously, man, you gotta talk to me. Maybe if you try explaining your reasons you'll see how dumb they actually are." Malcolm glares at them, and they wince. "Sorry. I'm chill now, promise."

Malcolm brings a hand up to his chest, and he rubs his thumb along the soft fabric of his t-shirt. "Peter is...good." He pauses, expecting a comment from Goby, but they're just watching him curiously, waiting for him to continue. He takes a deep breath. "I think Peter might be the best man I know. Not just, like, kind. I mean, he is kind, he's so fucking kind, but he's also just. *Good*. He's a good thing that's happened to me, and usually when that happens, I fuck it up."

"You don't know that you're gonna—"

"Yes, Goby, I *do* know I'm gonna fuck it up because I am literally already fucking it up. I'm keeping secrets, I'm avoiding him, I'm caressing his face one moment and then running away the next."

"You're doing *what* to his face?"

"My point is, I know I'm gonna fuck up with Peter because I am literally the epitome of fucked up. Either I can try to make something good happen between me and him and probably just end up losing it in the end, or I can stop anything from happening at all. Save us all a little heartache."

There's a moment of silence in which Malcolm just breathes, and Goby watches him. Goby scoots over until they're shoulder to shoulder with Malcolm, their legs spread out in front of them, and they lean their head down to rest on top of Malcolm's.

"I think I understand," Goby says softly. "But, you've already started something with him, Malcolm. Something special. You see that, right?"

Malcolm picks at a loose thread on his ripped jeans and mumbles, "Says who?"

"Says anyone with two functioning eyes, dude," Goby says with a light chuckle. "There's obviously something going on between you and Peter. You can't just decide it's not going to happen—it *has* happened. It *is happening*. And all this work you're doing to avoid heartache is just causing more heartache."

"Like...a self-fulfilling prophecy?"

Goby gasps, "So you *did* listen to my time travel infodump."

"I always listen to your infodumps. I may not remember everything, but I'm listening."

Goby lets out a happy noise, the vibration a comforting buzz against Malcolm's skull. "That's what makes you such a good friend, Malcolm. A good friend, and a good person, who definitely deserves to let good things happen to him."

"Yeah, yeah, I hear ya," Malcolm says. "Jeez, it's almost like you love me or something."

"I'll knife you."

Malcolm sputters out a surprised laugh, and he shoves Goby's shoulder until they topple over onto the ground. Goby stays on the floor, looking up at Malcolm with a beaming smile.

"You know, I used to do this same thing," Goby says. At Malcolm's confused stare, they explain, "The whole, 'running away because you're scared of losing things that make you happy' thing. Remember Rosalie?"

"Your ex?" Malcolm says. He hadn't heard about Rosalie in ages.

"Yeah. I had the biggest crush on xem, remember? But when I found out xe reciprocated, I got scared and drove all the way to the beach. Malcolm, the beach is *three hours away*. That's about as literal as you can get when it comes to running away from your worries."

"Why did you run away?"

"Malcolm, have you *seen* Rosalie? Xe was literally the hottest person on campus. I was dead sure I'd fall in love with xem and then xe'd just leave me for some supermodel-slash-professional-golfer from our rival school."

Malcolm frowned. "Then what brought you back? You guys dated for a while, didn't you?"

"Yeah, we did," Goby nods, lost in thought. "It was great, and I did love xem. But then we just kinda figured out that it wasn't meant to be. We had different ideas about our futures, and that was that."

Malcolm tries to imagine it, having something so good, being *in love*, and then just...walking away. "You don't regret it?"

Goby looks at him and snorts. "Aren't you supposed to get wiser with age?" Malcolm starts to argue that he's *barely two years older than them*, but they continue before he can get a word in. "It's okay to do things just 'cause they make you happy in the moment, dude. Maybe it'll hurt when the good things are gone, but that's okay too.

That's literally what life is all about. Loving things and being happy and, yeah, being heartbroken sometimes. Like, imagine going on a roller coaster with no dips? That'd be a boring ass roller coaster."

"I think that's just a train."

"Okay, smart ass, do you wanna live your life on a roller coaster or a train?"

"I kind of like Amtrak."

"You're making this metaphor more difficult than it has to be," Goby says, pressing their foot against Malcolm's arm. "Just live your dumb life and don't worry about what happens next, okay? Do some shit that makes you happy, even if it might hurt later."

Malcolm pokes at their leg, one of Jazz's stick n poke tattoos fading against Goby's calf. It was supposed to be a snail, but looks a bit more like a honeybun.

"Easier said than done."

30

Goby's gone when Malcolm wakes. He vaguely remembers making it to his bed after playing far too many rounds past midnight, the brightness of the TV screen digging into his eyeballs like daggers. The headache it gave him then must've stuck around, because there's pressure behind his eyebrows and along his cheeks that feel like his brain is trying to push out of his skull. He tries to lift his head for a brief moment, only for the world to tilt drastically to the left, leaving him with no choice but to flop back pathetically onto his mattress.

It doesn't take long to realize that he's sick.

He tries to take note of his symptoms through the fog in his mind. He's sweating through his clothes, the fabric sticky against his skin, but the few parts of his body that are left uncovered by the blankets are shivering against the fan in his room. He tucks himself further into the sheets, leaving only his face out in the open so he can breathe. He tries to sniff through his nose, only for his breath to halt suddenly against the blockage. He coughs wetly and takes in a shuddering breath through his mouth. It grates against his throat like sandpaper.

God, he's *really* sick. His eyes travel with little coordination around his room, dazed. He blinks, and when his eyes open again, Mona is kneeling beside his bed. He doesn't know how long she's been there.

"I guess I shouldn't bother asking why you aren't ready for work yet," she says. She places the back of her hand against his forehead. "Goodness, you poor thing. You're burning up. Why didn't you call for one of us?"

Malcolm grunts, trying his hardest to keep his eyes focused on Mona but failing. They go back to traveling around the room aimlessly, and when he looks back towards Mona again, the furrow in her brow has deepened.

"Geez, you're really out of it," she mutters, more to herself than to him. "Hang right here, I'll be right back."

Malcolm blinks again, and Mona's there with a cooled washcloth in hand and Goby at her side.

"What's goin on, dude?" Goby asks as Mona places the washcloth over Malcolm's forehead. It dampens some of Malcolm's hair, but he can't find the energy to move the few strands away.

"He's sick," Mona says. "He's burning up and I noticed he can barely focus his eyes on anything."

"Shit," Goby hisses. "I have to get to work soon. Can you watch him?"

"I've got work too, but I'll cover for Malcolm. "

Malcolm pushes at the sheets, dragging one leg to the edge of the bed with the slowness of a plague victim. "Work...I hav'tuh...go work..."

Mona pushes him back down onto the bed, cocooning the blankets around him. "Nuh-uh, doll, you're staying right here. I'll text Jazz and see if she can come by, maybe bring some medicine."

Goby holds up a hand before Mona can bring her phone out. "Don't worry about it. I'll take care of it."

Malcolm closes his eyes. He hears footsteps leaving the room, then Goby's voice speaking low. Not to him—to someone else. They might be on the phone. Before he can even try to figure out who it may be, he's slipping away once again.

• • • •

Dreams never quite make sense like they do in movies. In Malcolm's dream, he doesn't see his father's face, but he knows the body on the hospital bed belongs to him. Malcolm's there, sitting by his bedside, and then he's somewhere else, somewhere outside of his body, watching him and his father together. The skin on his father's hand begins to bleed over onto Malcolm's, like mud. Then the scene changes.

Malcolm's somewhere else now, somewhere darker and bleeker. The basement of a hospital. Or maybe this is just what hospitals look like now. His father is on a gurney, being rolled away from him. Malcolm runs towards him, pushing past hospital door after hospital door, and with each door that he opens the hall gets longer and longer, until the people taking his father away turn a corner and disappear. Then the scene changes.

He's on a bench, and his father is there. His skin is glowing and all his hair is intact, graying but healthy, and Malcolm knows the cancer hasn't touched him yet. His father holds out a closed palm, and Malcolm guesses, "Even." When he opens his hand, three marbles are resting in the middle. Malcolm blinks, and his father is gone. He doesn't dream again.

• • • •

There's something cool and refreshing pressed against his skin when Malcolm comes to. The washcloth must have slipped off his forehead in his sleep, because he can feel its dampness against his neck in a crumpled ball. The cool thing on his forehead pushes his hair out of the way, and Malcolm lets a relieved sigh slip through his cracked lips. He presses into it, wishing the satisfying chill would spread to the rest of his burning body.

Fingers weave through his hair, slicking it back, scratching at his scalp. Another sigh, but not from him this time. "What am I going to do with you?"

Malcolm wills his eyes to open, and after a few moments, they obey him. He smacks his lips together, wishing there were even an ounce of moisture to them. "Peter."

Peter holds out a glass of water. "Malcolm."

Malcolm tries to reach out to take the glass, but it takes a while, and his arms are shaking when they emerge from the blanket. Peter quickly places the glass on the nightstand and helps Malcolm sit up. He puts a hand on Malcolm's back and lets Malcolm use the other as a crutch for balance. Peter doesn't mention the clamminess of Malcolm's palms, thankfully.

"How did you get like this?"

Malcolm shrugs and tries not to slur his words together when he says with a waved hand, "There's'uh…bug goin' around."

"And you haven't been sleeping."

Malcolm furrows his brow as much as he can with what little energy he has. "How'd'yuh know that?"

"Goby told me," Peter says. He hands Malcolm the drink. "They said you're acting pretty out of it, even if you are sick."

"Don't like bein' sick," Malcolm says, punctuated with a phlegmy cough that causes Peter to wince. Malcolm downs a few gulps of the water, and Peter grabs at the glass gently.

"Not too fast," he says. "Just take sips. And no one likes being sick, dummy."

Malcolm gives Peter an irritated look but makes sure to slow down. The water feels good to his dry mouth, although swallowing is still difficult with how sore his throat is. He takes a few gentle sips, then lets the glass rest in his lap. He can feel his mind starting to drift again, the fog taking over.

"I can't tell if you're dissociating or just delirious from fever," Peter says, a little more worry in his voice than there was before. He still has a hand on Malcolm's back. "Can you name three things you can see?"

Malcolm lets his head flop to the side, looking up at Peter. He blinks slowly, trying to name what exactly he's seeing. "Pretty eyes."

Peter looks away, clearing his throat. "Delirious it is."

Malcolm starts shuffling again, slowly but surely scooting his bottom down the mattress, and Peter gets up to help him lay back down. Peter flips the pillow so Malcolm's head rests against cool cotton, and Malcolm smiles weakly in appreciation. When he looks at Peter, Peter is looking at the floor.

"You've been avoiding me," Peter says quietly.

Malcolm starts to shake his head. "Nuh-uh."

Peter's smile is almost amused, but it's mostly just sad. "I won't grill you for it now since you're sick and all, but just know that I've noticed."

Malcolm looks up at the popcorn ceiling, wishing he were in a better state of mind to give Peter the response he deserves. Instead, he inhales deeply, a mistake he regrets as soon as he starts hacking up a lung once again. He turns his head to the side so he isn't just spewing germs into the air. His body relaxes back into the mattress as soon as his coughing fit is over, and he puffs out a few uneven breaths.

"Ugh," Malcolm says with feeling. "Hate being sick."

"You've already said that."

"Reminds me of my dad."

"Your dad have asthma or something?"

"No," Malcolm says, eyes fixed on a small raised scar on Peter's knee. He wonders where it's from. He wonders how many more scars Peter has that he doesn't know about. "Had lung cancer."

Peter falls silent, and Malcolm knows he didn't miss the use of past tense. Peter looks down at his hands.

"Should I say sorry or is this one of those things that you want people to move past without mentioning it?" Peter asks. Malcolm would think he was being an asshole if it weren't for the genuine look on his face.

Oddly enough, Malcolm finds the fact that Peter even asked more touching than any response he's gotten before about his dad.

Usually when he drops that bomb it's all awkward 'sorry's or 'I had no idea.' That never made sense to him. Of course they had no idea, he never told them. This is the most honest reaction he's ever received about it.

Malcolm shrugs as best he can with his heavy limbs. "I dunno. Wha' ya wanna say?"

"I'm not really good at these things. I'm not sure if it'll be the right thing."

"If...If it's the truth, I don't think...it'll be wrong," Malcolm gets out. "Come on, we'll—" he pauses, catching his breath, "—we'll try again." Malcolm clears his throat, gathers whatever energy he has left, and says, "Peter—my dad's dead. From lung cancer, specifically."

Peter nods determinedly, taking a deep, albeit awkward, breath. "That sucks, dude."

Malcolm feels his face dripping into a slow smile, and then he snorts, which unravels into an uncontrollable giggle-slash-coughing fit. He covers his face with a hand, more in disbelief than in any attempt to hide his amusement.

"Shut up!" Peter shouts, a little distressed. "You said it wouldn't be the wrong thing to say!"

"It's not, it's not," Malcolm assures him, his words slurring a bit so it sounds more like he's repeating the word 'snot'. He forces himself to relax before he passes out from lack of oxygen. "That w's perfect. Ya hit the nail on the head, buddy. It does, in fact, suck."

"You're one confusing guy, Malcolm."

"Got that from *Firefly*."

"What?"

"My name," Malcolm explains, eyes starting to fall shut again against the weight of sleep. "Got it from...from *Firefly*."

There's a pause, and Malcolm wonders what Peter's face is doing. "The TV show? With the space cowboys?"

"Mmmm-hm," Malcolm says. Malcolm giggles a little deliriously. "Had a crush on the captain...so I stole his name."

"You are a nerd, Malcolm."

"Okay, Han."

Peter laughs, but it's lost through the haze of Malcolm's half-sleeping mind. He slips in and out of consciousness for what feels like ages before he's back again, this time due to a poke to his forehead.

He grumbles when he gets poked again. "Let me die."

"You're not dying, you're just stupid," Peter says. "Sit up and eat this soup."

Malcolm whines but follows the order. He cups the bowl in his hands, the steam soothing his irritated nose. "Careful," Malcolm says. "Remember what happened the last time you had soup around me?"

Peter shakes his head. "I'm gonna sit here until you've had all that, and then you're gonna get some rest."

"All of it?"

"All of it."

Malcolm blows a raspberry, bringing the soup up to his mouth slowly. He knows part of him is going to be drawing this out just to keep Peter here, and he hates himself for it. He's the one who's been avoiding him—he doesn't get to keep him too. He can't have both.

"You're ridiculous," Peter says when Malcolm takes a solid thirty seconds to sip at one sad spoonful of chicken noodle soup. He comes over to sit on the bed and grabs the bowl, bringing up the spoon to hover in front of Malcolm's mouth. "Open up."

"Now this is just sad," Malcolm says. "A man can't feed himself now?"

"Not my fault you're slow," Peter says, and nudges the spoon at Malcolm's mouth. "Open."

Malcolm furrows his eyebrows, now thoroughly embarrassed, but he obliges. He opens his mouth, and Peter feeds him the soup. It tastes marvelous, actually, but Malcolm's pride is hurt, so he doesn't let his face show any emotion beyond annoyance. That almost slips when Peter grins, though.

"Good job," he says once Malcolm's swallowed. It's supposed to be teasing, Malcolm's sure of it, but apparently his heart isn't getting that message. Malcolm opens his mouth for another spoonful and tries to convince himself he *isn't* paying attention to the way that Peter is just a few inches taller than him here, forcing Malcolm to tilt his head up to keep eye contact.

They go through the whole bowl that way, mostly silent except for the blood pounding in Malcolm's ears. Then the spoon scrapes the bottom of the bowl and Malcolm flinches.

"Sorry," Peter says, grimacing. "I hate that noise too." He gets up and leaves the room with the bowl, then returns with a small cup of some dark green liquid. "Lay down, doofus."

Malcolm groans but once again does as he's told. "Doofus...*you're* the doofus."

"Uh-huh," Peter says, then holds out the miniature cup. "Drink."

"We takin' shots?" Malcolm grins.

"Maybe another time, hot shot. Now drink."

Malcolm downs it, then sticks out his tongue. "Blegh. No. Bad. Bad taste."

"I know, hun, I know," Peter says. Malcolm thinks he imagined the pet name. "Lay down. This shit'll knock you out pretty quick and you're already dazed enough, I don't need you cracking your skull open on the dresser or something."

"So much faith in me," Malcolm bemoans, slowly settling into his bed. "I'm not...not *that* clumsy..."

"Mm, whatever you say," Peter says, and that cool feeling of his hand on Malcolm's forehead returns. He brushes his fingers through Malcolm's hair, and Malcolm is suddenly so grateful that he gets to feel this one more time before he messes up their friendship forever.

Sleep grabs at Malcolm with hungry fingers, pulling him under so quickly that Malcolm can't remember the words Peter says to him before he's deep in a dreamless slumber.

31

When he wakes again, his throat tingling from the gross aftertaste of medicine but no longer unbearably sore, a yellow sticky note catches his eye on his nightstand.

Malcolm,

Had to go to work. Please for the love of god drink water. And take another shot of that green stuff when you've woken up.

And <u>TEXT ME</u>. Bitch.

- Peter

Malcolm sticks the note onto his wall, slapping a few extra pieces of tape onto it to keep it there. He knows the record shop is closed, so Peter must be talking about his job at the radio station. That green stuff Peter gave him must have had the powers of gods in it, because he feels infinitely better than he did yesterday—or was that this morning? He turns to check the time, and startles at how long he's slept. It's still the same day, but it's almost time for Rebo's segment.

Should he even call in for Rebo? Peter said to text him, but he's not sure if he can do that yet. Is that even fair, to call Rebo when he's still kind of avoiding Peter? Fair or not, he knows what he wants to do.

He picks up his phone, shaking out his arm to get some feeling back into it after sleeping on it wrong for hours. He turns on the radio, checking the time. At 11pm, Rebo's voice rings through.

"Hello, hello, hello! Welcome, welcome, to the amazing, brilliant, *fabulous*—" There's a muffled voice, and Rebo says, "Alright, jeez, getting on with it. Hello listeners, I am your host, Max Rebo."

You could probably compare the effect Rebo's voice has on his body to a drug, Malcom thinks. The instant his voice comes through, Malcolm can feel his body relax, like it knows that that voice means 'safe.' He calls in.

"Hello, Malcolm," a voice that *isn't* Rebo says.

"He...llo?" Malcolm says. He had to give his real name for the screener the first time he called, but he didn't realize they would actually remember it.

"After all this time, you still don't know my name?" The woman says.

Malcolm's mind clears for a blessed second, and he says a fraction too loudly, "Kit! Of course, I remember your name. Rebo's supervisor."

"And friend," Kit says. "You know you call in here a lot?"

Malcolm nods his head despite being invisible to the woman on the other line. "Uh, yeah, I guess."

"Uh huh. And you know that means a lot to Rebo."

Malcolm feels a chill start to go through his body, and the guilt he had been staving off comes flooding back with a vengeance. "You know what, maybe I should just—"

"Kit!" Rebo's voice says over the radio and slightly through the phone. "Looks like my supervisor has someone on the line for me. Bring 'em over!"

"Just don't hurt him, please," Kit says to Malcolm, leaving him thoroughly dazed before she puts him through to Rebo.

"Welcome, caller!"

"You know it's me, dude," Malcolm says, trying to shake off that dunked-in-ice-water feeling Kit's words brought him. "Do you even get any callers?"

"C.K.!"

"What?"

"I'm trying it out. It's short for Clark Kent. Don't like it?"

Malcolm hums, pursing his lips. "Try it again."

"C.K.?"

"Nah, don't like it," Malcolm says. "Makes me sound like a frat boy."

"You're telling me you're *not* a frat boy?" Rebo says with a dramatic gasp. "There goes my whole mental image of you."

"Oh, don't tell me you've been thinking of me as some douchey backwards-cap muscle bro this whole time."

"I never said *anything* about muscles."

"Oh, you asshole," Malcolm laughs. Rebo chuckles on his end, and in that moment, Malcolm almost forgets why he ever wanted to stop talking to Peter. Then Rebo's laughter settles, and Malcolm hears something in his breathing that makes his shoulders tense.

"Speaking of mental images," Rebo says. "I was kinda thinking...maybe I wouldn't have to guess what you looked like if I actually, uh...knew?"

Malcolm feels his hands go cold. "What?"

"There's this shop I work at," Rebo says, and in his mind Malcolm shouts '*no, no, please, not now*.' "It's called Roisin Records. I thought—well, I dunno. I've had kind of a weird week and I just thought, hey, maybe it's time I finally get to meet my best pal, Clark!" He lets out a weak laugh that dies quicker than it started. His nerves seem to only make Malcolm's grow stronger. "I don't know how far away it is from wherever you live, but, you know. Maybe you can swing by?"

Malcolm's throat isn't sore anymore, but suddenly it feels as though he's lost his voice within the past five seconds. He opens his mouth, but only an odd strangled sound comes out.

"There's no pressure!" Rebo adds quickly, a little too loudly. "Honestly, it was just a thought. Just, if you happen to be around that area, then, uh...yeah. I just thought that might be a cool, ya know, thing to do. Maybe...maybe next Saturday?"

There's a muffled voice—presumably Kit. "*You work next Saturday!*"

There's a sound over the speaker like Rebo's put his hand over the mic, and his lowered voice saying, "Kit, I love you, but I might just have to take that day off if things go according to plan."

In the five seconds that Malcolm hesitates to speak, he tries to run through all of the many, many reasons why he should say no. He still isn't replying to Peter. He still hasn't told Peter anything involving Rebo and Clark. It is quite possibly the worst idea in the history of *ever* for Malcolm to actually say yes to Rebo right now.

"Okay," Malcolm's mouth says without his consent. His eyebrows furrow, marveling at his own audacity. "I'll see what I can do."

There's a crackling sound over the speaker, like Rebo's blown out a gulp of air he had been holding in. "Awesome," he says, sounding a little awed. "Cool."

"Cool," Malcolm says, and ends the call.

32

Malcolm can't remember the very first time he had a panic attack. One moment he was fine, then suddenly he was hyperventilating nearly every week in the abandoned restrooms in middle school. Sometimes he still can't tell when it will happen. Sometimes it's not until he's right in the middle of one that he'll realize what's happening. Sometimes, when he's lucky, he can see the signs before it starts.

He makes it a full 24 hours after Rebo's call before the reality of what he's done fully catches up to him. He listens in on the show the next night and brings his hand up to his phone a total of eighteen times, but pulls back before he can call in again. Rebo spends the rest of his segment sounding on edge. Malcolm feels nauseous.

"Jazz," Malcolm says into his phone.

"Malcolm? You sound like shit, dude, are you still sick?" Jazz's voice crackles through the speaker.

"No," Malcolm says. "No, I'm—" he sucks in a breath, and it hiccups in his throat.

"Malcolm? Are you alright?"

"I'm—" Malcolm tries to breathe again, but it feels like the air in his room refuses to cooperate with his lungs. "I can't—"

"Hang on, we're coming," Jazz says. "I'm going to FaceTime you, okay?"

"Mm," Malcolm says.

The phone lights up with the call, and he brings a shaky thumb down on the answer button.

"Hey, sweetheart," Mona answers. She's out of breath but makes sure to smile down at him. "Not a good night, huh?"

"Mm-mm," Malcolm shakes his head, his face crumpling. He hiccups again.

"It's okay, hun, it's okay," Mona says as she jumps into a car. Malcolm can hear Jazz cursing at the truck to turn on faster. "We're just a few minutes away, alright? I'm gonna use my phone to call Goby, is that okay?"

"Mm-hm," Malcolm nods his head. He brings a hand up to his chest, wrapping the other around his torso and squeezing.

He can hear Mona and Jazz talking, and a moment later footsteps come bounding down the outside hallway and into his room.

"Heeeey, buddy," Goby says, crouching down in front of him as he sits on the edge of his bed. "Mona and Jazz are on their way. I'm right here, it's alright."

"Guh—mm—*Goby*," Malcolm tries to say. He forgot what it's like sometimes, panicking this intensely. He can barely get his words out. He might be dying.

"You're not dying," Goby says before he can even voice the thought. "I know what you're thinking, but you're gonna be okay. We've been through this before, yeah? We can do this. You're gonna be alright."

Malcolm shakes his head.

"Yes, yes it is," Goby says. "It's gonna be alright. There—you hear that? Jazz and Mona are already here."

Goby's right, Malcolm can hear two more pairs of footsteps rushing into his room, and he tenses up.

"Chill, guys, we don't need a stampede right now," Goby says to them.

"Sorry, sorry," Mona says.

"Where the fuck did I put it..." Jazz mumbles, barely acknowledging their presence as she rummages through Malcolm's closet.

Mona mirrors Goby's position and kneels in front of Malcolm, palms up. "Is it alright if I touch you? Or no touching?"

Malcolm shakes his head. He's distantly aware that he's sobbing.

"That's alright, love, that's okay. Do you think you can talk yet?"

"He won't be able to," Jazz answers. "Can you guys get him to lay down?"

Goby and Mona do as they're told, helping Malcolm to fall back onto his bed with the least amount of touching as they can manage. Jazz shuffles quickly over to his nightstand, dragging a portable fan with her that Malcolm had forgotten he even owned. She plugs it in and turns it on high, pointing it directly on Malcolm's body.

"He's overheating," Jazz says. "See if he can take his sweatshirt off." Malcolm starts to shake his head, but Jazz says, "It's okay if you don't want to, but it'll cool you down faster. You know you're safe with us."

Malcolm eventually relents, letting the others help him undress. The air feels good against his skin, his neck and forehead burning from the panic and the lingering aftermath of his illness.

"Come on, deep breath, you can do it," Mona says, breathing in deeply through her nose. He copies her the best he can but chokes on the breath out. "That's okay, you're doing so well. Let's do another one, love. Deep breath. You've got this."

Malcolm follows her guidance, breathing in as deeply as his lungs will allow, and breathing out even more. The others do the same, until they've become a ring of deep breathing.

"Don't forget to stim if you need to, buddy," Goby chimes in gently. "It helps. I'll do it with you."

Malcolm glances at Goby, who has started to shake their hands in front of them like they're flicking water off their fingers. It takes a moment before his hands finally unclench against his body, but eventually he's able to move them, albeit weaker than Goby can do. He waves them weakly above his chest, his fingers limp and dangling.

Mona and Jazz glance at each other. They don't stim quite as often as Goby and Malcolm do, but after a moment they begin to follow along anyway. Mona wiggles her fingers in the air, and Jazz twists her wrists back and forth.

"This is nice," Mona says. "We should do this more often."

"Feels good, doesn't it?" Goby says.

"I feel like I'm conducting my own little worm concerto."

"That's certainly one way to view it."

They stay that way for longer than he can keep track of. Malcolm stares and stares at his friends, still breathing in sync, and now shaking out their hands together. It's an odd sight to anyone but him. His lips finally do their best to quirk up into a grateful smile (he thinks he's squinting more than smiling, really) and it takes a moment for the others to notice that he's winding down.

"How are we doing, Mal?" Jazz asks, who's added a small little hop to her stimming. Now it looks like she's dancing very lazily.

"Better," Malcolm says.

"Hey, we've got a word!" Goby says brightly, and the others give a quiet cheer. Malcolm chuckles, wiping the snot from his nose on his sleeve. Jazz cringes but says nothing.

"Are you ready to talk about what happened here?" Mona asks.

Malcolm looks at Jazz. She nods her head.

"Okay," Malcolm says. "I think it's about time I told you guys some things."

• • • •

It takes a bit to explain it all without sounding nuts. Jazz sits on the bed next to him, a steady force as he relays the information to those who had been left out of the loop. Talking to Peter, talking to Rebo, Peter helping him with his episodes, finding out Peter *is* Rebo, avoiding Peter in a last ditch attempt to run from his feelings and the guilt of lying to him about his identity, and now Rebo/Peter inviting Clark/Malcolm to meet in person.

It's a mess, and from the looks on Mona and Goby's faces, they think so too.

"And you were aware of all this?" Mona asks Jazz.

"Don't give me that look, baby, I had to keep his secret," she says. She turns to Malcolm and puts a hand on his shoulder. "He's really struggling with this."

"Well," Goby sighs, puffing their cheeks out and planting their hands on their hips with finality. "You have to tell him."

"What?" Malcolm says, startled. "Why do I have to tell him? Can't I just run away to the woods and live as a wolf-man?" Even the thought of telling Peter is bringing the panic from earlier back, and he grabs a fistful of his bedsheets.

"Hey, no, no," Goby stoops down and pats his hands. "It's okaaay, it's alriiight," they coo in a semi-sing-song voice. "It's no stress, dude, it'll be fine."

"It will *not* be fine," Malcolm stresses, stressfully.

"He deserves to know the truth, love," Mona says, coming over to sit on his other side so he's encircled by the whole group. "Even if that means he might be mad at you."

"And who knows," Jazz pipes up, "maybe he'll be happy about it."

"Happy?" Malcolm says, incredulous. "I've been lying to him for months, Jazz. Who would be happy about that?"

Jazz blows a raspberry. "Someone who's got a massive crush on you *and* Clark?"

"Oh, we're talking about that?" Mona says, eyebrows peaked. "I thought we were leaving that unsaid."

"Not like he would've figured it out," Jazz mutters.

"Are you joking?" Malcolm says. "Peter doesn't have a crush on me. On Clark, *maybe*, but he definitely won't anymore once he finds out who Clark really is."

"You've got some serious self-esteem issues to work on," Goby says.

"It's not a self-esteem issue, it's reality," Malcolm says sternly. "There's no guarantee he'll forgive me after all this time, and even if he does, I've still betrayed his trust. There's no way I'd have a chance with him after this."

"So what I'm hearing is," Goby says slowly, "you're going to tell him?"

Malcolm pauses. He looks between Jazz and Mona, who are both staring at him, waiting. He says to Jazz, "I thought you said I didn't have to tell him right away?"

"I believe the situation's changed, buddy," Jazz says, her lips downturning in a sympathetic frown.

Malcolm sighs, long and defeated. "I'll try," he says.

They all crowd around him in a hug, one that he has to fight his way out of once their combined body heat gets to be too suffocating. They trail out of his room one by one, ending with Jazz, who gives him a grin and a two-fingered salute on her way out. Malcolm turns to his radio.

He left Rebo's station playing despite never calling in. It's almost time for the segment to end, so Malcolm gives in to the masochist in him and turns up the volume a few notches.

"This is a song that reminds me of one of my closest friends," Rebo says, his voice lacking its usual energy. Malcolm can't help but feel it's because of him. "Sleep well and sweet dreams, everybody."

Malcolm's breath hitches in his throat, and he stares unblinkingly at the radio as the slow strum of "Cosmic Dancer" bleeds through the speakers. He stays awake long after the song has ended, but the tune plays on in his mind until morning.

33

He doesn't call into the station the next night either. He still listens, because he's pathetic, and part of him feels like he deserves to hear the ache in Rebo's voice and suffer with the knowledge that he's the one who's caused it.

He almost goes to Roisin Records about a dozen times throughout the week, always changing his mind at the last minute. The others give him looks, ranging from pity to exasperation.

"I thought you were done avoiding him," Goby said to him at one point, arms crossed.

"I am," Malcolm had said, and it was the truth. He just had no fucking clue how to go back. How to start fixing things.

Saturday approaches quicker and quicker, and Malcolm still hasn't decided if he can actually go. He knows he said he'd try, and he *will*, but what if that's a mistake? What if everything goes tits up and he loses everything he worked so hard to build between him and Peter?

On Friday, the night before the meet up, Malcolm still doesn't call into the station. Rebo's energy peaks at the start of the segment and steadily declines as the night goes on and Clark is nowhere to be found. Malcolm listens intently to every word Rebo says, half out of punishment, and half out of some twisted desperation to feel close to him. At the end of the segment, Rebo goes off his usual script.

"Hey, uh...I'm not going to say any names, but I'm sure it's obvious who I'm talking to right now," Rebo says, his voice monotone. It's what Peter sounded like that night in the kitchen, drained of energy, but it's not just a low social battery now. It's total defeat. "I'm sorry. I know I've probably scared you off with that offer, but...well, it still stands. If you aren't completely weirded out by now, of course. The offer still stands. But, you know, it's okay if you don't come. I won't be mad. In fact, we can pretend it never happened at all. I'm just...I'm getting this sinking feeling that that was the last time I'll hear your voice again, and I'm really, *really* hoping I'm wrong."

It's silent for a moment. Malcolm squeezes his eyes shut, curling around the pillow he holds against his chest.

Rebo lets out a breath. "Anyway. Sorry to end on a weird note—I promise not to make a habit of it. Goodnight, everybody."

Malcolm turns off the radio before anything else can start up. The silence feels thick and suffocating as soon as the hum of the speaker cuts out. Malcolm inhales once. Twice. Then grabs his pillow and hurls it across the room. It hits his closet door hard, nearly toppling over one of his dying plants.

He can feel his nostrils flaring, and he closes his eyes. He breathes in. Out.

He pulls out his phone.

i know what i have to do but i don't know if i have the strength to do it

He shouldn't be surprised when Peter answers. He knew he'd be awake.

last time i heard that line, my favorite character died. please tell me you're not killing anyone.

no death here. just having a crisis.

Three dots pop up on the screen, and Malcolm stares at it until they disappear again. He waits, but they don't return.

Malcolm turns onto his back, forcing himself to look away from his phone. Then he picks it back up and stares at the screen again. He shouldn't have texted him. He's always using Peter for help, but what does he ever do in return? God, even without all the Rebo and Clark business he's still a shit friend.

He stares at the screen for longer than he cares to admit before finally closing out of the messenger app; but just as he hovers his thumb over Spotify, ready to drown out his sorrows to Mitski, his phone vibrates with a new message.

come outside.

Malcolm blinks at the message. He runs over to his window, squishing his face against the glass to try and peek into the street, but he can't see anything clearly. He lets out a disbelieving laugh, his breath fogging up the surface, before slipping his feet into a pair of slippers and darting out of the apartment, shoving his arms into an oversized coat on his way out.

He scrambles down the steps as fast as his body will allow him, nearly missing a step when he sees Peter standing at the bottom. Malcolm slows down as he gets nearer, holding his breath until he's only one step above Peter.

"You just gonna stand there?" Peter says.

"Yeah," Malcolm says. "I'm taller than you for once."

Peter snorts, shaking his head as he makes his way to the curb. He sits down, and Malcolm has no choice but to follow.

"How'd you get here so fast?"

Peter shrugs. "I was in the area."

Malcolm squints at Peter's back as he approaches. His shoulders rise and fall quickly.

"Did you...*run* here?" Malcolm asks as he sits down.

"What? No," Peter says with the voice of a man clearly trying to hide the fact that he's winded. "I've never run a day in my life."

"You go on jogs all the time, dude."

"And *you* said you were having a crisis," Peter diverts smoothly. "Let's focus on that."

Malcolm blows a raspberry, eyes fixed on the street. "You know, normal people usually call first."

Peter looks at him. "Would you have answered?"

Damn. That's fair.

"I'm sorry," Malcolm says, turning his eyes to his shoes. "For the way I've been acting recently. I have been avoiding you, and I can't...I can't really explain why."

Peter purses his lips, and Malcolm squeezes his eyes shut. He doesn't want to see the disappointment on Peter's face; he can hear it clear enough.

"I can't say I'm not hurt," Peter says quietly. "I thought we were getting somewhere, man. I thought we were leaving all that stuff behind us—"

"We are!" Malcolm assures him. "I swear, we are. I was just...going through something. Trying to figure some of my shit out."

"Does it have anything to do with what you texted me about?"

Malcolm bites at his cheek for a moment before nodding his head.

"And you really can't tell me what's going on?" Peter asks.

Malcolm shakes his head.

Peter looks away. He purses his lips, runs his tongue over the scar on the top. "Okay. That's really annoying, but okay."

"I'm sorry—"

"No, shut up, I'm not mad," Peter says, poking at Malcolm's forehead. "I can be annoyed without being angry, dude, that's a thing that I can do. Relax."

Malcolm frowns. "You sound mad."

"I'm not mad. I've brought you candy in the middle of the night to cheer you up about a problem I don't even know about. That's not a thing a mad person does."

"You brought candy?"

"Oh, fuck, right—" Peter shoves his hand into his pocket and brings out a crinkled bag of assorted candies. "My roommate said I could have some. He didn't exactly clarify how many."

Malcolm laughs and opens his hand. Peter reaches into the bag and drops a massive handful into Malcolm's palm, laughing when the pile spills over his fingers and onto the ground.

"Jesus, I don't need that many," Malcolm says through a smile, cradling the remaining pieces in both hands. He brings his legs together to drop the candy into his lap, then picks through his options. "Oh, shit, I love lemon."

"You're insane," Peter says.

"You don't like lemon?"

"*No one* likes lemon."

"Everyone likes lemon. It's like, the prime candy flavor."

"Have you hit your head? Are you concussed?"

"I'm a lemon lover," Malcolm says solemnly. "It's who I am."

"We can't all be perfect."

"You're rude, you know that?"

"You like it, though."

Malcolm shuts up pretty quickly after that, and he knows he's lost the argument. Was it even an argument? It doesn't matter. Peter won.

When Peter speaks again, his teasing tone is gone. "I need you to know that you're brave. Braver than you think, at least."

Malcolm stays quiet, but he wills himself to look at Peter.

"Whatever you're scared to do," he continues, "you can do it. You can do anything. And if everything goes to shit, then I'll be right here to help pick up the pieces." He falters. "Me and everyone else. We're all here to help."

Malcolm forces in a deep breath. "And what if you change your mind? What if, after everything is said and done, you won't want to have anything to do with me?"

Peter shakes his head. Then he shuffles around until his body's facing Malcolm's and brings his hands up, one on his shoulder and one cupping his neck. Malcolm thinks his heart stops completely. His gaze flickers between Malcolm's eyes and somewhere below them, and Malcolm doesn't allow himself to hope that it's somewhere in the vicinity of his mouth. "I wasted a ridiculous amount of time hating you, Malcolm," Peter says. "I'm not going anywhere now."

Peter's words are so sure, so concrete, that Malcolm almost believes him. And that almost-belief is just enough for Malcolm to make his decision.

He needs to meet Rebo.

34

"You're doing the right thing, love," Mona says. Her hand is in Malcolm's. Goby holds onto his arm on the other side as Jazz leads them towards Roisin Records. Their footsteps echo against the wet asphalt, and Malcolm hops over a puddle left from the afternoon's rain.

"Yeah," Jazz says, turning around and walking backwards in order to face Malcolm. "We know this isn't easy, but we're proud of you."

Goby nods in agreement, tightening their hold on Malcolm's arm. Malcolm purses his lips.

"Thanks guys," he says. "If I puke, please don't make fun of me."

"No promises," Jazz says.

"Jazmine," Mona scolds.

"I'll wait the appropriate amount of time before making fun of you," Jazz corrects herself.

"I'll take it," Malcolm says. They all halt as the front of Roisin Records comes into view like the final boss in a video game. It's packed.

"Where the fuck did all these people come from?" Goby asks, marveling at the decently sized crowd spilling out of the front doors and lingering along the sidewalk.

"They must be from Rebo's show," Malcolm says, eyes wide. "He mentioned the shop on the air. I guess he's gained more of an audience than I thought."

"Atta boy," Goby says proudly.

"Are you gonna be alright with the crowd?" Jazz asks. "Not gonna, you know..." She mimes an explosion, and Malcolm rolls his eyes.

"I'll be fine," Malcolm assures her. "And if I'm not, I can always hightail it out of there."

"Alright then, now that the escape plan's in place," Mona says, and squeezes Malcolm's hand. "Are you ready?"

"Fuck no," Malcolm says.

"Great. In you go," she says, and tugs him toward the entrance.

Malcolm sputters and stumbles forward. "You guys aren't coming with me?"

"Don't worry, dude," Goby says, hiking up their voice as Malcolm walks further away. "We'll be close by just in case you need us, but we think this is something you need to do on your own. You know?"

Malcolm frowns. He turns back towards the shop. "I know."

• • • •

The inside of the shop is uncomfortably tight, with two or three people filtering in and out of the doorway every few seconds. The music playing overhead just barely drowns out the white noise of the crowd. Malcolm clocks it as something from the Bee Gees, but can't focus enough to determine the exact song.

He spots Peter at the desk, manning the station with ease. No one is actually buying anything. Malcolm realizes, quite suddenly, that they may not be here for the shop at all. They might just be here for Rebo.

Maybe they're here for Clark, too, he thinks.

Malcolm dismisses the thought as quickly as it came and makes his way to the desk. He smooths down his hair and brushes some nonexistent dust from his pants, then stops in front of Peter.

"Busy tonight, huh?" Malcolm says.

Peter startles, like he hadn't even noticed Malcolm's steady approach. "Oh, hey man. Yeah, shit, it's packed as hell."

Malcolm glances around the store at the sea of customers. Many of them are treating the shop like a lounge, standing around the rows of records to chat with their friends. There's a lot more teenagers than he expected there to be.

"Are you alright with how packed it is?" Malcolm asks. "It's a bit, well—crowded."

"I'm fine," Peter says, then points to his ear. Malcolm finally notices the small plug inside of it. "These bad boys filter out excess noise so I don't get overstimulated."

"Oh, sick," Malcolm says with genuine interest. "Maybe I should get a pair."

Peter laughs, despite it not being that funny, and the sound of it is emptier than usual. Malcolm can't help but feel like Peter's pushing himself more than he should. He hasn't looked at Malcolm once since he came in, and the few sentences he's said seem to have drained him more than they should.

"Are you sure you're alright, man?" Malcolm asks, leaning in a bit closer. His nerves have mostly escaped him now, replaced instead with cautious concern. "You seem kind of...spooked."

"I'm alright, really," Peter says, looking at Malcolm for the first time since he came into the store, but he looks away just as quickly. "I'm kind of expecting someone to show up tonight. But we haven't met before and my dumbass didn't ask for an *identifier* of some sort, so..."

"So it's up to them to make themselves known," Malcolm says. The nerves have returned with vengeance. He hopes Peter doesn't notice him wiping his palms on his jeans.

"Yeah, pretty much," Peter says. He sighs, then shakes his head. "Sorry, I haven't even asked—how are you doing? How did your thing go, the one you were so stressed about last night?"

And now is his chance. It's the perfect opportunity, a smooth segue into his big reveal. *It's happening right now*, he could say. *It's me. It's me, it's me, it's been me all this time. Are you happy? Are you pissed? Am I anything like who you'd hoped I would be?*

"I'm—" Malcolm's voice cuts out, stuck in his throat like a chunk of ice. He clenches his teeth together.

Three deep breaths, and I'll say it, he tells himself.

He breathes in once, and he imagines himself grabbing his nerves by the throat and hurling them out of a window.

He breathes twice, and he feels the smallest ounce of confidence he can muster begin to grow and expand inside him. He can do this. He knows he can. Peter deserves the truth, and Malcolm deserves to tell it.

He breathes one more time.

"Malcolm?" Peter asks. His eyes are so kind, and he looks so concerned, and Malcolm hears Rebo's voice for once.

"I'm...still working on it," Malcolm says. His confidence deflates like a balloon.

Peter just smiles at him, and Malcolm hates himself all the more. "Don't worry, man, it'll work itself out."

"You have more faith in me than I do," Malcolm says.

"Good thing you have me around then, huh?" Peter says.

Malcolm looks down at his shoes. "I don't think I tell you that enough, actually," he says. When he looks back up he finds Peter staring at him curiously. "I'm really grateful you're my friend, Peter. Like—insanely so. I wish I could be as good of a friend to you as you are to me."

Peter's eyebrows crease together. "What? Dude, you're an amazing friend. Don't say that."

"I'm really not."

"You really are. You're an asshole sometimes and you're confusing as hell, but you're a good friend."

Malcolm scoffs. "You have helped me so much in the short time that we've been friends. What have I done to help you?"

"I think you need to refresh your knowledge on what exactly a friendship is, moron," Peter says. Malcolm forgot how easily Peter seems to make insults sound like pet names. "I'm not your friend just because I might get something out of you. I know you'd help me if I needed you, but that's not why I'm your friend, or why I even consider you a good one. You're a good friend because you make me happy."

Malcolm blinks at him. "I make you happy?"

"Obviously," Peter says. "I think all that self-deprecating bullshit in your head is clouding your perception. Like, what did you do when you found out how much I mask myself in public, huh? You didn't make me feel bad for it or even push me to stop masking completely, because you knew that was too much. You didn't just give me empty words of sympathy. You just...gave me the space to be myself, if I ever needed it." Peter stops a beat, as if waiting for Malcolm to process his words. "Do you even know how much that meant to me? I didn't even realize how badly I needed a place to be myself until you gave me that, Malcolm. You're like..."

Peter trails off, trying to find the words. Malcolm waits.

"You're like home," Peter finally says. He nods to himself, happy with his word choice. "Yeah. That's what you are, Malcolm. You're like my home."

Malcolm hopes that his heart doesn't fail on him, but it feels dangerously close to giving out. Peter's still looking at him, and after all this time it still feels like staring into the sun, so he says the first thing that comes to mind that'll break him out of this trance.

He clears his throat, and says in a slightly wobbly voice, "That's kinda gay, man."

Peter barks out a surprised laugh. "You're shit at this."

"You just called me your home, dude! My brain is malfunctioning!"

"I didn't know I had such an effect on you," Peter says, leaning his arms against the desk, and *fuck*, great, he's back to being the flirty friend. Malcolm can't survive flirty Peter, not tonight of all nights. He's too weak to pretend it doesn't do something to him. So he doesn't pretend. Malcolm bites at his cheek, scratches the scruff on his jaw that he forgot to shave, then says just loud enough for Peter to hear, "Yeah, you did."

Peter seems startled, for the brief second Malcolm can get himself to actually look at him. His surprise melts away into something closer to wonder, his mouth still open just slightly from the aftermath of his smirk. His voice is warm and subdued when he says, "Well, I guess I know now."

Malcolm wishes for all the world that he had something smooth to say in response, but luckily his phone saves him from having to think of one. Unluckily, it makes him jump when it starts ringing violently in his pocket, which is embarrassing to do in front of the guy you kinda sorta maybe just confessed your feelings to in a super vague roundabout way. He apologizes and fishes the phone out of his pocket.

The briefest shock races down his back when he sees that it's his mother calling. But, as he looks back at Peter, he finds for the first time that he isn't tempted to answer. Not even a little. He mutes the call and tucks his phone away.

Peter's looking out into the crowd again when Malcolm turns his attention back to him. Peter purses his lips, and seems to come to a decision.

"Okay, I'm calling it," Peter says. "He's not coming."

The panic from before races back into Malcolm's body in one quick motion, fast enough to make him dizzy. "W-wait," he says, "maybe you just have to wait a little longer?"

Peter shakes his head with a frown. "Nah. It's late. If he was going to show up, he'd be here by now."

Malcolm frowns. "Was this like...a date?" He's not sure if he really wants to know the answer.

Peter gives him a considering look, then shrugs. "Honestly, I don't know. It might've been. But it didn't have to be." He pauses, seeming to think to himself. "Maybe I should've let him know that. Maybe that's what scared him off."

Peter starts to raise himself up onto the desk, and Malcolm yelps, rushing forward to make sure he doesn't fall and break his neck. Peter straightens up once he has his footing, giving Malcolm an appreciative nod before turning towards the crowd.

"Alright, folks!" Peter shouts, his palms cupped around his mouth. "We're closing up! Everybody buy whatever you're gonna buy and then make your way out!"

There's a chorus of disappointed grumbles, and Malcolm feels each one like a personal punch to the gut. They were waiting for him, he can see that now. They were waiting for the big reunion of Rebo and Clark. He let them all down too.

The shop empties slowly but surely. Peter watches them filter out, and Malcolm wonders if he's still looking for any sign of Clark.

"Hey," Malcolm says, and nudges Peter's arm. "You wanna go on a walk or something?"

Peter takes a moment, still watching the store slowly empty out. The music overhead has been turned off. Malcolm realizes that he's never been in the store this late at night. Now that it's lost all the commotion from the crowd, it feels kind of like when he would come back to school after a field trip. The buildings would be drenched in shadows cast from the orange street lamps, not a teacher in sight aside from those still leaving the buses. Back then, he always felt like he wasn't supposed to be there. He tries not to feel the same way now.

"Yeah," Peter says. "I could go for a walk."

35

Walking is usually one of his favorite activities. It clears his mind, reminds him to enjoy the charm and beauty of Bugswick. It's harder to enjoy, however, when all he can focus on is just how badly he's fucked up. *Again.*

He had his chance. He was *so close* to doing the right thing and revealing himself. Peter would have finally known who he really was—Malcolm and Clark, one and the same—for better or worse. The truth would've been out. But he couldn't even do it when the opportunity presented itself. It didn't even just present itself, it was shouting in his face, "*Hey, now's the time, dickhead!*"

Now would just be a sour time to do it. Right after he disappointed everyone like that? Leaving Peter in the dust? No, he can't do it now.

He *will* tell him. Just...later.

"Wish there weren't so many lights out here," Peter says. Malcolm shakes himself out of his pity party and glances at Peter, who's walking with his hands in his pockets, his eyes pointed at the sky. "All this light pollution washes out the stars."

Malcolm hums in agreement, albeit distractedly. He's never really paid much attention to the stars, but he tries to see the sky through Peter's eyes. (It doesn't really work. It just looks black to him.)

"Are you sure you're alright?" Malcolm can't help but ask. "It's just us now. You can tell me if you're not."

Peter keeps his gaze to the sky. "I'm fine. Honest," he says. "Disappointed, I guess, as anyone would be. I was...really excited to meet this person."

Malcolm kicks at a pebble on the ground, and Peter kicks it after him.

"Maybe I was looking for something too good to be true," Peter mumbles. "My fault for getting my hopes up."

"Hey, no," Malcolm says sharply. "That wasn't your fault. It's that dick's fault for standing you up. He's a fucking idiot and he doesn't know what he's missing." The irony in his statement isn't lost on him.

Peter laughs. "I think you're more mad about this than I am."

"You should be mad!" Malcolm near-shouts, but when Peter shushes him through a giggle, he can't help but smile too. "That was so fucked up! You should be angry! How are you not angry?"

Peter shrugs. "Maybe part of me is—but, you know. I get it. This guy...he's got some issues."

Malcolm tries not to sound like he's taken it personally. "Yikes."

"We *all* have issues, I'm not trying to shit on him," he says. "I just...I get it, you know? I understand why he may not have wanted to show up. So, no, I'm not mad. I guess I just wish he had told me he couldn't do it instead of just...running away." Peter throws a smirk in Malcolm's direction. "Sounds kinda familiar, huh?"

"Oh, fuck off," Malcolm laughs. Peter doesn't know how close he is to the truth.

"I guess I just have a type," Peter says.

Malcolm bites down on his smile. He shouldn't be smiling. He shouldn't be enjoying this moment, so soon after he's fucked up so immensely. But that's the effect of being around Peter Tollemache lately: Malcolm can't help but be happy around him.

"Are we going to the park?" Malcolm asks once he recognizes the trail they've headed down.

"Yup. The fountain should be on, if I remember the hours right," Peter says.

"I don't remember a fountain being here..."

"It's one of those ground fountains, the ones that shoot water up from the ground and get you soaked. See?" Peter points, and Malcolm hears the *swshhh* of the water being sprayed into the air before he sees it. It turns off, and the splattering of the water droplets falling to the earth hits his ears.

"Isn't that for the kids to play in?" Malcolm asks.

"Mhm," Peter says. "And tonight it's for us."

"Oh. Oh, no. Nuh uh."

"Yuh huh," Peter says, nodding his head with a devilish grin. "C'mon, dude, I just got stood up. You have to do this."

Malcolm groans. Of course he was going to do it.

"That's my boy," Peter says, and Malcolm vehemently wishes for God to strike him dead.

Peter makes his way towards the fountain, and to Malcolm's horror, he begins to strip off his shirt. Malcolm gets stuck staring at the muscles of Peter's back for a solid five seconds before he wills himself to speak.

"Hey, yo, I didn't agree to stripping!"

"I'm not stripping completely!" Peter argues. "I hate wearing wet clothes. Can't exactly take my pants off in public, though, so this is the best I can do. Are you coming?"

Malcolm groans again, pressing his palms against his eyes. "Fine. *Fine.* God." He wiggles out of his hoodie and t-shirt, throwing them onto the nearest bench in a messy heap next to Peter's nicely folded shirt.

Malcolm belatedly realizes that he hadn't hesitated to show his chest.

"C'mon!" Peter shouts, grabbing Malcolm's hand and dragging him into the middle of the fountain. They lay flat on their backs, faces to the sky. They're surrounded in a circle of water spouts, and Peter must have memorized the timing of the water, because he counts down from three, and the water goes soaring into the air.

"*Wooooooo!*" Peter yells, and the loud spraying of the fountain almost drains him out, but Malcolm can hear him well enough.

Malcolm laughs, and when Peter whoops again, Malcolm joins him with a loud holler. They shout and laugh and scream together, drowned out by the roar of the water before it stops and sends the droplets spraying onto their faces. It's refreshing, feeling the water against his bare chest. His pants are soaked through already, but he can't find it in himself to care.

And Peter's still holding his hand.

Malcolm looks at their hands joined together. Peter's hand is bigger than his, but Malcolm's is rougher. That surprises him. He figured Peter would have calluses built up from all of the instruments he's sure he plays. Malcolm always imagined him playing bass. Wait, does he play anything at all?

"Do you play any instruments?"

"What?"

"Instruments. Do you play any?"

"Uh, a little? I play the keyboard sometimes."

"Oh. Cool. I used to play the trombone."

Peter laughs. "Cool."

He's thinking too much. He needs to stop thinking so much, but speaking from experience, trying to stop his thoughts usually just makes it worse. If anything, they seem to go even faster just out of spite. But then Peter's thumb rubs across Malcolm's, and his thoughts halt entirely.

Malcolm drags his eyes away from their hands in a show of great strength, only to settle instead on Peter's face.

"Hey," Peter says. The fountain sprays again, and he laughs. It turns off, leaving behind fresh droplets of water on his nose.

"Hey," Malcolm says. He swallows. "When you—earlier, when you said, '*I guess I know now...*'" Malcolm trails off for a moment, but Peter stays silent, waiting for him to continue. "Did you mean that? Did you really not know before?"

Peter's face goes soft, his lips still quirked up in the smallest of smiles. "Know what?"

"Fuck off, you know what," Malcolm says, and Peter's smile grows.

"It's hard to tell, sometimes," Peter admits. "Not just with you, but with anyone. Sometimes I think I know how someone feels, but it's...tricky, I guess. And you're a bit of a wild card as it is, so, no. I didn't know for sure."

"But you do now?" Malcolm says. He gulps down what remaining saliva he has left in his mouth. He's not quite sure what's possessed him to ask this in the first place. "You know?"

"I think I do," Peter says, his voice dropped to a whisper. "I hope I do." The fountain goes off around them, but neither of them look away, even as the water falls against their bare chests and faces. The fountain cuts off. Peter's eyes flicker across Malcolm's face, from his forehead to his chin, until they finally settle, undoubtedly, on his lips.

"Peter," Malcolm breathes.

"Malcolm," Peter says.

"No, wait—*Peter*."

Peter stops. He had started to lean in, and that's when the alarms in Malcolm's brain finally start to blare.

"Are you okay?" Peter asks. Fuck him for being hot *and* respectful.

"I shouldn't do this," Malcolm says. "I can't—I can't do this."

"O...kay," Peter says, understandably confused. "I guess I...didn't get that right then?"

"No! You did! You got it right. I do feel that way, I do. I—I *really* like you, Peter."

Peter blinks at him. "Alright, I'm lost."

"I just can't do this to you," Malcolm says as he starts to sit up, dragging his hand away from Peter. "This isn't—it's not *fair*, god, I can't believe I did this, I—I have to go. Fuck, I really have to go."

"Wait, wait—Malcolm!" Peter shouts, but Malcolm's already grabbed his clothes and started to run.

"Fuck fuck fuck fuck fuck fucking shit fuck," Malcolm chants to himself. He can hear Peter calling after him still, but he doesn't let up. He stumbles as he tries to put his shirt and hoodie back on, gasping when his head finally fits through the hole at the neck, his wet hair plastered against his forehead. "Shit fuck shit fuck *shit*."

"*Malcolm!*"

He runs faster. He runs and runs, and he's almost crying by the time his apartment comes into view, but he refuses to break down before he's in the safety of his room. He's going to have to face the others and tell them what happened. He doesn't want to see the disappointment on their faces too.

He climbs the stairs two at a time, chest heaving. That's the fastest he's run since high school P.E., and his body's aware of it. He's ready to make a beeline to his room and pass out on his bed as soon as he enters the apartment—but when he steps through the door, he's greeted by someone's back.

Goby, Jazz and Mona stand in front of a woman, each of their faces varying degrees of panic. Their eyes dart over to him at his entrance, and their panic only grows. Jazz has his name halfway out of her mouth, sounding almost like a warning, before the woman finally turns around to face him.

She grins at him, her lips a thin line, like an open wound. She spreads her arms wide, welcoming, suffocating. "Hello, sweetheart," she says, and there's a spot of lipstick on her professionally whitened teeth. Malcolm does his best to swallow the bile that rises in his throat.

"Hey, Mom."

36

"You really need to get that phone of yours checked out, darling. You didn't answer my call," his mother tuts at him.

"I'm sorry," Malcolm says weakly. The empty 'I-don't-exist' feeling started to creep back into his body the moment he realized who exactly was in his home. Part of him wishes it would just hurry up and take over already. He'd prefer dissociation over this.

"Rita," Jazz says stiffly. "What are you doing here?"

"Jazmine," Rita coos. "Forgive my manners, I would've given you a hug already, but *somebody* was being awfully rude about my visit."

"This is our house," Goby says, sounding colder than Malcolm had ever heard them before. "You just showed up with no warning. Sorry we didn't prepare a fruit basket."

"Is it so bad for me to wish to see my only child?" She says, sighing when she turns back to scan Malcolm. She shakes her head at the state of his clothes. "Why are you all wet? Really, darling, don't you stand out enough with your..." She gestures to his whole body, his *masculine* body, and he feels himself go cold. "Oh, don't give me that look, you know what I mean."

He does. He wishes he didn't. He glances at the others and finds himself glad that his mother can't see their faces. They look, quite frankly, insane. He's never seen Mona so furious. Jazz looks downright murderous.

"Who's this?" says a new voice, and Malcolm spins around fast enough to make himself sick.

He left the door wide open, and now Peter's standing at the entrance, soaked to the bone, chest heaving and looking for all the world like the most confused man on Earth.

"Oh, well, aren't you handsome," Rita purrs.

"*Mom*—"

"That's your mom?" Peter says, straightening up. "Shit. Oh, fuck—sorry for saying shit. Sorry for saying it again. I'm Peter." He sticks out his hand, and Rita chuckles.

"So charming," she says, giving his hand a flirtatious shake. "It's lovely to meet you, Peter. I'm Rita. Rita Clark."

Goby freezes. Mona's eyebrows shoot up. Jazz's head falls in defeat. And Malcolm—he can't breathe.

"Clark?" Peter says, his voice quiet, barely reaching Malcolm's ears. "Like...Clark Kent."

Malcolm squeezes his eyes shut.

Rita chuckles, albeit awkwardly. "Yes, I suppose so."

Malcolm forces himself to look at Peter, and regrets it immediately. Peter's looking straight at him, his eyes wide and wondering, questioning. Malcolm could pretend he doesn't know. It could be a coincidence, for all Peter's concerned. But he's just so *tired* of lying. He's tired of pretending, of letting everyone down again and again.

So he lets Peter see it. He lets him see the truth on his face.

It's me. I'm him. I'm sorry.

Peter's face clears of all confusion in an instant. Malcolm's lip wobbles, and he clamps down on it with his teeth, his eyes clouding with tears. He presses his hand to his chest, willing himself to breathe. Peter's jaw clenches. Malcolm closes his eyes.

"Is something wrong?" Rita says awkwardly. He thinks he hears one of the others shush her.

"Yeah, actually," Peter says in a low rumble. "I've heard a lot about you."

Malcolm hesitantly opens his eyes, but finds that Peter isn't looking at him anymore. His gaze has locked onto Malcolm's mother instead, stepping over the threshold of the apartment until he's standing in front of Malcolm—in between him and his mother.

Malcolm doesn't ever remember telling Peter about his experience with his mom—not enough to warrant this kind of reaction. He remembers, however, telling Rebo.

"I think it's best if you leave," Peter says, his voice nearly a growl. "Now."

Rita gapes at him, her finely plucked eyebrows disappearing beneath her bangs. "Excuse me?"

"You heard me."

"How *dare* you speak to me like that," she hisses, her voice trembling with barely contained rage. "I drove for miles to see my *only child* and you have the audacity to treat me like some *enemy*."

"Peter's right," Mona says, moving to stand next to Peter. Goby and Jazz migrate over as well, until they're grouped around Malcolm like a protective shield. "Leave, Rita. Now."

Rita huffs out a furious breath, her face an ugly red from anger and humiliation. "I cannot believe this. I'm trying to be a good mother, and you all want to stop me from that?" She locks her eyes on Malcolm. "Are you just going to stand around and let your friends treat me like this—"

And Malcolm's deadname begins to slip from her mouth. It's just the beginnings of a syllable, barely even a full word, but it's enough to send Malcolm's heart into his stomach.

And then Jazz is in front of Rita, and her hand has slapped her clean across the face.

"His name is Malcolm," Jazz spits.

The room falls silent. Rita's frozen in shock, her hand pressed against the glowing red of her abused cheek. When she starts to regain herself, her face beginning to morph into a look of predatory fury, Mona steps up in front of Jazz. Her height is enough to intimidate anyone into submission—she knows how to use it to protect her girlfriend. (Or protect someone else from Jazz.)

Rita stands down, gaping, before turning once again to Malcolm.

"Malcolm," she whispers. "My son. Please."

Malcolm had always yearned for the moments where his mother would validate his identity like that. Use his name, call him *son*. He'd hold those moments close to his chest, like a rare four leaf clover. But he sees them for what they are now. It's not love, or acceptance; it's manipulation. Just a tool to get him to come back to her side.

Malcolm walks forward, and the others part for him. Rita looks hopeful.

"Leave," he says. He refuses to show any emotion when he speaks. Rita's face crumbles. "Come back here...and I will never speak to you again."

"Malcolm, please, I'm *sorry*—"

"He said to leave," Peter says. Malcolm doesn't dare look at him, but he feels it when Peter's hand slips into his own. Malcolm squeezes tight, grateful for the anchor.

Jazz says, "Don't make me kick your ass this time," and Mona looks close to chastising her, but stays silent in the end.

"I'd listen to her," Goby says. "She sewed spikes into the toes of her boots. They hurt."

Rita glances down at Jazz's feet to confirm. She pales at the shoes before glancing nervously back at the group. She looks at Malcolm one last time, but when he refuses to show any sign of backing down, she groans. "Fine," she says. She starts to head toward the door. "But when you come to your senses and realize these friends of yours will lead you nowhere, I'll be here. That's what a good mother does."

And Jazz seems to be tired of her talking, because she takes one giant breath before letting it out in a booming bark. A *literal* bark—like a dog. Rita jumps at the noise, but Jazz doesn't let up. She steps forward, and barks again and again, getting closer into Rita's space until she finally leaves the apartment in a startled hurry.

"Nice one, babe," Mona says.

"Danke," Jazz says.

"Can you teach me how to do that?" Goby asks. "That was freakishly realistic. You sounded like my gran's Great Dane."

"Your gran has a Great Dane? Isn't she, like, five feet tall?" Mona asks.

"Yeah, but she could also bench press you and Jazz at the same time," Goby says.

"Sick," Jazz says. "Would she?"

Peter interrupts their conversation when he asks, "Malcolm, are you okay?"

Malcolm blinks. He was very close to full dissociation by the end of that whole scene, and he still doesn't feel completely himself. So much has happened in such little time.

He hears his mother's car roar to life and drive away.

"I'm going out," Malcolm says.

Peter looks like he's ready to argue, and Malcolm doesn't blame him. Malcolm has run away so much tonight already, but he just can't stand being in one place right now. Jazz seems to sense this and, being the absolute blessing that she is, places her hand on Peter's shoulder and says, "It's okay, Mal. Go."

He gives her a nod in appreciation. Then he looks to Peter.

"I'm sorry," he says. He hopes Peter understands he's apologizing for everything.

• • • •

He loses track of how long he wanders for. The streets blur together. After a while, it starts to feel more like he's playing a video game than walking his actual body. He only starts to wake up from his haze when his feet begin to blister, and his chest begins to ache. It feels like he's walked the perimeter of the whole town by the time he eventually finds himself on a bench outside Roisin Records. Of course he'd come here.

He licks his lips and tastes salt. He's not sure when he started crying, but it explains why the world's become so blurry. He wipes the tears across his cheeks, remembering what Goby told him about tears being naturally good for your skin.

"My skin better be damn gorgeous after this," Malcolm mutters to himself with a sniff. The stuffiness of his voice makes him cringe, and he wipes his nose on his sleeve. It's gross. He's too tired to care.

He takes out his phone and pulls up Spotify. The *Electric Warrior* album is already pulled up on his Recently Played list, sitting just a few rows down. He clicks on the only song he's actually listened to on the album.

"Cosmic Dancer" quietly filters out of his phone speakers, and he turns up the volume a few notches. He draws his knees up to his chest, willing himself to remember the breathing exercises Peter did with him to this song. The memory pulls at his chest, fierce and unforgiving. It hurts, and it helps; and he wishes, not for the first time, that he hadn't let things go so far.

"Fuck," Malcolm whimpers.

He pats the rhythm of the song against his chest, his arm held tightly between his torso and his knees, his fingers tapping softly along his sternum. When the song ends, he plays it again, turning the volume up higher.

The streets are empty save for a few passersby. He spots the silhouette of Mr. Lu closing up his shop down the street, but Mr. Lu doesn't see him. Malcolm wonders if he has a pet waiting for him at home. Mr. Lu has never mentioned a pet. But then again, Malcolm's never asked.

"I'm a real asshole, huh?" Malcolm says.

"Maybe just a little."

Malcolm startles and swivels his head around. Peter wanders over to him, his hands in his pockets, the picture of nonchalance.

"Scooch," he says, and Malcolm scoots over to make room for Peter. "Somehow, I had a feeling I'd find you here."

Malcolm feels his cheeks go red as Peter glances up at the Roisin Records sign. Malcolm rests his chin on his knees and stares out at the street. "I'm guessing you pulled the short straw?"

"Huh?"

"The others. They told you to check up on me, right?"

"Malcolm, I spent the past thirty minutes trying to convince Jazz to let me come find you," Peter laughs. "I'm pretty sure she only let me leave because I was annoying her to death."

Malcolm blinks at the ground. He turns to stare at Peter, eyebrows furrowed. Peter notices his confusion and sighs, long and exhausted.

"Look," Peter says. "I'm not going to pretend I'm not...really fucking confused. But I'm not upset." Peter pulls a hand out of his pocket, using it instead to twirl the string on his jacket around his finger. He pulls up his legs until he's sitting cross-legged on the bench. Now neither of them have their feet on the ground. "I should've known, really. I mean, it's fairly obvious, when you think about it. I *knew* your last name, dude. I heard it in college—hell, I saw it every time you gave me your credit card to buy something at Roisin. But it just...didn't click, I guess. Not until tonight."

Malcolm closes his eyes. "I know what you mean. When I found out about you being Rebo...I was almost angry at how oblivious I'd been. I mean, of *course* it was you."

Peter turns to look at him, and Malcolm can see it in his periphery, but he doesn't dare look back. He's still a coward, even in these moments. "How long?" Peter asks. Malcolm hangs his head lower. "The look on your face, back at the apartment—you already knew I was Rebo. I mean, I figured that out pretty quickly. You didn't seem surprised. You just seemed...sad." Peter takes a breath and asks again, quieter than before. "How long have you known?"

"Way too long."

"How long, Malcolm?"

Malcolm forces himself to look Peter in the eye. No point in lying any more. "Since that day at the burger joint. Your sister called you Max Rebo as a kid. Wasn't too hard to connect the dots after that."

Peter's silent for a moment. Then he falls back against the bench, his head tilted up to the sky. He blows out a gust of air, and the fog from his breath drifts up into the night until it disappears completely.

"Shit," Peter says. "I guess that makes sense."

"Yeah."

Peter rubs his thumb over the seam of his jeans. Malcolm stares at it. There's a freckle on his wrist that Malcolm never noticed before. "Why didn't you just tell me?" Peter asks, finally. The million dollar question.

"I don't know if you've noticed, Peter, but I'm kind of an asshole," Malcolm says.

"Being an asshole right *now* isn't going to help me forgive you."

"Well, maybe you shouldn't," Malcolm says. "What do you want me to say? That I was scared? That I was so fucking scared of getting close to you, especially since I had already opened up so much to you without even *knowing it was you*, that I did the only thing I thought to do and pushed you away? Well, there you fuckin' go. I was so scared of getting close to you and hurting you somehow that I just went ahead and made it happen anyway." Malcolm stands up, his muscles too tense for him to stay sitting any longer. "And don't even get me started on the fucking mommy issues! You can imagine how badly that asshole screwed up my self-worth; and dude, that's only the tip of the iceberg when it comes to how fucked up I am so, honestly, Peter, I should be asking *you* why you aren't running for the goddamn hills right now. I mean *fuck*, man, I cursed you out the first time we met, and I don't even *remember it!*"

Peter blinks at him, his eyes wide and eyebrows raised to his hairline. He takes a breath and says, "You've been holding that in for a while, huh?"

Malcolm growls. "Fuck you!"

"Why are you yelling at me!"

"Because you're not!" Malcolm cries. "Why the fuck aren't you more angry, asshole!"

"You're yelling at me because *I'm not angry?*" Peter asks with a finger to his chest, and he finally stands as well so he and Malcolm are at equal eye level.

"*Yes!*" Malcolm says desperately. "I fucking lied to you, Peter! I lied for *ages* because I was too chicken shit to do anything else, and you're just okay with that?"

"Of course I'm not okay with that!" Peter says, his anger finally, blessedly rising to his face.

"Well then prove it!" Malcolm shouts.

Peter swipes a hand across his nose, clenching his jaw before swiping his tongue across his teeth. It's been a while since Malcolm's seen him do his signature *I'm-pissed-the-fuck-off* move. Peter sniffs once, turning his body almost as if he's about to leave, before stepping up into Malcolm's space and poking him hard in the chest.

"Yeah, alright," Peter says. "I'm pissed. I am, I'm fucking *pissed*, dude, cause what the fuck? You lied to me, you avoided me, you made everything so much more complicated than it had to be!"

"Yes, yes, fucking *exactly*. Be pissed!" Malcolm says.

Peter backs off in an instant. "No, fuck off, don't tell me how to feel!"

"Wh—" Malcolm groans. "What the fuck! We were just getting somewhere! Are you mad at me or not?"

"*Why*, Malcolm?" Peter shouts. "Why do you want me to be mad at you?"

"Because I *deserve it*. After everything I've done, I deserve you yelling in my face! Hell, I deserve a punch to the neck but lord knows you're too fucking nice to do that."

"Believe me, I'm tempted," Peter mutters.

"Then *do it!*"

"No!"

"*Why not?*"

Peter stomps up to him, and for a second Malcolm's certain he's finally snapped. Malcolm's eyes go wide for a split moment before he clenches them shut in preparation for the hit. But the hit doesn't come. He feels Peter's hands fist the collar of his hoodie and jerk him forward.

And Peter kisses him.

Malcolm's hands fly upward, but his brain has fried to the point of uselessness, so he leaves his hands awkwardly hovering near Peter's shoulders. He hasn't closed his eyes yet. He's pretty sure this is what shock feels like. And Peter's still kissing him.

Until Peter pulls back with a smack of their lips and says in a breathy voice, "You gonna kiss me back, Clark?"

So he does.

37

Malcolm had tried not to think too much about what kissing Peter would be like. He was sure that it was just unnecessary torture to imagine a scenario that couldn't possibly ever come true. Thank fuck he was wrong about that.

The kiss had started out blazing, the tension from their argument still present, bleeding out from Peter's mouth and into Malcolm's. Peter fought without saying a word, moving his jaw in a way that forced Malcolm to tilt his head back (and *damn* the inch Peter had over him). His hands grasped at the sides of Malcolm's face, keeping him where he wanted.

But the fury of the kiss didn't last long. Peter's hands relaxed the longer their lips moved together, and his palms slid down from Malcolm's face to his shoulders, then his chest, until they settled on Malcolm's waist. He flexed his hand, drew Malcolm closer to him, and Malcolm followed with ease.

Malcolm thinks he made a noise of some sort; a whimper that was either from pleasure or from relief. He still couldn't quite believe this was happening.

Actually, that's something he should probably ask.

"Wait," Malcolm says against Peter's lips, putting a hand against Peter's chest. Peter stops immediately.

"Are you okay?" Peter asks, catching his breath. His lips are swollen. Malcolm has a very hard time not looking at them.

"I just—I need to ask. What is this? What does this mean?"

"I think you know that."

Malcolm laughs breathlessly. "I hope I do. I'd really like it if you said it out loud, though."

Peter grins, his thumb rubbing against Malcolm's waist in soothing strokes. "I was so torn up about having feelings for both you and Clark. I thought—I thought I'd have to choose, and I didn't really want to. I guess maybe the reason why I was so oblivious this whole time is because...the thought of you two being the same person was just too good to be true." Peter swallows, and Malcolm's eyes flicker down to the bob of his Adam's apple before returning to Peter's face. "I like you, Malcolm. I mean, I *really* like you. That hasn't changed. I'm not really sure it ever will."

Malcolm feels a grin break out across his face, uncontrollable. And then his whole body starts to slump.

"Whoa!" Peter says as Malcolm headbutts his chest, slumping into him so that Peter has to hold him up. "Malcolm? Are you alright?"

"Yeah," Malcolm says with a light chuckle. "Yeah, I'm fine. Just. Holy shit, a lot has happened tonight. I'm a little overwhelmed. I think my body's just catching up with my brain."

"Understandable," Peter says. "Let's get you home, buddy."

"Peter?"

"Yeah?"

"I like you, too, if that wasn't completely obvious."

"Good to know," Peter says, a little cheekily.

"Yeah. So please never call me buddy again."

Peter barks out a laugh, brilliant and bright, and they begin their walk home.

• • • •

They've been walking in silence for a few minutes when Malcolm feels a finger brush against his knuckle. He looks down to see Peter reaching out towards his hand, somewhat hesitantly. Peter isn't looking at him.

"This alright?" Peter asks.

In lue of a response, Malcolm unfolds his hand and intertwines his fingers with Peter. Malcolm glances over at Peter to see him beaming down at his shoes.

"You had your tongue in my mouth and this is what gets you flustered?" Malcolm says.

Peter throws him an incredulous look, his cheeks blazing, and he shoves Malcolm's shoulder. He still doesn't let go of his hand, though.

"Don't be so crass!" Peter says.

Malcolm laughs, and Peter laughs, and it feels so, *so* right.

• • • •

"Hey, Peter," Malcolm says. They've been walking for ten minutes now. The apartment isn't that far away, but a silent agreement was made that they'd be taking the long way there. "Did you like me or Clark more?" Malcolm asks, and Peter's eyebrows raise. "Before you knew we were the same person, obviously."

"Tricky question," Peter says, looking out into the empty street. Malcolm appreciates that Peter takes his useless questions seriously. "I liked you both a lot. Like, *holy shit*, a lot. But I definitely liked you more."

"Really?" Malcolm cuts in, dubious.

"Oh yeah," Peter says. "In fact, I've probably been crushing on you for longer than we've even been friends. You're kind of hot, dude." Malcolm snorts. "But seriously. You're just—you're amazing, Malcolm. Sure, Clark was you, but it's nothing compared to the you I got to be friends with in person. Your laugh, your smile...you're just so...*you*. You know? Clark got real with me about the tough shit, but then again, anyone can do that when they're just a voice on the radio. Now, with *Malcolm*..." he grins over at Malcolm. "I could see the real him. And I wanted that."

Malcolm kind of stumped at that. "Really?"

Peter nods.

"I thought...I dunno, I thought Clark was more real than me," Malcolm says. "*Because* of all the 'tough shit' I told you about that I didn't tell you in person."

"The tough shit isn't what makes you *you* though, Malcolm. Your mom doesn't make up your identity, your trauma doesn't define who you are. In person, I got to see the full picture. I could see your struggles, I could see your strengths, I could see your passions and your fears. I could see what a dick you are when you're trying to hide the fact that you like someone." He nudges Malcolm, and Malcolm snickers. "You were real. Realer than anything Clark was."

Malcolm stops, forcing Peter to stop as well with a tug of their hands. Malcolm blinks at Peter, breathes in deep, and plants the world's quickest kiss on Peter's lips.

Peter grins, his eyes flickering between Malcolm's. "What was that for?"

"Just, you know," Malcolm says. He shrugs. "Yeah."

"Yeah?"

"Yeah."

"Okay." Peter says. They start walking again. "What about you, huh? Did you like me or Rebo more?"

"Oh, Rebo, for sure." Peter makes an affronted noise, and Malcolm laughs. "No, but—I *was* more drawn to Rebo at first. He was just...real. I think I liked him so much because you let yourself be more free over the radio. You didn't have to hide as much when you were just a faceless guy on the air. But then you came over to my house, and..."

"Oh shit, you totally fell for me that day," Peter says with a teasing smirk.

Malcolm glances at him. "Yeah, I think I did."

Peter looks away, bashful, and Malcolm does the same.

"I mean," Malcolm says, "I definitely already had a crush on you before that point. You saved my cat, dude."

"You liked me way back then? I barely talked to you!"

"Well, yeah, but you *saved* my *cat*. That's hot, dude, I couldn't help myself."

"You're ridiculous."

"You're cute."

"Jesus," Peter laughs, and covers his face with his free hand. It feels good to be the one making him flustered for once. He didn't think it would be this easy. "You're having fun, aren't you?"

"Yeaaah, a bit," Malcolm concedes with a slow, tired blink. "Gotta make up for lost time."

Peter squeezes Malcolm's hand. "Good thing we've got plenty of it."

"That was so cheesy, man."

"Only the best for my boyfriend."

"Your *what*—"

"Oh, look, we're here!" Peter shouts too loudly, and he yanks Malcolm towards the building before he can get another word in.

We're talking about that later.

38

Malcolm thought he had been done with crying for the night; but then he returns to the apartment to find that his friends have turned the whole living room into a giant blanket fortress, and they've pulled up one of his favorite movies on the TV.

"Oh, what the fuck," Malcolm says through the incoming water works.

Goby looks up from where they had been stabilizing the fort, using heavy books to keep the sheets weighed down. "Remember when we did this in my dorm my freshman year? Made a fort so big it made it all the way into Janet Marley's room."

"I don't think we'll get that big this time," Mona says, "but this'll have to do. Jazz is out getting the ice cream. Pistachio, right?"

"Yeah," Malcolm says, his lips wobbling. "God. I love you guys."

Mona and Goby rush over to him with their arms spread wide, and he falls into their embrace easily. After a moment he feels a third weight collapse into his side, and he realizes that Goby must have dragged Peter into the group hug. He's definitely getting snot on someone, but no one seems to care.

The door opens behind them. "Oi, the fuck?" Jazz says. "You couldn't have waited on the group hug until I was back?"

"You hate group hugs," Malcolm says with watery laughter.

"It's a special occasion," Jazz says, and shoves her way into the group until she has her arms wrapped tightly around Malcolm's middle. "Sorry for slapping your mom," she says, her voice muffled.

"No, you're not," Malcolm says.

"No, I'm not."

"I wish I'd done it first," Goby admits.

"Don't we all," Peter says.

"I know I'm usually the one who chastises the use of violence," Mona says, "but in this case, I'm afraid I must agree."

Malcolm laughs, burrowing further into the embrace. It's probably the longest group hug they've ever had, but he can't find it in himself to let go. "I should have stood up to her a long time ago," he admits softly. "I couldn't have done that without you guys. Thank you."

They all coo and say he has nothing to thank them for, although he'll always disagree. Mona smacks a wet kiss to the side of his head, and Goby ruffles his hair. It's strange being on the receiving end of that one, and Goby laughs at his disgruntled face.

Malcolm insists that they start the movie over. He can't just watch *The Holy Grail* from the middle—it's blasphemy, basically. The others don't seem to mind.

"You know, I've never seen this," Peter says when he and Malcolm are sitting on the couch. Malcolm desperately wants to collapse into Peter's side and stuff his face into Peter's hoodie until he's all he can smell, but he keeps himself still, sitting upright on the couch. Lady Governor meows next to him, and he feels her judgment.

"You've *never* seen *Monty Python and the Holy Grail?*" Goby asks indignantly. They turn to Malcolm, eyes wide. "Are you sure about this one, Mal?"

Malcolm snorts. "Yeah, I'm sure. He'll be watching enough *Holy Grail* to last a lifetime if he plans on sticking around."

"And he is sticking around, right?" Jazz asks, her eyes fixed on the TV so she can pretend she's not interested in the answer. Malcolm turns to Peter. He can't answer this for him.

"Yeah," Peter says. "I'm not going anywhere."

Mona has set herself up horizontally in the chair next to the couch, and she tips her head against the arm of it until she's looking at Peter upside down, a warm grin spread across her face. "Welcome to our sad little gang, Peter. Happy to have you."

"Thank you, Mona," Peter says with a pleased smile.

"Yeah, just wait until Jazz gets comfortable enough with you to fart on your hand when you steal her seat on the couch," Goby says with an ounce of bitterness that implies they're speaking from experience.

"I'd do that now, I don't care who you are," Jazz corrects. "My spot is my spot."

"I love when you get all protective," Mona says dreamily. "Very sexy."

Malcolm glances at Peter, who's watching the group with a mix of curiosity and amusement. Goby makes a disgruntled noise before taking Jazz's hand and plopping it on their head, and Jazz allows it without a blink, her conversation with Mona never breaking. Malcolm knows Goby does that as a pressure stim, but he wonders what Peter thinks about it. He tries to imagine seeing their odd little family from a stranger's point of view—but Peter isn't a stranger anymore. He's one of them.

"Having regrets yet?" Malcolm asks.

Peter smiles. "Not a single one."

Peter suddenly grabs the sleeve of Malcolm's shirt and pulls, and Malcolm topples out of his stiff position on the couch with an ungraceful squawk. He finds himself messily pressed against Peter's side, with Peter's hand already wrapped along his torso. Malcolm's ears burn, and Peter laughs.

"You had your tongue in my mouth and this is what gets you flustered?"

Malcolm gapes, his own words thrown back at him, before Goby's suddenly pressed into their space with wide eyes.

"Y'all kissed?" Goby shouts, unnecessarily. They're literally inches away. "And that wasn't the first thing you said when you came back?"

"Sounds like it was *more* than just a kiss," Jazz says.

"It's been a busy day, alright?" Malcolm tries to defend himself. It's unsuccessful.

"Leave them be, Goob, you're embarrassing them," Mona says.

They don't leave them be. Both Goby and Jazz fight to get the full story out of Peter and Malcolm, poking and prodding until Malcolm has to shove his shirt collar over his face to hide his embarrassed flush. Mona, bless her beautiful soul, manages to wean them off with the promise of enchiladas the next time she goes grocery shopping.

Malcolm peaks up at Peter, worried that Goby and Jazz were perhaps being too overwhelming. He knows they can all be a lot sometimes. But Peter seems to be perfectly content, an affectionate look in his eyes as he laughs at the group's antics. It doesn't feel strange, Malcolm realizes, to have Peter here. It feels like he's always been here—like this is where he belongs.

"Peter," Jazz says, flinging an almost accusatory finger towards him. "I have a question for you, and it is of the utmost importance."

"Yes?" Peter asks. Malcolm expected him to be nervous about Jazz's sudden seriousness, but it's like Peter knows, somehow, that this is nothing to be afraid of.

"Peter Tollemache," Jazz says, then snaps her fingers together like the starting horn of a race. "Favorite ice cream. Go."

"Shit," Peter says, "that's actually kind of hard. I have a few—"

"You have to pick!" Jazz says. "Go, go, go!"

"Um, chocolate—*fuck*, wait, too basic—"

"Three! Two! One!"

"Neapolitan," Peter calls out quickly.

"Final answer?"

"Final answer." He nods his head with an air of finality.

"Mister Tollemache," Jazz announces, "you have gained my respect. Neapolitan is the correct answer."

"I didn't have your respect before?"

"Bring the man his cream of choice!" Jazz hollers, ignoring the comment. "Gooberson! The cream!"

"Quit calling it cream," Malcolm says.

"The *cream!*" Jazz says again, pointing her finger to the sky.

Goby fetches the ice cream dutifully, presenting the tub to Jazz like a precious treasure.

Malcolm glances back at the kitchen, where a couple other tubs of ice cream remain. He can't quite make out the flavors. "Did you get—"

"Yes, I got pistachio, stupid," Jazz says quickly. "I'm your best friend, you think I'd forget your favorite?"

"I was just checking!"

"Never doubt me, Clark!"

Malcolm feels Peter's quiet laughter against his neck, the low vibration of it humming against his back where it's comfortably settled into Peter's side.

"Is this amusing to you?" Malcolm asks.

"Yes, very much so," Peter says. "But I also just keep forgetting that the whole Clark thing is real. God, that really was you this whole time."

"Crazy, right?" Goby chimes in. "And this asshole didn't tell us for months!"

"Actually, I found out before he did," Jazz says, picking at her nails absentmindedly. "I'm just smarter than you all." Mona flicks her on the forehead, and Jazz winces.

"Wait, how did *you* find out before Malcolm?" Peter asks.

Jazz smirks. "You remember when Clark brought a friend onto the show?"

Something clicks in Peter's brain, and his mouth falls open in disbelief. "*You're* Ludo?"

Jazz dips her head in a mock bow. "At your service."

"Holy shit!"

Goby pouts. "How come you got to go on the show and we didn't?"

"I'm a bit disappointed, too," Mona admits.

"I'm sorry guys, but I had to force my way in," Jazz says. "It was great though, I wish you had heard it. It was *so* obvious who Rebo was, and he totally had a crush on Malcolm back then too."

"Oh my god," Peter mutters, bringing a hand up to cover his face. "I don't remember what I said. Oh, god, please don't tell me it was that embarrassing."

"You were all, *oh, I wanna be this guy's friend so bad, but he's so mean and so, so hot,*" Jazz reenacts, throwing her arm over her forehead dramatically. Goby cackles loudly, toppling over onto the rug.

"I would never say that on the air!" Peter argues.

"Ah, but you were *thinking* it," Goby interjects from the floor.

Peter grumbles. "Well, *yeah*."

Malcolm's eyebrows jump to his hairline. He shoves himself upward so he can fully turn towards Peter. "You thought I was hot back then?"

"I thought you were hot, like, always," Peter admits with the faintest blush. "Didn't we establish this?"

"Keep establishing it," Jazz laughs, "it's fun to see him go red."

"Scoundrels," Malcolm says, flopping back into his place beside Peter. He cozies up a little closer than he was before, hoping the others don't notice. (He thinks Peter does, because he squeezes Malcolm's hip.) "Menaces. Fiends. Every single one of you."

"Hey, I didn't do anything!" Mona pipes up.

"Don't act like this isn't entertaining to you!" Malcolm says.

"Oh, now, that's a different story."

39

It's near morning when the gang finally winds down, falling asleep in odd spots around the living room. Malcolm's used to their living room slumber parties; what he *isn't* used to is Peter holding him close on the couch, his soft snores ruffling the edges of Malcolm's hair. Lady Governor is settled near Goby, facing away from their face so that her tail flicks over their open mouth. Malcolm bets she's doing it on purpose. Mona and Jazz aren't cuddling each other to death for once, but their hands stay clasped in their sleep.

The movie has stopped playing, and Netflix asks if they're still watching. Malcolm slowly detaches himself from Peter's hold. Peter makes a soft noise of complaint, and Malcolm has to fight the urge to fall right back into his arms. He turns off the TV instead and heads to the kitchen.

Nothing quite feels real, still. A miserable day turned into an even worse evening, which then turned into one of the best nights of his life. And now it's quiet.

It's been a long time since the quiet nights have felt as peaceful and content as this.

There's movement by the couch, and Malcolm grins at Peter when he stretches and makes his way over to the kitchen.

"Hey," Malcolm says, leaning against the fridge.

"Hey, yourself," Peter says, his voice still rough with sleep. He stands opposite Malcolm, his hip resting against the kitchen island. "Hm. I."

"Our places were swapped the last time we were here."

Peter smiles. "How poetic."

"Did I wake you?"

"Nah, not on purpose. I think I just missed you."

Malcolm snorts. He looks away so he doesn't have to see Peter's cheeky grin. "That's the cheesiest thing I've ever heard you say."

"It's only gonna get worse from here, sweetheart."

"*Sweet*—" Malcolm chokes on his words, his stomach doing some crazy flips that make him feel simultaneously nauseous and giddy. He slaps his hands over his face. "Jesus, Peter."

Peter laughs, though he tries his best to keep it quiet, checking to make sure the others aren't disturbed. He settles down after a moment, and Malcolm watches him, knowing there's something he's waiting to say.

"Spit it out, Peter," Malcolm says when it becomes obvious he needs a push.

Peter chuckles, more nervous than before. His eyes have fallen to the floor, and his fingers tap against the counter at an irregular rhythm. "What I said...right before we got to the apartment. That didn't freak you out, did it? I wasn't really thinking at the time."

Oh. The boyfriend thing.

Malcolm thinks for a moment. "Well. Did you mean it?"

"I didn't mean to say it."

"That's not what I'm asking," Malcolm says. He holds his arms against his chest, trying to hide that he's starting to shake with nerves. "Did you mean it then? Do you still mean it now? Is that...is that what you want?" *With me, of all people?* He catches his tongue before he says it.

Peter's eyes soften, his head tilting. He shrugs, as if the answer is obvious. "Of course I mean it, Malcolm. I want that more than anything. I have for...longer than I realized, honestly."

He kind of wants to shout, or maybe cry from how amazing it feels to hear Peter say it. But he holds himself back; still cautious, still disbelieving. "Are you sure?" Malcolm asks. "I mean. You know me, Peter. You've seen me at my absolute worst. You know probably better than anyone else at this point just how difficult I am to deal with."

"It's not difficult," Peter says immediately, standing up straight. "It's not, Malcolm. You're not."

"That's a lie," Malcolm snorts. "You can admit it's a pain to have to pick me up from my mess all the time."

"The only thing that's a pain," Peter says, "is having to watch you tear yourself down like this. You're more than a chore I have to check off, stupid."

"I'm just making sure you know what you're signing up for."

"Do you know what *you're* signing up for?" Peter asks in return, spreading his arms wide in a challenge. "You haven't even experienced all the ways I'm fucked up."

"You're *not* fucked up," Malcolm says sternly.

"Uh huh, you say that now," Peter says, stepping closer. He quirks his head to the side playfully. "I get the sensory overload thing too, dude. You think it's always easy to deal with?"

Malcolm squints. "I'm sure I can handle it."

"Sometimes I scream, you know," Peter says. "Total bloody murder. You're lucky if you get a warning."

"Good thing you've introduced me to those noise reducing earbuds," Malcolm says. "Easy peasy. What else have you got?"

"I can't do dishes," Peter says, shuffling even closer, tapping Malcolm's leg with his foot. "The wet food makes me gag."

Malcolm grins. "Sometimes I'll space out during an entire conversation and you have to repeat it all over again, and sometimes I forget to pay attention the second time around."

"My gran had dementia, I've got the patience of a saint," Peter counters.

"I'm definitely attracted to Megamind and I'm not sure what that says about me."

"The blue dude with the big head?"

"Uh-huh."

"We can get you a doctor," Peter says, and Malcolm giggles. "Sometimes I sing the same single phrase in a song over and over again, for *days*. Drove my mom nuts."

"Once again, noise reducing earbuds," Malcolm retorts. "Come on, man, give me something difficult."

"Fine," Peter says with a defiant nod. He takes a breath. "Sometimes I don't leave my bed for days." Malcolm's smile falters with the change in tone. Peter isn't looking at him anymore. "I don't shower, I barely eat—it's a miracle if I even talk. You'll need a notepad to communicate." Malcolm lowers his arms, his heart feeling dreadfully heavy. Peter's still smiling, but Malcolm can sense his anxiety. Peter clears his throat. His voice is more cautious than before, struggling to keep its playful tone. "You're not the only one with problems, sweetheart. I think it's important you know what you're getting into."

And Malcolm realizes, as Peter's eyes flick nervously around the kitchen, that Peter isn't the better of the two of them. Neither of them are. They're both fucked up in their own incredibly human ways. Peter has issues that Malcolm doesn't even know about. But he wants to know. He wants to know everything.

"I know what I'm getting into," Malcolm says. He takes Peter's hands, and places them along his waist. "And *you* know what you're getting into. I see that now."

Peter's breath leaves him in a stutter. "Yeah?"

"Yeah. No more self-deprecating shit," Malcolm says. He scrunches his nose. "Well, I'll try my best. You might have to help me get out of that mindset."

"I can do that," he says with a nod. "You'll get sick of hearing me talk about how wonderful you are all the time."

"I might not always believe it."

"That's okay," he assures him. "I'll just keep saying it until you do."

"That might take a while," Malcolm sighs. "Like. A long, long while."

Peter hums thoughtfully, and brings his hand up to cradle Malcolm's face. He leans down and places his lips against Malcolm's hairline, and Malcolm's surprised to find himself suddenly blinking away tears. He doesn't remember the last time he was handled so gently. Like he's something to be protected—something to be cherished. Something worth holding onto.

"However long it takes," Peter whispers against his skin. "I'm not going anywhere."

"You can't promise that," Malcolm whispers back, letting his eyes flutter closed. He feels a tear slip down his cheek, and Peter's thumb catches it.

"No one can promise tomorrow, sure," Peter says. "But I promise not to ditch at the first sign of trouble. I have no intention of leaving anytime soon."

Malcolm wraps his fingers around Peter's wrist, keeping his hand in place against Malcolm's jaw. "I'm not leaving either. I promise. I'll wash all the dishes so you don't have to touch the wet food. I'll build a soundproof room for you to scream in when you need to, if that's what you want. And I'll make you food on your low days, although you might prefer Mona to do that. But I'll still be here, Peter. I promise, I promise, I promise."

Peter sniffs, and Malcolm realizes he's crying.

"I'm sorry," Malcolm starts, "Was that too mu—"

Peter presses their lips together before Malcolm can finish. His lips taste like salt, but Malcolm doesn't mind. It's a little messier than the first kiss they had, and more emotional than any kiss Malcolm's ever had before, but he kisses back with equal enthusiasm. Peter has one hand cupping his face, and the other pushes against Malcolm until his back is pressed firmly against the fridge. Malcolm tries to keep up the best he can, moving his hands when he realizes they had been stuck clutching at Peter's shirt collar.

He slides a hand over Peter's chest and tugs the hair at the base of his neck, and Peter pulls away with a gasp, although that wasn't Malcolm's intention. Peter presses their foreheads together, and their breath mixes in the air between them.

"Sorry," Peter pants, although Malcolm can't imagine why he's apologizing. "Got a little overwhelmed. Had to let it out somewhere."

"Buh," Malcolm says, a little dazed. Peter laughs, and his free hand presses firmly into Malcolm's hip. Malcolm clears his throat, and when he talks his voice is higher than he'd like it to be. "Yeah, uh—no, yeah, for sure. I get it. No problem. Good, uh—good outlet. Good...good job."

"Thanks," Peter says. "You too."

"Shut up."

"So touchy," he teases, leaning back in.

"Hey, dickheads," Jazz calls from the living room.

Malcolm shoves Peter on instinct, and Peter nearly slips against the hardwood floor but thankfully catches himself on the counter. They both stare with wide eyes at Jazz, who's thankfully the only one awake. Less thankfully, she's definitely not happy about being the only one awake.

"You literally have a room for this shit," Jazz says, her tone low and murderous. "Use it, or I'm torching your collectible *Doctor Who* underwear."

"Roger," Malcolm squeaks.

"You have *Doctor Who* underwear?" Peter asks.

"Shut up, it's collectable."

"God, you really are a nerd," Peter says, mystified, as Malcolm drags him over to his room. "I've never been more attracted to you."

"If I hear anything out of that room," Jazz calls out again, "I'll blast the Crazy Frog song outside your door and board up all the windows so you can't kill yourself to escape it."

"So *violent*," Peter says, only slightly concerned.

"You get used to it," Malcolm says, locking the door behind them.

Peter grins. "Can't wait."

40

"Welcome, caller, to the Max Rebo Show! Who do we have with us tonight?"

"Hey, Rebo! My name's Fe. I've been listening to your show for a while, and I've noticed that you have yet to talk about something I've been dying to hear. Did Clark ever show up when you invited him to your shop? First he ghosts the show for days, and then he comes back without a single explanation! You're killing us here, dude."

"Well, firstly, dear caller, I'm amazed that you remember all that—that was months ago. *Several* months ago. Do I have a new stalker? I didn't think I was popular enough for *two* stalkers."

Another voice comes over the line, muffled. "You're more popular than you think, *Rebo*."

"Not denying the stalker part, I see."

"*Who was that? Holy shit, was that—*"

"Caller, I'm gonna have to let you go, but rest assured, all your questions will be answered if you stick around for the rest of the show. Today's segment, as you will soon find out—*shut up, you look fine, they can't even see you*—it's a *very* special segment! Friends and fiends, put your hands together for the one, the only, *Mister Clark!*"

• • • •

After that night—*The Night*—the night that everything changed—Peter didn't bring up the Rebo show right away. Neither of them brought it up, but Malcolm could tell he was dying to know whether or not "Clark" would be calling in again.

When Malcolm called in the following weekend, he could practically feel Peter smiling into the microphone.

"*Hey, stranger,*" Rebo had said.

"*Hey yourself,*" Clark said.

And they had come to a mutual understanding, over that call, that they wouldn't mention what happened between them. Not yet, at least. That was something they wanted to keep for themselves, at least for now. Although Kit was decidedly vocal about her confusion.

"*What the fuck!*" Her voice was far away and muffled over the air, and it was enough to send both Peter and Malcolm into hysterics.

And apparently, Kit wasn't the only one who was dying to know what happened.

Now, Malcolm's sitting across from Peter, a heavy pair of headphones over his ears and a giant mic settled in front of his face. Peter wiggles his eyebrows across from him.

"Friends and fiends, put your hands together for the one, the only, *Mister Clark!*"

"Actually," he says, "my name's Malcolm."

"Bah, Rebo and Malcolm," Peter scrunches his nose. "Not as catchy. Two double-syllable names—too clunky."

"You're insufferable."

"Apparently not enough to keep me from gaining a following," Peter says.

That's the cue.

"Yeah," Malcolm clears his throat as he pulls up his phone. "Who knew people would enjoy the sound of your voice this much? The Rebo Show twitter has gained thousands of new followers over the course of just a few months."

"I didn't even know I *had* a twitter. Thanks Kit!"

"*I haven't forgiven you!*" Kit shouts through the glass. Malcolm laughs when she shoots him a particularly sour glare.

"Kit's peeved I kept Clark a secret," Peter says. "I'm sure many of you feel the same. So, we're here to lay it all out in the open. Once again, dear listeners, I would like to introduce you to Clark—not just as my favorite listener in the world and our special guest on the show tonight, but also..." Peter smiles, almost giddily. "...as my boyfriend. Malcolm."

Kit throws her hands up into the air, either in triumph or complete exasperation. Malcolm has a feeling it's both.

Malcolm's phone starts to buzz in his hand. Notifications start to pop up on the screen, more than he's seen on his own phone before.

"Malcolm and I actually knew each other this whole time, funny enough," Peter says.

"Uh, Rebo."

"We went to college together. Isn't that insane?" Peter continues. His eyes go soft, and he laughs. "We *hated* each other. Well, sort of."

"Rebo."

"It's a long story, guys, but it's a good one. Maybe I'll tell it some time. But yeah, surprise, we're totally a thing now. Hashtag, uh, ReboClark. No, that's lazy. Clebo? Gross. Rebark? Maybe."

"Rebo! *Look at this.*"

Peter finally snaps out of his rambling, grabbing his own phone from where Malcolm had it pushed in front of Peter's face, the Rebo Show's official twitter already pulled up. Peter's eyes light up, and his mouth opens in shock.

"Oh, shit."

"People are going nuts," Malcolm says, mystified, as he scrolls through twitter on his own phone. @reboshowforreal has been tagged thirty times in the past two minutes, and it just keeps going.

cleo @dabislut

listening to @reboshowforreal and almost crashed my car. I'VE BEEN WAITING FOR THIS FOR MONTHS???? SOMEBODY SEDATE ME

|

matty matt @cryptidmatt

Replying to @dabislut

WHAT WHAT'S HAPPENING??? BREATHE BITCH

Malcolm lets out a disbelieving chuckle as he scrolls through all their mentions. Peter looks up at him, and they share an equally mystified smile. Peter shakes his head and goes back to the phone.

"'My life is complete now that #rebark is real,'" Peter reads out loud. "'I can die happy.' Well, don't do that."

"In all caps, '#rebark is real, shut the fuck up, I'm eating dirt,'" Malcolm reads from his own phone. "That's…a compliment, right? That sounds like something Goby would say. Also, are we really sticking with Rebark?"

"Wait, this one is different," Peter says, leaning over so Malcolm can read it from Peter's phone.

Howard Lu @howielu

Very proud of my boys… Miranda taught me Twitter for this. Glad you finally figured things out… About damn time you did. Many congratulations, Malcolm and Peter… Mention my shop on your show once in a while, would you? Winky face… @reboshowforreal @malmalmal

"*Mr. Lu?*" Malcolm squawks.

Peter laughs, loud and a bit hysterical. "Oh my god. Holy shit, we have fans. We have *shippers*. Oh my god, what is happening?"

"I told you people like your show, dumbass," Malcolm says.

"People like *us*," Peter corrects. "We make a good team, Clark."

There's a knocking from the glass, and Malcolm and Peter look over to see Kit pointing to the phone. Someone's calling in.

Peter picks up, smooth as ever. "Howdy, howdy! Welcome to the Max Rebo Show, who do we have here?"

"*Um, hey,*" the caller says, and Malcolm and Peter both seem to clock onto their shy demeanor pretty fast. Their voice is high and breathy, undoubtedly nervous from the way it shakes. "*I can, um…I can use whatever name I want on here, right?*"

"Of course," Peter says, his voice changing just slightly, his energy settling. Malcolm's amazed at the way he changes his tone so quickly to fit what he thinks the caller needs. "We'll call you whatever you like, as long as it's radio appropriate."

"Even then, we'll probably still say it," Malcolm says, to Kit's dismay.

The caller lets out a breath. "*Um. Can you call me Ivan?*"

"Of course, Ivan," Peter says. "Very nice to meet you! That's a nice name."

"*Thank you. I, uh, picked it myself.*"

"Same here," Malcolm says immediately. Peter smiles at him, soft and secretive. "Feels good, yeah? Better?"

"*Yeah,*" they say. "*Much better.*"

"Did you have something you wanted to talk about, Ivan?" Peter asks gently. "No pressure to hurry, we can always just chat about our days. I saw a skunk on the way to work."

The caller laughs, and Malcolm can hear them relax. "*I just wanted to call to say…uh, well, you guys…you sort of really helped me. I've been keeping up with the show since I found it a few months ago, and it's helped me so much. To know that people…people like* me…*can be this successful, and happy—well, it just helped me get through some really tough times.*"

Peter's staring at the table, looking slightly stunned. Malcolm reaches over and grabs his hand, rubbing his thumb over the top. Peter's eyes have gone misty, and Malcolm can feel himself getting choked up too. He feels that distant urge to run away, the urge he used to always give into, and he pushes it away with a gentle hand.

"There have been so many times where I just felt so alone. But you guys are such an inspiration, a-and I wanted you guys to know that. Thank you, Rebo. Thank you, Clark. Thank you so much."

"Oh, god," Peter says, his voice wobbly. "I did *not* expect to cry on the air. Thank *you*, Ivan. You are just as much of an inspiration to us as you say we are to you."

"Really? I-I haven't done anything special."

"Not true, man," Malcolm says. "You're being you. In a world like ours, that's brave as hell. Keep being you, Ivan, okay? Promise me that. No matter what anyone says, just keep being you."

"And if you can't be you anywhere else," Peter adds, "you know you have us. Call in any time, Ivan. You can be yourself here. Always."

There's a sniff on the line, and a shaking breath. "*Thank you. Thank you.*"

Soon after Ivan leaves, another call comes in.

"Busy day," Peter says with another disbelieving laugh. Malcolm has a feeling it'll take a while for the show's popularity to fully sink in with him—with either of them. "Welcome, caller! What's your name, what's your hobby, what's your favorite muppet?"

"*Hey! Uh, Stephanie. Crochet, right now. And—um, Kermit, I think?*"

"Basic, but understandable," Peter says. "Mine's Gonzo. What brings you in today, Steph?"

"And Stephanie," Malcolm cuts in, "would you mind telling us how long you've been listening to the show?"

Peter blinks at him, but Stephanie answers before he can comment.

"*Oh, ages. I've been here almost since the beginning.*"

Peter lets out a gust of air, sinking into his chair a bit. "Oh, wow."

Stephanie continues. "*I've been wanting to call in for a while, but honestly, I kinda thought the calls were just for Clark.*"

"What!" Peter exclaims, and Malcolm's not sure whether to laugh or blush. "Why would you think that? I had other callers!"

"*Yeah, like, two.*"

"Okay, moving on," Malcolm interrupts, ignoring the way Kit has started shaking with laughter in his peripheral vision. "What did you want to talk about, Stephanie?"

"*Well, I guess I just wanted to ask you guys what you had planned for the future. Y'know, now that you guys have 'met' and everything.*"

"Oh," Malcolm says. He's surprised that anyone was interested in their lives outside of the show. "Interesting question. Rebo?"

"Nuh-uh, go ahead, Clark. I know you've got an answer in your head, I can see it on your face," Peter says, leaning back in his chair with a grin. He waves his hand in front of him. "The floor is yours."

"You're unbearable, you know that?" Malcolm says, and Peter smiles even wider. "I guess...I have some thoughts."

"Mhmmm," Peter presses. "Go on."

Malcolm sighs. "I sort of had this idea, a little bit ago, but it's kind of stupid." Malcolm half wishes that Peter would interrupt, but he waits for Malcolm to continue, curious. "I thought, maybe, it would be cool if we had this kind of—bar-slash-record shop? Like a combination of the pub and Roisin. And we could...I dunno, we could be in charge of it. Together. I guess."

There's silence for a moment.

"*Wow,*" the caller breathes, and Malcolm jumps. "*That's so romantic.*"

"Christ, I forgot you were still here," Malcolm says, his hand pressed to his chest.

"*Language!*" Kit yells.

"Our listeners wouldn't be here without our language!" Malcolm counters, leaning away from the mic. "It's hip and relatable!" Kit gives him the finger.

Malcolm looks at Peter, finally, and finds him staring at him with wide eyes. "You would want to do that?" Peter says, a genuine question. "You'd wanna run a shop together? You and me?"

Malcolm feels his neck heat up, and he shrugs, suddenly remembering just how many people are listening to them right now. "Of course, I would. Lord knows your annoying ass would keep me busy on the slow days, at least."

"*He's being mean to hide his vulnerability.*"

"Bye, Stephanie!" Malcolm says abruptly, ending the call. "Didn't think my therapist had this number, goddamn."

Peter cackles, his eyes soft and adoring. "What would you call it? Our little bar-slash-record shop?"

Malcolm hums, pretending to think. He already has a written list of names hidden in his bedroom, but Peter doesn't need to know that. "Would 'Rebo and Clark' be too on the nose?"

Peter often tries to keep his true feelings under wraps when his emotions get intense. Malcolm's learned that over the past several months. He keeps a calm demeanor, still terrified of being '*too much*' sometimes, despite how many times Malcolm has said he's *never* too much for him. But Malcolm can see the way he melts now, ever so slightly. Peter smiles, and it's the smile he only does for Malcolm, the one that makes Malcolm want to take a page out of Jazz's book and start looking at hand crafted rings already.

"'Rebo and Clark,'" Peter says, testing out the feel of it. He says it like an answer. "Yeah...yeah, I like that." And Malcolm knows he means it.

41

FRIDAY, JUNE 15TH
KARAOKE NIGHT
SING YOUR HEART OUT!
COME FOR THE DRINKS, STAY FOR THE TUNES!
(OR VICE VERSA! WE DON'T JUDGE!)
REBO & CLARK

Bonnie Tyler's "Total Eclipse of the Heart" is a sing-along requirement for all pub patrons.
NO Journey before 10pm. Free drink for every Backstreet Boys song.

• • • •

"Why did we let Goby make the posters?" Peter says, staring at the flyer in his hand as he leans against the bar. "I like Journey."

"Well, it worked," Malcolm says as he fixes yet another long island. "Can't complain when the pub's this full. I've already made more tonight than I have in the past week."

"That's because you're cute," Peter says. "Bat your eyelashes a little more next time and maybe we can go to that fancy restaurant I like for our next date night."

"Am I just a piggy bank to you, Mr. Rebo?"

"Of course, Mr. Clark," he smirks. "What, did you think I was here for the personality? The looks?" He leans in as he says it, and Malcolm shakes his head.

"Mm, foolish of me," Malcolm mutters.

"Very."

Peter presses a quick kiss against Malcolm's lips, and Malcolm's sure he would've taken his time if they weren't both on the clock.

"Don't you have records to be selling?" Malcolm says, raising an eyebrow. Peter finally taught him how to do it right, and he's been taking advantage of it every chance he gets. "Can't have you neglecting our customers just to flirt with the bartender. What would the owners say?"

"I don't think they'd mind," Peter says, and he glances back at the section of the room where the majority of the records are held. It's definitely not what people are focusing on tonight—they probably should have just closed it up for the night, but Peter refused. It's a *bar and record shop combo, Malcolm, we need to provide what our customers expect.* "I've got Ivan keeping watch of things, he'll be fine."

That was one of the many recent developments included in their new and shiny life. One day, a kid just a few years younger than Goby showed up at the shop, nearly shaking with nerves. He introduced himself as Ivan, and Peter recognized his voice instantly as the boy who called in all those months ago. Ivan admitted that he moved here recently in hopes of finding people like him, remembering how Rebo and Clark had talked about their own friends. After several minutes of Ivan obviously dancing around what he really wanted to ask, Peter finally blurted out, "Would you like to work here?" He admitted that Ivan wouldn't be able to work with the drinks until he's 21, but he can work with Peter and the records, and they pay decently enough for Ivan to afford living here—and Malcolm nearly stepped in to keep Peter from rambling before Ivan cut him off himself, tears in his eyes, to say he would love to work here.

That had been so long ago. Rebo & Clark had just opened, squeaky clean and waiting for the charm of dirty old Bugswick to give it some character. Ivan slipped into the routine of their life as easily as the store did. He was still nervous around Peter and Malcolm's friends, unsure if he really belonged; but just the other day Malcolm found Ivan and Jazz talking in the back room about how to tell a queen bee apart from a drone, laying on the floor while Pink Floyd played over the speakers, and Malcolm knew that he had nothing to worry about.

Malcolm realizes, suddenly, that a familiar voice has been singing in the bar, and he looks up to find both Goby and Jazz on the stage. Goby sings with a strong and steady voice, while Jazz half shouts the lyrics into the microphone. The screen behind them displays the lyrics to Buzzcocks' "Orgasm Addict," and Malcolm flushes in embarrassment.

"Oh, for fuck's sake," Malcolm mutters. "Why am I friends with them? Mr. Lu is literally right over there. I'll never be able to face him after this."

Mona hollers from the other end of the counter, "*That's my girlfriend!*"

Malcolm groans.

"Relax, Malcolm," Peter laughs. He tugs at Malcolm's shirt collar, flattening out wrinkles that Malcolm *knows* aren't there because he ironed the hell out of this shirt before tonight's event. "And Mr. Lu is 87 years old, he's definitely heard worse than this."

Malcolm blows a raspberry, slumping against the counter. Peter looks at him, the smallest hint of worry in his eyes.

"I'm fine," Malcolm assures him before he can ask. "No overload yet. I promise, I'll let you know if it gets to that point. I know the drill."

The drill, of course, is for Malcolm to alert the nearest member of their group if he notices any warning signs of an episode. He is to go straight to the back room, no questions asked, for as long as he needs. If it's past the point of prevention, the gang practically forces Malcolm to take the rest of the shift off. So far they haven't needed to do that, thankfully. But it's nice to know they have a plan in place.

Once, Peter needed to do it for himself. It was a bit terrifying, actually, to find Peter sweating and holding his head in the back of the shop. Malcolm had never had the roles reversed like this, at least not with Peter. He sat next to Peter, a little lost on what Peter needs when he's having these issues. He remembers Peter telling him, long ago, that it's different for everyone. Then Malcolm felt a nudge at his leg and looked down to see Peter holding his phone out to him, hands trembling. It was already open on the notes app. "*Panic Plan for Peter*," it said.

He's learning, still, how to help. He's so used to being the one everyone has to look after, the one who always *takes* more than he can *give*. Peter knows so much about people, about how to take care of them. He handles everything with so much patience and grace. Malcolm's scared he isn't doing it right, sometimes. He had told Peter that once, after ages of pressing and prodding from Peter.

"You're doing everything right," Peter had responded. "It's okay if you don't know what you're doing right away. You're willing to learn. And that's more than a lot of people can say, Malcolm."

Malcolm had never thought about it that way before. When he worries about messing up, he tries to remind himself of that. He's learning. He may have a ways to go, but he's learning.

Peter pats at his hand now, anchoring him in the present. "Hey."

Malcolm rubs his thumb against Peter's, letting him know he's with him. "Hey yourself."

"Do you ever look around and just..." he shakes his head, glancing around the pub in wonder. "Just think about how fuckin' lucky we are?"

Malcolm looks around. Goby and Jazz are trying to get another spot on the Karaoke list, arguing over which song to choose while a line forms behind them. Mona's brought Terrance the stick bug out—Malcolm's sure the poor thing's having a heart attack with all this commotion—and she's showing him to a patron that genuinely seems more interested in the bug than Mona for once. Ivan has poked his head out of the back to nod along to the man on stage singing Bon Jovi.

Malcolm turns back to Peter, whose hand still rests securely against Malcolm's, warm and sure.

Malcolm smiles and says, "Every damn day."

Epilogue

Y*ou've reached the voice mailbox of*—RITA CLARK. *Please leave a message after the beep.*

• • • •

The message begins with distant noise, as if a party were happening close by. There's the sound of a throat clearing; then a voice, clearer than the music in the back.

"Hey, Mom. You didn't answer, which isn't much of a surprise. I'm kinda glad you didn't, though. I probably would've just hung up. Also, sorry it's loud, someone started 'Total Eclipse of the Heart.' It's a whole thing. Uh, anyway.

Listen. I just wanted to say...you don't need to worry about me. Not that you do anyway. I know you say you do, but I'm kind of done believing all the shit you say.

I want you to know that my life is the best it has ever been. If you don't listen to anything else I say, at least remember that. It's taken me years to get here, and one of the biggest turning points was letting you go. Not just you, but the idea I had of you. The mother I wanted you to be. Someone who loved me, not just in spite of my differences—but because of them. You've never been that person, Mom.

But you know what? I've found people like that. It took me a while to figure it out, but I don't need to waste my time crying about you when I have people like them in my life. I'm so loved, Mom. I'm so fucking loved.

And you know what? I wanna thank you. Because you showed me what the wrong kind of love looks like. Now I know when to stay the hell away from it. That was never the love I deserved. But what I have today? That...that is what I deserve.

I don't know for sure if Dad would be proud of me or not. You don't know that either, no matter what you think. Neither of us can know for sure. But I know people who are proud of me, and they're here—and they're all that matter."

A different set of voices, more distant than the first and clearly intoxicated.

"*Get fucked, Rita!*"

"*Jazz, that's a private conversation!*"

There's a laugh against the receiver.

"*Yeah. What Jazz said.*"

End message.

Don't miss out!

Visit the website below and you can sign up to receive emails whenever M. Dean Wright publishes a new book. There's no charge and no obligation.

https://books2read.com/r/B-A-KCSU-EJJAC

BOOKS 2 READ

Connecting independent readers to independent writers.

About the Author

M. Dean Wright is a queer, trans, "auDHD" author who wrote *Welcome, Caller* between his undergraduate college courses and work. Currently persuing his Bachelor of Fine Arts in Art Studio, Wright still plans to stick with his passion for writing as long as he has stories to tell...which is always.

When he isn't writing, Wright can be found sketching, reading, or binge watching Doctor Who. He also loves to spend time with his family and their two pets: a chaotically playful puppy named Parker, and the exasperated old cat who has to deal with her, Charles Bartholomew Wright.